KING'S QUEEN

LARGE PRINT

MARIE JOHNSTON

LE PUBLISHING

Copyright © 2021 by Marie Johnston

Editing by Razor Sharp Editing

Proofing by MBE, Judy's Proofreading, and Deaton Author Services

Cover Art by Shanoff Designs

All rights reserved.

No part of this book may be reproduced in any form or by any electronic or mechanical means, including information storage and retrieval systems, without written permission from the author, except for the use of brief quotations in a book review.

The characters, places, and events in this story are fictional. Any similarities to real people, places, or events are coincidental and unintentional.

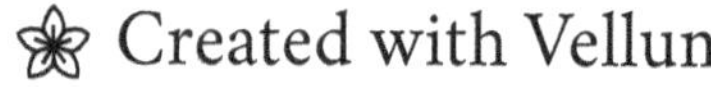 Created with Vellum

When Aiden King asked me out four years ago, I went from mousy librarian to wife of the most wanted bachelor in Montana in four months flat. No longer the nerdy girl from the wrong side of the tracks, I was a CFO's wife in a mansion by the river—and my husband was the man of my dreams. I almost couldn't believe my good fortune.

Turns out, I shouldn't have believed it. After years of rattling around that mansion alone while Aiden put in long hours at the office, I learned his secret: he'd needed to marry someone, anyone, to fulfill his trust requirements, and the nerdy girl from the wrong side of the tracks had been an easy target.

I never thought I'd be the girl asking a handsome millionaire for a divorce. Now, my pride and I just want to limp back to my family and start over. But to do that, I'll have to swallow one question. If the trust

only required him to be married for a year,
why has it been four years since we said
I do?

CHAPTER 1

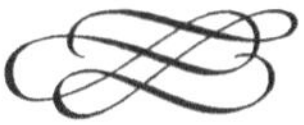

iden

FOUR YEARS and six months ago...

MY OFFICE DOOR WHIPPED OPEN. Grams appeared in the doorway like an avenging angel in a business suit. Emilia Boyd never looked like she was relaxed and happy, but today her eyes were narrowed, her mouth pinched. The office LED lights gleamed off her silver bob. "Aiden, meet me in your dad's office."

My fingers hovered above my keyboard. I was in the middle of compiling a five-year historical financial report for King Oil's stakeholders. "Now?"

She just gave me a look that told me to quit being stupid, of course she meant now. Patience wasn't one of Grams's virtues.

I saved my work. I had the process of compiling various historical reports down to an art, but it was still time-consuming. One of many time-consuming tasks I had on my list to get done before the next board meeting.

Grams had left my door open, and I stared at it for a moment. What was Grams doing here? Why the urgency? My dad, Gentry, was the CEO of King Oil, and I was the CFO. Grams wasn't here on a work matter, or we'd know about it.

Oh, Grams wasn't completely out of the game. King Oil had been hers, founded by her and my grandpa DB under a different name decades ago. Now she stayed on as president of the board of directors. Our monthly meeting had been last week. It didn't mean she stayed out of the day-to-day operations, but she'd retired enough to give Dad and me breathing room at work.

I had no doubt we'd have to pry her cold, dead fingers away from the building before she ever retired completely.

If it was a family emergency, Dad would've known before Grams. My brothers and I didn't get together often, but we'd call Dad before Grams. She had been a steady part of our lives, but unless it was a milestone like high school or college graduation, she only bothered when it came to work. Her motto was "live and let live, unless you're talking about King Oil."

I rose from my desk and turned, my gaze roving over the wall of windows at my back. Through the tint of the glass, the blue Montana sky taunted me. It was the middle of spring. This used to be my favorite time of the year.

Calving would be over. I'd work cattle with my three brothers, and there'd be mud pits all over our land that four boys could get into way too much trouble in. Those days were over. Sometimes I returned to King's Creek to help my youngest brother, Dawson, work the cattle, but it was never often enough. The best I could do was take my daily runs outside instead of on the treadmill, listening and reading some of the many messages that bombarded my various inboxes.

I tore my gaze from the beautiful weather that would be perfect to ride horse in, straightened my tie, snapped my suit coat to discourage any wrinkles from sticking around, and walked out the door.

Dad's assistant, Phillip, wasn't at his desk. He was the only help we were allowed in the inner office. Phillip was good, but we could use three more Phillips. I bypassed his desk, planted front and center of the elevator. He didn't miss who came and went, and more importantly, he could stop them from intruding on me and Dad. The other office in the corner was the one Grams used. I wouldn't be surprised if she sometimes sat in there because she had nothing else to do. This company was her life.

Grams was pacing the length of Dad's office by the time I entered and shut the door behind me. Another man in a gray pinstripe suit sat across from Dad.

Our family lawyer, Ellis. What was so critical that he'd driven from King's Creek to Billings to tell us in person?

"Hi, Aiden." The creases in his face were deeper than the last time I'd seen him. Age or stress? Both?

"Have a seat," Dad said. His expression was serious but he gave no other indication that he knew what this meeting was about. I sat in the chair next to Ellis. Grams continued to pace behind us.

Dad reclined in his seat and tented his fingers. "Go ahead and tell Aiden and me what this is all about."

Ellis licked his lips and the lines around his eyes deepened. "It's come to my attention…" He huffed out a breath. "I mean, there was no way to give myself a reminder. This was years ago."

"Tell them, Ellis," Grams demanded.

"Yes. Right." He pinched the bridge of his nose. "Before she died, Sarah put some money in a trust for each of the kids." His gaze darted between me and Dad.

Ice crystals crowded my veins. Being reminded of Mama's death was never easy, as if I didn't think about it every day. I erected a mental block before I could be sucked into the past, to the day Mama had been killed and the dreary months afterward.

Dad's brow furrowed, but I didn't miss the beat of sorrow in his eyes. "A trust?"

Dad didn't know about this?

"The terms, Ellis," Grams snapped.

Ellis jumped, but adjusted his weight to another butt cheek to hide it. "A rather sizable sum of one hundred million dollars was set aside for each of the kids."

For me and my brothers? That was a lot of money. I made an excellent wage as King Oil's CFO, but not one hundred million dollars.

"From the partial sale of King Oil. *Years* ago." A storm raged in her eyes. Grams had loved Mama—her only child. And she loved money. Mama was gone, but this money wasn't. "I gifted it to her to put into a trust. But I never thought…" She waved her hand at Ellis. "What was she thinking?"

Ellis licked his lips again. He'd need an entire tube of ChapStick before this meeting was done. "It's payable on each kid's thirtieth birthday. However." A shadow rippled over his features, and the already diminutive man shrank in his chair. "The stipulations require that each boy be married for one year before the trust is paid out. If that boy has already been married for the requisite year, or gets a divorce sometime after, the money will be split in half. It is exempt from any prenuptial agreement."

I snorted. Married. Did my job count? It was the only girlfriend, fiancée, or mistress that I had.

Grams's glare bore reality into me. I would turn twenty-nine later this year. Was I expected to get married and get this money?

How the hell would that work? I wasn't seeing anyone. I didn't really date. I'd go on a date here and there. I worked my ass off, but sometimes I wanted to get laid too. That was the only reason I dated. My work was all-consuming. I'd been groomed for this job since I was…since Mama had died. My grandparents had founded this company. My dad had worked for it since I was born.

I was the oldest. It was my job to continue in the family's footsteps.

Mama's casket had barely been lowered into the ground when Grams and DB had told me that the fate of the ranch rested on my shoulders, and that my brothers were looking up to me. Dad had the company to worry about.

I'd done it. I'd raised my three younger brothers and run the ranch that Mama had managed from when I was thirteen until I'd left home at eighteen. Then I'd poured myself into the company. Because that had been what was expected too.

Now that included getting married?

I wasn't against the idea, but the few times I'd tried to see someone, I'd been left disappointed. They wanted to date Aiden King, the prince of an oil empire. Aiden King, the face that graced the billboards with his dad—only once, but that had been more than enough. Aiden King, the guy who'd built a big house to go with that massive paycheck.

They'd heard about the private jet. They'd heard about my salary. They'd seen the local magazine feature about the custom home I'd built outside of town along the Yellowstone River. They wanted the lifestyle. Not me. And certainly not my schedule.

"That's not the worst of it." Grams's heel dug into the carpet. If she wasn't careful, she'd shred a hole in the material.

Ellis's head did a passable imitation of a bobblehead's. "Right. Um, if the stipulations aren't met, the trust will go to Daniel Cartwright, or his daughter, Bristol, if Danny has passed."

The money would go to the neighbor responsible for Mama's death?

"Sarah set this up?" Dad's incredulous tone made it clear I wasn't the only one losing their mind.

Ellis tipped his head. "She did. Made me draw up a confidentiality contract as soon as she entered my office. Attorney-client privilege wasn't enough for her. Truth be told, I forgot about it not long after. Your kids all turned out to be decent young men. I had no doubt they'd each find someone and get married." He cleared his throat and his eyes darted to me, then skated away.

None of us were married, or even close to it. My brother Beck hadn't been in a relationship that lasted longer than six months. Was he seeing someone now? I didn't talk to him enough to know.

Xander was somewhere in the world. He could be married, but I doubted it. That'd take commitment and Xander didn't commit to anything, much less anyone.

Dawson had come the closest with his college girlfriend, but he'd been running the family ranch for almost two years now. And that college girlfriend was long gone. He dated, and that was it. He never mentioned anyone special.

"You need to get married, Aiden." Grams stared me down like she'd tasked me with saving the world.

"Grams." I didn't want our seedy neighbors to get the money any more than she did but this was my life she was talking about—and someone else's. My future wife's.

"Emilia." Patience laced Dad's voice. He

was good with Grams. He'd married Mama right after high school graduation. She'd been pregnant with me and they'd been too scared to go against Grams and DB when they'd laid out how it was going to be. Get married. Mama, stay home and keep the ranch going. Dad, start at the oil company. Because of all that, Grams and Dad had history. He could handle her moods and redirect her ire.

She shook her head. "DB and I worked too hard for that money." Grandpa DB was long gone, which was for the best. He had a worse temper than Grams and this news would've put him straight in the hospital. "We trusted Sarah with that money. It was our legacy to pass to our grandkids," she hissed. "I'd been too busy to deal with it. I should've known better."

Should've known that Mama had a tender heart that wasn't driven by the bottom line? Yeah, Grams should've known. But this trust didn't make sense.

Grams stabbed a finger at me. "You're

the oldest, Aiden. If you do this, you can show your brothers that this money is rightfully theirs and they'd better do what they need to in order to keep it in the family." A disgusted sound left her. "And keep it away from the damn Cartwrights."

"Now, let's talk about this." Dad had learned to be part politician. But he wasn't dragging me out of the office, grabbing the first single woman we passed, and hauling us to the altar like I was sure Grams wanted to. Dad eyed Ellis. "Is there nothing we can do?"

"Every contract has loopholes but Sarah paid extra to minimize them, and…you're running out of time." No wonder Ellis was so nervous. Grams's fingers twitched like she wanted to wrap them around his neck and squeeze. "Additionally, if Danny were to hear about this and we didn't do everything to the letter…"

Dad's expression darkened.

Grams radiated rage, her hands fisting. Dad's jaw clenched and his shoulders tightened. I could practically see his blood pressure climbing. This news was hard on them.

Grams was right. I was the oldest. It was up to me to set the example. To pave the way for my siblings, like I'd done with the company.

Dad cleared his throat. "I can't argue that what you decide to do, Aiden—"

"Which had better be finding a wife," Grams snapped.

"—will dictate how your brothers handle the trust. But"—Dad shot Grams a quelling look she ignored—"the decision is yours. No matter what."

No matter what.

The survival of the ranch. It's up to you, Aiden.

Raising my brothers without our increasingly absent father. It's up to you, Aiden.

It's a family company. We need to keep it that way. It's up to you, Aiden.

It's up to you, Aiden.

Fuuuuck.

If I didn't get married, my entire family would be pissed at me. I'd be pissed at me. Danny Cartwright didn't deserve the mud in his driveway, much less one hundred fucking million dollars. He was the reason we'd lost Mama and had to deal with this trust in the first place.

And if I married? If I married just for the money, would that be what my brothers did? Would they sacrifice their own happiness and find someone who'd say *I do* for millions of dollars? Worse, what if the public learned of this trust? My brothers would be pursued by all sorts of gold diggers. It was hard enough to find meaningful relationships as a King.

It's up to you, Aiden.

"I'll take care of it." It was what I did. All three heads swiveled toward me. I lifted a shoulder. "That money's ours. I'll make sure it stays in the family." And I'd make sure news of the trust stayed within the family too.

"I can't imagine this is what Sarah wanted." Dad's tone oozed disappointment.

But it was. Ellis had the signed proof of it. And Dad was leaving the decision up to me—because I always made the right one. I came through. It was what I did. I was the oldest; I had to set the example.

My chest tightened. "Mama made the trust for a reason. She had to know that if something happened to her and she couldn't give us the money, we'd do everything possible to keep Danny from getting it." Mama had been softer toward our troubled neighbor than any of us, but she hadn't been blind. "I'm not going to let her down."

Mama had been taken away from us and it had nearly destroyed our family. I wasn't going to let this trust destroy my brothers' chance at happiness.

Kate

. . .

TWO MONTHS LATER...

HIS VOICE LEFT ME BREATHLESS, like I'd run three miles instead of walking from the parking lot to the conference room where our King Oil tour group was being greeted.

I didn't run. I liked a brisk walk, but if anyone saw me running, they'd better sprint because something was on fire or chasing me. Yet my heart hammered worse than any sprinter's.

Had Aiden King always had that deep of a voice? Had I ever heard the CFO of King Oil talk before? He'd murmured "good match" to my brother during wrestling matches in high school, but he'd never been the center of attention.

Oh, he'd been the center of *my* attention. If staring were a crime, I'd have been on top of Montana's Most Wanted list.

Aiden King.

Another speaker started talking. Aiden's dad, Gentry. The CEO's voice was deep too, but with a mature timbre, as he told us about when King Oil headquarters had moved out of his hometown of King's Creek, Montana, to the sophisticated new office building in Billings.

I should be taking notes. It would be a good research topic for work. I could present on it. But I already knew all the details. When it came to Aiden King, I had paid attention. I hadn't outgrown that lovesick teen from my brother's high school wrestling matches.

I was in the back of the group. As soon as I'd heard King Oil had extended an invite to the public library staff for a private tour, I'd been a puddle of anticipation. For six weeks, I'd heard about other civic bodies around Billings being personally invited for a tour. First, the city council. Then the city maintenance department. City zoning and planning. All departments that worked directly with King Oil. The company gave generously to the library each year, but I didn't think we'd get an invite. Until King Oil HR had contacted the library director.

I'd given myself a pep talk. This was a King Oil tour, but that didn't mean that Aiden would participate. He probably had better things to do with his Friday night. But he was helping to lead the tour with Gentry and the head of HR.

I was twenty-eight and old enough not to act like a fourteen-year-old with a crush. Instead, I had gotten up this morning and blown out my hair. I'd had to learn *how* to blow out my damn hair first. And I'd had to rewash it and try again. Twice. Then I'd stood in front of my hole-in-the-wall closet and stared at my clothing choices. How obvious would it be if I showed up for the tour all *oh, this old thing?* in a brand-new outfit that made my bank account choke?

No, I would work with what I had, though at least my new non-frizzy hair wouldn't stand out. What did I own that wasn't stereotypical staid librarian? My coworkers dressed in various interpretations of business casual, and I wasn't any different. I usually wore slacks or leggings and an oversized sweater. In the summer, I wore a blouse—in a pattern if I wanted to be wild.

Reaching for a frilly shirt that would look cute with plain black leggings, I frowned and paused. My hand hovered over the fabric. The top had a faint floral print. As a lifelong wallflower, I did not need to wear flowers on my top as I hovered in the back of the crowd.

But Mom's smoky voice had drifted through my head. "Fuck them."

And here I was, fucking them in my floral shirt as I stood next to the dang wall. Standing at the back of the group, I could barely see Aiden through the crowd of coworkers I normally adored but was a tiny bit ragey at right now. Not cranky enough to crowd my way up front and look at Aiden's perfect face up close, though. I could stare back here without being creepy. I hoped.

Aiden shifted and I edged to the right. There. A gap.

He was speaking again and my belly quivered. That voice. That face. Dark hair gelled mercilessly into place. Eyes with a slight perma-squint that made whomever he looked at feel like one thousand percent of his attention was on them. I'd never survive that look. His shoulders were wide. Did he still have his wrestling physique?

Duh. It was better. A stacked but sinuous upper body with powerful thighs that could flip an opponent in a split second. That description was probably stitched into his suit. *For the stacked but sinuous man in the business world.*

His gaze roamed the crowd, lingering only long enough to make each person feel seen. He was over six feet tall, but he couldn't see me tucked in the back of the group.

I could see him, and that was what mattered. It was just *wrong* how well that suit fit him. Black suit, black slacks. Light gray shirt. Simple, packing a powerful statement, one that said *I can crush you physically or financially, and only I will decide.* That thing must be custom tailored. With that wide chest tapering to his narrow waist and long legs, he couldn't buy off the rack.

I snorted quietly. He could buy the whole rack. The whole store. The Kings were loaded.

Others might see money when it came to him, but I'd always seen dogged determination. Aiden King knew what he had to do and he worked at it until he accomplished the task. He'd been like that when he'd faced my brother on the wrestling mat. It didn't matter the opponent. The grim determination in Aiden's eyes had said he wasn't thinking about the girls swooning over him in the stands. He wasn't thinking about the party he'd be going to that weekend. He was planning his win. He was envisioning it. And he'd execute it.

He had that look now.

My body didn't care. My knees shook like the time he'd walked past me after pinning my brother Jason. His gaze had skipped over me, but my teen mind insisted he'd lingered.

Aiden King lingered on nothing, definitely not me.

I jumped when Aiden clapped his hands together, the corners of his eyes pinched like he was smiling but his lips hadn't quite gotten the message. God, that was sexy. His intensity was thrilling. What was it like for the women he dated?

Jealousy shredded me until I was a brick of cheese ready for Mom's tater tot hotdish. I bit my lip to keep from snarling.

This man was not mine. He'd never remember me; I'd never given him a reason to. He might recall Jason, but he wouldn't know who I was.

I shuffled through the tour with the rest

of the group. Being librarians, we were a quiet and respectful group. It was a job that had called to me after the chaos that was my childhood. It was a job where I fit in, where I could contribute to the world in my own low-key, nerdy way. I wasn't in charge of a multibillion-dollar company, but that was fine with me.

I considered Aiden's tall, straight back as he led us through the wide hall to a room with dioramas and landscapes scattered with oil wells.

Was he happy being the CFO? He had to be making sick money. He had to go home with a sense of accomplishment. He was the reason this company stayed afloat, him and his dad. Surprisingly, I'd been able to pay attention while his dad had described their organization. I'd expected a long list of vice presidents, but beyond him and Aiden, there hadn't been any.

The headquarters was a work of art. From the outside, the glass encased nearly the entire structure, gleaming a deep brown, like oil. Inside, it was open, spacious. An environment that stimulated creativity and boosted morale as long as the leaders didn't quash it. By the time we wound back around to the conference room, the space had been filled with various water choices—spring, sparkling, and flavored—and finger snacks like wafer cookies, meat and cheese, and oh god, were those miniature muffins?

I had a serious weakness for muffins that I was not going to expose in front of Aiden One Ounce of Body Fat King.

I crept through the line, trying not to ogle the treats like I was Cookie Monster's second cousin Muffin Maniac. *Don't get the muffins. Don't get the muffins.* They weren't jumbo muffins. One little bite wouldn't be worth it.

Okay. *One muffin, but don't stuff the whole thing in your mouth.*

I grabbed a bottle of water and two mini muffins, one blueberry and one chocolate.

Few of my coworkers had taken any. I

couldn't let the Kings think they'd made a poor choice. Muffins were never a bad choice.

When I turned, I didn't see where Aiden or his dad had gone. Some of my coworkers were single, and since they'd chattered for days about this tour and how hot the King men were, I wouldn't be surprised if they'd glommed on to Aiden as if he were the lead singer of a boy band.

The jealousy roared back, along with searing anxiety. I had a few single coworkers. What if Aiden hit on them and I had to go to work and hear about his suave pickup lines? Seriously, all Aiden had to do was crook a finger. Even worse, what if I had to listen to someone gush about a date with him? Or…*more*? I had no idea if Aiden was a player or not. There were rumblings about Gentry, but I hadn't cared. I'd hung on every detail of Aiden in the news, but it was a good thing news clips weren't sustenance or I would've starved.

I knew that he hadn't married, but that was about it.

Yeah. I so wasn't going to stand around and awkwardly wipe muffin crumbs off my boobs while Aiden got hit on.

I was edging out when a wall of heat hit me from behind. "Are you Jason's sister?"

I froze, one muffin getting crushed in my hand. It was him. Was he talking to me? I had a brother named Jason. Oh, god. Was Aiden talking to *me*? I turned around and had to look up. He was that close. All heat and just enough cologne to encourage me to lean closer and sniff. Almonds and anise. What guy wore that combo?

Aiden did. And it was intoxicating.

My heart clambered into my throat. He was hotter up close. The cowlick I remembered from wrestling, the one that had pushed against his protective headgear after a match, was flattened into the comb lines of his hair. For a fleeting moment, I wished I could see it again.

His eyes were a dark brown with sooty

lashes, but I caught a few glints of yellow. Subdued, like the cowlick. The way he focused on me and only me… My knees quivered.

"Um, Jason? Yeah." I could kick myself.

I steadied my breath. Calm down, Kate. He's asking to be polite. King Oil wants the support of the community. It's his job to talk to everyone.

Wait! He knew I was Jason's sister. He… knew who I was?

A smile spread across those lips. Lips that had an arrogant tilt when nothing but confidence oozed from him. His smile was a heady combo of pleased and predatory and my heart pounded like I'd been cornered and wanted desperately to be ravaged.

Those lips moved. I'd never fixated on a mouth like this. Maybe during those uncomfortable dates when men went in for a kiss and I thought I'd rather make out with a jellyfish, the kind that stung, rather than kiss a dud again. "What a small world. Kate, right?"

My eyes went wide. *He knew my name?* "Yes?"

I had to quit sounding like I was asking him a question.

His smile grew wider, his gaze more intense. "It was cool the way you were always there for Jason." He leaned closer and my breath stalled. I was inches from Aiden King. Inches. His heat curled around me as gentle as a caress. "I admit to being a little worried that you were watching for my weaknesses and would tell him all my secrets."

Jason's wrestling was a comfortable topic, one I missed talking about. "You mean like how you preferred double-leg takedowns over single leg? And that if you didn't think you could pin your opponent, you'd rack up as many points as possible instead?"

He shoved a hand in his pocket, making his suit crinkle just right. If a photographer were around, they'd circle him and snap pictures that magazines would buy for thousands of dollars. "I knew it."

Breathing around him was exquisite torture. I hadn't expected talking to him to be so easy. "Busted."

"How is Jason?"

"Working for you, actually." I lifted a shoulder. "In a roundabout way. He's at the refinery."

"Does he like it there?"

I detected nothing but genuine concern, deeper than small talk. How was this guy so perfect? "Yes. And he has two young boys—who are already wrestling."

"And you? How've you been?"

Well, this moment was the highlight of my decade, so how did I answer? "Oh, you know. Busy with work. You?"

"Same." I was prepping myself for the inevitable *I'd better get back* or some other polite brush-off when he tipped his head down. The world consisted of only me and him. "Would you like to go out sometime?"

My lips parted. Had I heard him right? I looked around. My coworkers were talking among themselves in small groups and a few were gathered around Gentry. Aiden hadn't been asking someone else out. He'd asked me. "Yes?"

The corner of his mouth lifted. Was that a beat of triumph in the depths of his brown eyes? "Good. Can I have your number?"

I rattled it off before I could wake up from the best dream of my life. He didn't write it down.

Would he remember it? Or was he a player? Was knowing he could have me tripping at his feet enough?

I didn't care. I would float on this high for weeks.

"I'll call you, Kate." The promise in his voice set my knees quivering. This guy was potent.

"Sure." I sounded pathetically breathless.

Two people were edging around us to leave, and he turned to ask them about their tour. The loss of his heat was like a rug being yanked out from under me. My head was spinning but I managed to stay upright.

I tossed my crushed muffin in the nearest garbage and peeled the wrapper off the second one. I waited until I was in the hallway to stuff it in my mouth. Sweetness bathed my taste buds. Muffins, my old friends. The effect was diminutive compared to the excitement zinging through my bones.

Aiden King was going to call me.

Can I have your number?

He could ask for anything and I'd give it to him. I was that lost to his magnetism. Always had been. If a guy like that wanted to be with me, I would never give him up.

THE LAST TWO months of my life couldn't be real. This stuff didn't happen to me.

This weekend, Aiden had flown me to

catch a show on Broadway. Freaking Broadway.

Mom had always wanted to go to a show on Broadway. But Dad had chosen to use his extra money on his mistresses. My stepdad, Randall, would love to take her, but going to the movie theater had been challenge enough while raising three kids and working long hours.

Aiden had made it happen for me. Two months into dating, and we were walking through Times Square, living my mom's dream. Mine too, aside from a visit to the New York Public Library. Nine divisions and eight of them were special collections. Forget about the materials inside—which I couldn't—the architecture alone would be stunning. Aiden might get bored while I gushed over the library's shelves and what was on them, but well, I was a librarian.

But we weren't at the library. At the moment, I was his date and in Times Square. I would summon as much sophistication as possible. The sun had set, but people swarmed the sidewalk, and horns and sirens blared around us. A concrete jungle. He had my hand in his as we wandered with the crowd filled with gawkers like me and locals who walked as if life was too busy to slow down and enjoy the TV screens anchored above—monitors taller than my apartment building.

I was in New York. With a guy who could pass for a Disney prince.

I'd had a nice college boyfriend. He'd treated me well. We'd been barely more than good friends and then we'd gone our separate ways. I'd tried dating after I was done with my master's degree and had settled into my job at the library.

Of the handful of men I'd met, two might've had potential. We'd gotten serious enough for me to learn that one lived in his parents' basement for a reason—he'd dug himself into such a financial hole he couldn't even afford to live in his car because it'd gotten repo'd. I'd broken things off when I'd envisioned a future that resembled my mom and dad's before the divorce. The other had started acting like my oldest brother, Matt, after our parents had divorced. Brash tempered with little self-control. A toxic mix. Mattie might've matured into a decent guy, but the guy I'd been dating hadn't seemed interested in changing.

I refused to be the girl who waited for a man to change.

Now there was Aiden. Controlled. Responsible. Dedicated. Hardworking. We'd been dating for two months. He'd taken me to restaurants that I'd never been to despite being born and raised in Billings. When I'd mentioned how interested I was to try real Wagyu beef, he'd flown us in the company jet to Seattle. Last week, he'd flown us to Chicago. We ate at restaurants that I'd been underdressed for in a simple black dress. The women around me had worn diamonds that cost as much as all my college degrees combined, and we'd had wine that was older than my mom.

When I gushed to Mom, she'd warned me in her smoker's rumble, *You'd better find out if he's a real diamond or a hunk of coal, Katie-bear, before it's too late.*

If too late meant hopping into bed with him, that ship had sailed. It had sailed long and hard.

Our first date, he'd kissed me on the doorstep of my apartment building. A long, passionate kiss. Literally swept me off my feet. He'd even growled when he pulled away, like he might heft me over his shoulder and up the three flights of stairs to my bedroom.

The second date had ended with just a kiss, but it'd been a *plastered against the door and holy shit is that his erection?* kiss.

He'd made his move on the third date, like I'd hoped he would. He'd been respectful and part of me hadn't expected to hear from him afterward. Had I been too boring? Unadventurous? Would my curves scare him off? The best sex of my life might've been his worst.

He'd sent flowers to work the next day. Two dozen red roses.

I was a lilies girl, but two dozen red roses were beautiful and fragrant and made me feel like a princess as much as this trip had.

Aiden was not a hunk of coal. He was crude oil. Rich and complex. Crude oil could be split into several different products and Aiden's personality was similar. When it came to work, he was serious. Nothing came before work, definitely nothing in his personal life. When he was with me, he was *with me*. He was relaxed and had a sly sense of humor that was subtle and unpredictable. His default was solemn, but I didn't think it was innate. I think he'd made himself that way, and considering the way he'd lost his mom and how he'd dedicated his life to his family's legacy, I couldn't blame him.

My heels pinched my feet, but we weren't going to walk far. I had to work tomorrow at noon and Aiden was cognizant of my schedule. Another admirable trait. The biggest financial responsibility I had at work was spending our budget on reference items for the library. Aiden controlled billions of dollars and hundreds of workers' livelihoods. Despite the difference between our work roles, he never acted superior.

In the center of Times Square, he led me past a woman in orange boy shorts with pasties on her boobs. She strummed a guitar next to a guy in nothing but an orange Speedo as he held another guitar.

Aiden tugged me close. His long coat was secured around him, but his heat still seeped through me. "Are you enjoying tonight?"

"Are you kidding? It's Broadway." My smile was wide, but sheer grit kept me from wincing. These shoes. It was the third time I'd worn them. After our third date at a restaurant where I was the only woman not in stilettos, he'd asked me out again and I'd gone shopping. Dating Aiden meant a new wardrobe that included fewer cardigans and more A-line skirts and heels. Anything to suggest I had an ounce of flair in my body. "It's amazing."

He stopped and faced me, searching my gaze like he sensed the blisters I wasn't mentioning. Were expensive heels more comfortable or were my feet just heel intolerant?

People swarmed around us. Fluorescent lights of all different colors scattered over his hair, managing not to get absorbed by his dark glossy strands.

He took both my hands in his. "Kate, I've really enjoyed being with you."

I waited for someone to jump out and tell me it was a lie. That was the feeling I'd had for the last two months. Aiden's name popping up on my phone. Aiden picking me up from work or my apartment. Aiden taking me to his magnificent house, a place that would be my dream home if it were possible on a librarian's salary.

He squeezed my hands. Was I supposed

to respond? I echoed him. "I've enjoyed being with you." Understatement of the century.

Relief passed through his gaze as if he'd been worried the plain librarian who'd grown up in the trailer park would turn down the hot, rich oil exec who'd grown up ranching, making him impossibly more attractive. "It might be too soon, but I love you, Kate."

My small gasp was lost in the noise of the city. "Aiden." He loved me? Me?

Did I love him?

I'd been infatuated with him for half my life. Most of it had been a schoolgirl crush, even as I'd stepped foot into the King Oil headquarters the night of the tour. What would I call it now?

I thought of him all day, every day. I lived for the moment I'd see him again. He was considerate, had good values, and loved his family. I hadn't met his brothers, and I'd only seen his dad during the tour, but Aiden talked about them. His love and dedication to them were obvious in the warmth of his voice and the way his usually intense stare would relax. He showed me glimpses of humor, love, and respect.

Who was I kidding? I'd been in love with him since he'd asked me out. Since he'd picked me out of the crowd of my coworkers and remembered me a decade after the last time he'd seen me.

"I love you too. You're everything I ever wanted. I grew up hearing how awful it was for Mom, with my dad and how he'd lied—" Aiden's expression flickered and a small furrow bisected his brows. Oh, crap. I was rambling and talking about my parents' failed marriage as soon as I admitted that I loved him. Way to pull the plug on the romance, Katie. "I'm sorry. The only thing that has to do with us is that I know what I want out of a relationship, and it's you."

Tension drained out of his body and a smile spread across his face. I was grateful he had ahold of my hands. A full smile on his handsome, chiseled face was devastating. It was brighter than the three-story screen above us.

"I know what I want out of a relationship too, Kate. And it's you."

The movies didn't show princesses swooning. To be fair, Snow White had been lying down. I had a second to collect myself before he reached into the breast pocket inside his suit jacket.

"Believe me when I say I've never been in love before, Kate. And I don't want to wait to start my life with you." He withdrew a ring with an obnoxiously large diamond. Light sparkled from its many facets as he kneeled in front of me. "Will you marry me, Kate McDonough?"

My hand flew to my mouth. Tears peppered the backs of my eyes.

This was a dream. A fantasy.

I'd been that girl. I'd written Kate King across my notebooks when I was supposed to be studying for a civics test. I'd hugged my pillow at night and wondered what it would be like to feel his strong arms around me. And when I'd lost my virginity in college, I'd inappropriately thought of Aiden. If my first time had been with him, would it have been as lackluster, or purely spectacular?

I was dimly aware that some people had stopped to wait for my answer. A handsome prince in his impeccable black suit down on one knee in front of me in my clearance dress and unforgiving heels.

It was like a scene out of a romance novel. I tried to summon the name of a specific book, but I couldn't. Any with a handsome man kneeling at the damsel's feet would do. Those damsel's heels probably weren't sporting three new blisters. And I wasn't Snow White, nor was I in a forest. An NYC pigeon would crap on me before it cleaned my house.

My answer was the same no matter what. "Oh, Aiden. Yes." My hand shook as I held it out.

He slid the ring on. The fit was perfect. How had he done that?

The weight of the cool stone on my finger was unusual. God, this thing was huge. I didn't know much about diamonds other than I couldn't afford them, but this ring was what an oil exec's wife would wear.

I was going to be that wife. I was going to wear this gigantic ring and live in a big house, but none of that mattered. The man of my dreams had asked me to marry him. And he was everything I'd hoped he'd be and more.

If the last two months were anything to go by, then I couldn't wait for our life together.

CHAPTER 2

iden

PRESENT DAY...

I HOOKED a finger around my tie, wishing for the ten thousandth time I could loosen it. Tension rippled across my shoulders, tightening muscles that screamed to break out of this constraining white button-up shirt.

But in a small community where everybody felt free to drop in, I couldn't risk a haphazard appearance. As the chief financial officer of King Oil, I wasn't the face of the company, but I was the backbone. I had to look like I could run a billion-dollar organization.

Even if it came with a suit and shoes that I'd rather trade in for blue jeans and cowboy boots.

Another notification pinged. An email. I had a quick bell sound for my IM. A chime for the group chat program employees used. And a visual alert that streamed across my computer screen when an app on my phone had a notification.

Another ping. And another.

Most days, I could ignore them and answer when I had a spare minute. I excelled at prioritizing. Some days, like today, I fantasized about closing all my accounts until my electronics were blissfully quiet. But then those people would come hunting for me and I'd rather keep people out of my office so I could get shit done.

Thanks, Grams. As the board president of King Oil, Grams got what Grams wanted, and she was every inch the micromanager, from her brilliantly bleached teeth to her thousand-dollar alligator-skin boots. She expected Dad and me to run the company the same way. The inner office, as we called it, had one assistant who didn't have time for more than fielding phone calls and scheduling meetings. There was Kendall, but she was Dad's executive assistant. She took the burden off him more than me. She could do half my job with her eyes closed, but I wouldn't wish this schedule on my worst enemy, much less my dad's second wife, the woman who'd turned him back into the dad I'd grown up with. The dad before Mama died.

Another ping.

There was a knock at the door. Phillip opened it and popped his head in. "Kate's here to see you."

Kate could walk in whenever she wanted, but she wouldn't. My wife was too respectful of my job. She was a damn saint for putting up with my hours.

"Let her in." I leaned back in my chair, easing the pressure between my shoulder blades. Anticipation crawled in my gut. I put my elbow on the armrest and leaned my chin on my hand.

Kate slipped in, giving Phillip a flash of a smile. Phillip closed the door behind her. My tension vanished at the sight of her, and the way her hips swayed made me want to say fuck this job and carry her out.

She wore simple black trousers and a loose-fitting knitted sweater. The deep blue enhanced the amber color in her hazel eyes. Her light brown hair brushed her shoulders and I restrained myself from yanking her over the desk and onto my lap to bury my hands in the soft strands of her hair. To capture that gasp that left her every time I kissed her full lips.

I changed position before I could tent my trousers like an unprofessional jackass. I could have all the fantasies I wanted of spreading my wife over my desk and losing myself in her soft body, but I'd never indulge. This job was too important. Too many people counted on me.

She took a seat, sitting like a timid mouse. I was watching her like a hawk, but I couldn't help it. I always left in the morning when she was still asleep, and many times she was already asleep by the time I got home.

Her brows knitted together. Worry pinched her eyes. I'd been too busy checking her out to notice something was bothering her.

I sat straighter. "Everything okay?"

She held a manila envelope in her hands. She spread one hand over it and the emotion in her eyes thickened. Worry? Fear? Sorrow?

"We need to talk."

"All right." I checked the time. "I have a

meeting in ten minutes." I could push it back. Kate hardly asked me for anything, so yeah, I'd be late.

Annoyance crossed her face, but she covered it, evening out her expression. I leaned my elbows on my desk. Something was wrong.

She glanced at the envelope in her hand, a deep emotion I couldn't identify buried in her eyes. I knew my wife, but this was foreign territory. I couldn't read her expression, I couldn't tell what she was thinking. I didn't like this twist.

She let out a steady breath and met my gaze. "What's with the trust?"

Ice washed through my veins. *Shit.*

The trust. Full of stipulations I should've told her about but…hadn't. And my brothers sensed I hadn't, so they hadn't said a thing either. Nor had their spouses. Years had gone by and Kate hadn't found out about the trust and I'd continued to gamble on not telling her.

Kate was smart. I respected her too much to bullshit her. Ironic, since I should have showed her the utmost respect by telling her about the trust before I proposed.

I was a man who dealt in numbers, who waded in reality, who made the tough decisions others wouldn't. Kate finding out had been inevitable, yet I'd tempted fate and now fate was flipping me off.

"Mama set it up." Tightness crept across my shoulders, bunching muscles that would take days to relax. "She, uh, she made some rules in order for us to get it."

"Like marrying before you turned thirty?" Her voice was nothing more than a whisper but it echoed between us.

"Yes." Words clawed their way into my throat. *I was the oldest; I couldn't fail. It all depended on me. How could I tell you that I had a hundred million reasons to propose when I did? And that I'd done it after you'd told me how I didn't lie to you like your dad lied to your mom?* I stuffed them down like I always did.

I'd hurt Kate enough with what I hadn't said.

"And what else?"

"We had to stay married a year." I swallowed hard. Speaking the rules out loud, to my wife, left a sour taint on my tongue. "Though we've been married for four," I pointed out. *Lame.*

Hurt resonated in her expression. "And if you hadn't married, you'd have lost it?"

"To the Cartwrights, yes." The neighbors my family had feuded with for generations. Until Bristol Cartwright had married my youngest brother, Dawson, a month ago.

"Why didn't you tell me?"

"It didn't matter." I uttered those words with the same finality I did in the boardroom, but they sounded off to my ears.

She tilted her head and those intelligent eyes pinned me in place. Eyes that had seen through my salary and my lifestyle. Eyes that had always seen down to the real me. "You don't think that marrying me before you lost a ton of money mattered?"

"We've been married for four years." As if repeating it would make it all better. The trust had stipulated a year, but I'd held on to Kate for longer.

She huffed out a gust of air that might have been a laugh. "Four years. I hardly see you and we live in the same house."

Another ping. Another email. I tried to ignore the way the notifications intruded on my time with my wife. "My hours—"

"And we're millionaires? You mentioned a trust once, acted as if it were insignificant." She shook her head and pressed the back of her hand against her mouth.

"It is insignificant. It doesn't matter." The trust had seemed to matter so much when I'd first learned about it. Now, it was nothing. My brothers were happily married and for all the right reasons.

A chime. Goddamn messages.

"You keep saying that," she snapped and

I blinked. Kate was the most even-keeled woman I'd met. The lack of drama around her made her my oasis, one I hardly saw in my vast desert of work. "But it does matter. It matters because hearing it from someone who's not even a part of the family sucks. It sucks a lot." Pain brimmed in her eyes. "And everyone knows?"

Thanks to my job, I could always answer hard questions. "Yes."

She let out a sob and sucked it back in, her back ramrod straight. "I'm so stupid."

"Kate, you're not—"

"You married me right before—" She squeezed her eyes shut and sniffled. I know what she'd meant to say. We'd married right before I turned twenty-nine. I'd learned about the trust, asked her out two months later, proposed two months after that, and we'd married shortly after. Before I'd turned twenty-nine.

She rose and thrust the folder at me.

I scowled at it. I wouldn't like what was in that thing. Not one bit.

She dropped it. "I filed for divorce." A tear spilled out of each eye. "Um, in Montana, we can file through the mail. We just have to notarize everything." Her voice wavered but she took a steadying breath while my world caved in around my ears. "Since I signed a prenup, it should be pretty straightforward. I have what I earned. You have everything else. The house is yours of course. I make a decent wage at the library, and I have a retirement plan, so no need to worry that I'm going to fight you for anything."

"You get half," I mumbled. Why did I say that? I didn't want her to go, but I'd kept the specifics from her long enough. She needed to know everything. Another ping. My email could go fuck itself. "Of the trust. We've been married over a year. You get half. Fifty million."

The amount meant nothing to me. The trust meant nothing. The urge to tell her that nearly choked me, but then I'd have to explain why. She might be angry with me, but I couldn't have her leave me because I was pathetic.

"Fifty mil—" She blinked and another tear snaked down her cheek. "Good thing we've been married for four years, then."

Her bitter sarcasm stoked my desperation. Divorce? No. It wasn't possible. "Kate—"

"Goodbye, Aiden."

Panic clawed in my gut. "Aren't we going to talk about this?"

"If you wanted to talk about this, you would've by now." She turned away from me.

I'd had so much time to tell Kate everything. But I hadn't. Talking had gotten me nowhere and there had always been a reason not to. Wrong time. Work. My brothers. Now…four years, gone. Just like that.

I stood. She had no idea how many times I'd wanted to tell her. To bury myself in her arms and spill everything. I needed more time. "Kate."

My wife walked out the door and out of my life, softly closing the door behind her.

No. This wasn't my life. I planned. I researched. I deliberated. I went home to Kate. But she dropped divorce papers on my desk and vanished?

"Kate!" I hadn't raised my voice in so long, it cracked at the end. There was no reply as the world imploded so quietly inside the office that had become my prison.

I could go after her, but Kate would hate being the center of drama like that. My feet stayed rooted to the floor. "Kate!"

Another ping, followed by a ding.

A roar ripped out of me, scorching my throat as it banged off the walls. I yanked my screen off the desk and heaved it across the room. It hit the wall, but I couldn't tell if the clatter was coming from the plastic bits that went flying or my heart.

Kate

STALE CIGARETTE SMOKE SURROUNDED ME. Mom had quit smoking in the trailer house ten years ago, but smoking in the attached one-car garage when it was chilly out didn't offer a lot of ventilation. The smell matriculated into the house. I found it oddly comforting. An old scent that reminded me of home and simpler times.

Mom patted my back as I sobbed in a heap on the floral sofa that was older than I was. *They don't make 'em like that anymore,* her rough voice said each time I offered to buy her a new living-room set. I could still afford to buy her a living-room set. Even without the trust.

Fifty million.

I inhaled a shuddering breath and let another sobbing moan echo off the walls.

"Aw, hell, Katie." Mom didn't have a nurturing bone in her body, but she rubbed my back. If I couldn't go back to my home, this was the only place I wanted to be.

My family was the definition of trailer trash, but they told the truth, no matter how crude and decorated with swear words it was. A few "ain'ts" never hurt anyone.

At least my empty marriage with Aiden had shown me how much I missed the loud, crass love my parents and brothers showed each other.

"I don't understand why you have to divorce him," Mom said.

"Mom!" I wiped my eyes with my sleeve and sat up. "He lied."

She flopped one purple sweats–clad leg over the other. "It's a lot of money."

I sniffled and grabbed a tissue. "He treats me like crap," I mumbled as I wiped my nose.

She narrowed her eyes and leaned toward me. "What?"

"He treats me like crap."

"You never told me about that."

I never talked to anyone about my

marriage. I might've had to admit it was failing otherwise. I might've had to reevaluate how my own personal Prince Charming had turned into the Wolf of Wall Street. I'd never seen the movie. I didn't know if it was an accurate parallel, but dammit. I'd married Aiden King!

And I was divorcing him.

"Do I need to send Mattie after him?" Mom's tone was menacing, like she was asking if she needed to order a hit. With my oldest brother, Matt, that could be the same thing.

"No, Aiden wasn't abusive."

"Then what?"

"He ignored me." I was a forgotten accessory when we went out. I was there, but if someone else was talking to him, he focused on them—an endearing trait for everyone but the wife losing one hundred percent of his attention.

Mom cocked a brow. Her way of telling me to elaborate. An effect of having a daughter that was her polar opposite.

"If we went out and another woman struck up a conversation with him, he talked to her. And I just sat there." Like a knockoff designer purse. Everyone knew I was a cheap imitation failing to look like the real thing.

"Fuck. Him."

"Right?" And this was why I came home. Nobody crapped on a McDonough. "And he worked all the time. I thought I could live with it, but then I found out about the trust. If that weren't bad enough, to learn he's staying married to me to keep me from getting half…" Another wave of tears gathered in my eyes.

"You gave him four years. Fight him for the money, Katie."

"I signed a prenup." I'd insisted. I hadn't wanted anyone to think I was marrying an Oil King for his money. I loved Aiden. Not his job, or his cash. The joke was on me. "Half the trust is supposed to be mine, but I don't want it."

She grabbed my hand. "Honey, you put

your life on hold for him. Don't walk away with nothin'. If you don't take it, I'm sending both Mattie *and* Jason."

I wished I hadn't brought up the trust. I'd wanted our marriage to be authentic, but in the end, I'd only fooled myself. "Aiden beat Jason in state wrestling, remember?"

"Pfft. That was years ago. Jason does hard physical work all day. Aiden sits behind a desk."

Aiden still had more muscles. More abs. So many abs. He worked out every morning—weekends too. And he fit in another workout most days. My husband punished himself in the gym.

It must've been better than spending time with me.

How stupid could I have been? Had I really thought he'd singled me out during the tour King Oil had given to the library staff because I was that alluring to one of the most wanted bachelors in the country?

The coiled strength. The quiet power.

He hadn't gloated when he'd dominated my brother, a promising candidate for state champ. Aiden had evaluated him until it was time to wrestle. Then he'd methodically worn my brother down and won.

When it was over, he'd shaken hands and walked away. No boasting. No arrogant grin. He'd done what he'd come to do. That should've been my first sign that he was all business and had no time for regular folk—like his wife.

I collapsed backward onto the other armrest. "I was stupid."

"Girl, you ain't been stupid a day in your life." Mom tapped her fingers against her knee. She was jonesing for another smoke.

I should take the money. I had to be able to afford her health care when her lifelong smoking habit put her in the hospital. Jason and Matt each had kids to take care of.

I had no one.

I was thirty-three. I had the career I'd worked for. But my long-held mental image of a husband and kids had fragmented into a pixelated mess that day I'd chatted with Taya at her coffee shop in King's Creek and learned about the trust. The day I'd removed my rose-colored glasses and seen my marriage for what it was.

Nothing.

"I was stupid for Aiden. His whole family knew, Mom."

"Fuck them." She said it so automatically, I doubt she realized when those words left her mouth. It was the McDonough family motto.

"I thought they were…" My in-laws were wonderful. Thoughtful. Witty. Each of them led interesting lives.

"Your shiny new family that was perfect?"

I scowled at Mom. Did she think I ignored them as soon as I'd gotten married?

Had I?

As a kid, I'd wanted to prove that I wasn't a walking stereotype of poor and trashy. I'd worked to talk more like my teachers—one happened to live in the same trailer park. I'd idolized Mrs. Vance. She'd spoken eloquently and happily discussed the classics with me—and how much we'd disliked many of them. Mrs. Vance hadn't stomped through town like she was permanently irritated, like Mom. She'd floated and worn colorful cardigans and T-shirts with witty sayings. She'd been a peaceful lake in my turbulent homelife.

Then there'd been Aiden and his family. The Kings were the opposite of how I was raised. Wealthy, with wide-open spaces. Aiden's brothers were all good people. I had considered their wives friends. But I'd never fit in. Perhaps it was the secret they'd all kept from me that had made me flounder like a fish out of water when I was in their company.

"I liked them, Mom. But I was never one of them."

"You're as good as any of 'em."

How many times had Mom told me that growing up? *They're no better than you, Katie.*

My family dealt out body slams and half nelsons, not witty retorts, but the sentiment was the same. It'd given me the confidence to be the brainiac in class, the nerd no one invited to their party. No matter how different I tried to be, I always had a place in my uncouth family.

"You're as good as any of them too," I replied. Mom and my stepdad, Randall, had worked as hard as any of the Kings. Probably harder. And the return had been less. So much less, but they'd carved out a comfortable niche in this double-wide on the edges of Billings.

Mom arched another penciled-in brow. "That why you brought your *deb-o-nair* husband over so often?"

Aiden had been to exactly one Thanksgiving at my parents' place, and he'd spent most of the time working on his phone. He'd have brought his laptop, but he knew my brothers' reputation from their high school wrestling days and surmised that my two nephews and only niece would be just as rambunctious.

The holidays we didn't go to King's Creek, I hosted at our house. *His* house. "I didn't want to get crap from Matt about Aiden working all the time."

I don't want to think about what you gotta do to get that guy's mind off work, Katie-bear.

Aiden's mind was never off work, so whatever I had to offer hadn't been enough.

"Is it just working?" Mom asked carefully, her tone asking if Aiden had cheated on me. If the answer was no, Mom wouldn't bother with Jason or Matt. She'd hitch up her sweats and charge to the King Oil headquarters building herself.

I twisted my fingers together. "I think so, but it's not like I really know him." I'd thought I had. I'd thought I'd understood him and I'd been willing to accept what he was like. But after that morning at the coffee shop when I'd learned that my husband was so dedicated to the family he'd married a near stranger to guard its money

—I wasn't sure how much I really knew him.

Long hours. Work trips. Meetings when he couldn't be contacted.

My stomach churned. Would I know if he had a mistress, or another family entirely? I'd trusted him. And I'd been wrong.

Mom sucked her tongue against her teeth. "Men are known to think with the wrong head. Have you talked to him about the way you're feeling?"

When would I have talked to him? Would he have cared? "I thought he was a good guy. That was all I wanted. To find a good guy like you found Randall." My stepfather had married Mom and moved us from a dilapidated single-wide trailer to this double-wide when I was two. Randall was quiet, introspective, and a man of his word. "But maybe he's more like Dad."

"He ain't like your dad." Mom snorted and switched the way she crossed her legs. "You'd know better than me."

Would I? Handsome. Charming when he needed to be. More experienced. I'd fallen hard just like Mom had. Only Dad had been more obvious. I'd only been a toddler when my parents divorced. Jason was only ten months older than me, and Mattie was four years older. Mattie remembered the fights. Mom's crying. He and Jason adored Randall, and so did I, but they'd taken to protecting Mom's feelings like Randall did. Which was why I had a relationship with our dad and my brothers didn't.

I loved my dad, but I'd heard all his faults. I knew that he contacted me when he was in town and left my brothers out. Dad went for easy affection, part of his issues with marriage. He would have to work for it. Aiden wasn't like Dad. But lying by omission was still lying. And just because he didn't argue with me didn't mean he wasn't sleeping around behind my back.

My insides twisted. Thinking about

Aiden with another woman tore me in two. It wouldn't be hard for him. The way he looked. The way he dressed. The confidence that oozed from him.

As Mom would say, *That boy'll attract 'em like fly paper tossed into a shit pile.*

I sniffled and swiped the tissue across my nose. "Do you mind telling Randall for me? And the guys? Tell them not to mob Aiden?" I didn't have the emotional bandwidth for talking my siblings off the edge of a cliff. Randall wasn't volatile like my brothers, but he had a protective streak when it came to me and my brothers.

When I had told my family I was marrying Aiden, Randall had pulled me aside and grilled me about how Aiden treated me. At the wedding, he'd split his time between beaming at me and studying Aiden.

"Yeah, I can do that. You need time to think and those boys can make it hard." Mom cleared phlegm out of her throat. "So where are you staying?"

I'd had enough time to think, but Mom had always liked Aiden and the way he devoured her cooking. I fiddled with my tissue. "Can I crash here for a while?"

"Here? You can afford to go anywhere."

"I told him I didn't want any of his money." My wages were funneled into a savings account that I now had to learn to live on.

"What would a McDonough have if it weren't for pride?" She sat forward and slapped her hands on her knees. "All right. I'll get the extra room ready, but, Katie—I don't want you staying here for long. Not because I don't love having you around, but because I know the lows you hit after divorce. I'm not going to let you get stuck there."

Another reason why I'd come here. "All right, and I'll get the room ready." It was my old bedroom anyway. My niece stayed in it when she slept over. "It'll give me something to do."

I'd taken the day off work. My

coworkers thought I had planned a long weekend. No one but the lawyer and Mom knew about the divorce. I'd have to tell my coworkers eventually. At least taking off my ring wasn't an issue. I'd quit wearing my ring a year after I was married. It'd been distracting at work, garnering comments from patrons. I'd told Aiden I was afraid I'd lose it, when the truth was, I just hadn't wanted to force another grin and laugh when someone commented on how heavy such a large diamond must be. Aiden wasn't the only one guilty of lying; he'd just done it first. So today, I'd lie in my old bedroom and wonder why all the fairy tales I'd read growing up couldn't be real.

CHAPTER 3

iden

Four years ago...

I was in Dad's office to update him on development expenditures and plan for the board meeting we'd usually prep for over the weekend. But I was getting married this weekend.

Nerves spread through my stomach. I

never got nervous. I was always prepared. But this wedding was out of my comfort zone. A lot depended on Kate saying "I do," and it wasn't just money. As worked up as Grams had been, I couldn't let her down. She'd called me more in the last six months than all the previous years of my life combined.

Then there were my brothers. How would they react to me failing to secure the trust that Mama had left for us? Word would get out and then we'd have to deal with rampant gossip in King's Creek. Hell, in all of Montana. Which would pale to the hell storm Danny would create if he got the money.

And Dad. Me getting married was supposed to help his stress, but the furrow in his brow was back now that I'd mentioned I'd be driving to King's Creek tonight with Kate to help Dawson prepare the house for the ceremony. The disapproving looks Dad had been giving me since I'd told him I'd proposed to Kate and she'd said yes were pushing the limits of my patience.

"Say it, Dad."

He didn't act surprised, or abashed that I was onto his not-so-subtle scowls. "It's just money, Aiden. Don't start your marriage with a lie."

He assumed that I hadn't told Kate about the trust. I hated that he was right. I refused to get into how I felt about Kate with anyone. I couldn't talk to my dad or my grams or my brothers about it. I couldn't talk with them about anything, really. Not since Mama's death. I hadn't been allowed to then, and the words just wouldn't come now.

Grandpa DB's voice resonated in my head, like it so often did. *Jesus, Aiden. You're the oldest. If your brothers saw you out here crying, what do you think they'd do? Hold yourself together.*

And Dad had been working all the time. When he hadn't been working, he'd been out having a good time. Getting lost in success and women. He hadn't cared about how any of us were feeling, how we were dealing with Mama's death.

Would I like to tell my brothers about Kate? About how I'd met her and what I thought about this wedding? Sure. And it'd go something like, *Look, there's this girl. She's lovely in every way. She grew up in a trailer park, so I took her to places I don't give a shit about but impressed the hell out of her so that when I popped the question weeks after asking her out, she'd say yes. Take notes. You'll all be turning twenty-nine soon enough.*

"My marriage, my business. My *money, my business.*" My business had been serving this company. My work was in the public eye, fodder for the media, my coworkers, Grams, and my brothers. Kate was my business and I wasn't letting anyone else in it.

"You let your grams make it her business."

I scoffed. "Not even Grams can force me to marry." Force? No. Badger? Maybe, but I understood all her one hundred million reasons. "Kate's a nice girl. What are you complaining about?"

"Exactly. She's a nice girl. How do you think she'll feel to know you're not with her because you love her?"

This lecture was rich coming from my father. He chewed up nice girls and spit them out without so much as a backward glance. He didn't know me, but he assumed I didn't love her? He hadn't even bothered to ask.

If he had, I wouldn't have told him anyway. He'd lost his chance to be involved in my private life. "Women are a means to help us get what we want. Isn't that what you've always taught us?"

His recoil at my words was satisfying. "I loved your mother, and when she died—"

"Did you? Or was it because you walked right into a multimillion-dollar job and a marriage once she got pregnant? Because you sure jumped into her best friend's bed quick enough after she died. And then everyone else's." Years of repressed anger threatened to explode. I'd been left behind at the ranch with three grieving brothers while Dad had buried his sorrows in work and other women. I wasn't going to let him weigh in on how I acted with Kate. "Women got you through your grief. Women got you through your midlife crisis. Women get you through the stress of your job. So, Kate is going to help me get what I want, and if you don't want to see her hurt, then don't tell her."

The words were cold, emotionless. If that'd work to get him off my back and keep my secrets from Kate, then I could live with it. That didn't stop more words from clamoring on my tongue. To tell Dad everything. To ease his fears. To explain that Kate meant more to me than a ton of money, but that the restrictions of the trust made me little better than her dad. But the words went unsaid. I'd learned a long time ago that talking was a waste of time.

PRESENT DAY...

THE DOORBELL RANG through the house while my phone buzzed to alert me that someone was at my front door. On any other day, it'd be just another notification, one of many, that I'd get at the office.

I worked most weekends, but Kate had served me on Friday. I hadn't been into the office since I'd shattered the monitor. Dad had suggested in a way that sounded more like an order that I go home and process what had happened while he cleaned the mess and kept my private life private.

I filed for divorce.

How convenient I lived in one of the few states that let us divorce quietly. By mail.

Would getting served at my house have been better?

I sighed and hit the button to unlock the

front door. I didn't bother to see who'd come to visit me. I wasn't up for talking. Besides, Kate wouldn't ring the doorbell.

Would she?

When I'd gotten home two days ago, the bed had been made, like always. But the laundry basket had contained only my clothing, and her part of the closet had been cleaned out. Her toiletries were gone from the bathroom. Her toothbrush no longer stood in the holder opposite mine. She'd never put her toothbrush in the slot next to mine. Always across. I'd wanted to tease her about being afraid to swap germs. But I never had.

There were a lot of missed opportunities when it came to Kate.

The front door opened and closed. I pried my eyes off the TV to see who the poor bastard was that thought I'd be any sort of company.

My brother Beck ascended the stairs, his head clearing the half wall that cut off the split-level flight of stairs from the front door. His cowl-neck sweater and jeans told me he wasn't in town for business. He'd come because of me.

His gaze found me right away and swept down my wrinkled black slacks and the button-up shirt that was hanging open and missing half its buttons. I'd tried to undo the top two but my fingers had fumbled and I'd just ripped the damn thing open.

"Aiden? Shit."

I turned my focus back to the TV. I'd picked a show where the characters were having a shittier time than I was. *Shameless* I think it was called. It also had double digits of seasons so I didn't have to expend the brain power to find something else. Endless *Shameless*.

Beck didn't move from the top of the stairs. His stare bored into me.

"That bad?" I asked dryly.

"Not good."

I didn't have to look at him to know that he was taking in the empty beer bottles at my feet. Those were from yesterday. The empty vodka bottle on the end table was from Friday night—no, Friday afternoon. The Ararat brandy I kept for Dad had run out Saturday morning. And I'd drunk all the beer the rest of Saturday. Good thing I didn't keep much alcohol in the house. My brothers drank beer and they weren't over very often.

So today, I let the hangover steep me in suffering. I wasn't fit for going out in public.

"Have you at least eaten something in the last twenty-four hours?"

I screwed my face up, but my head throbbed. "Maybe?" At some point, I'd stuffed leftover lo mein and an egg roll in my mouth when I'd gone to the fridge for a new beer.

Beck let out a frustrated sigh and went to the kitchen behind me. He rustled around, opening cupboards and banging plates. Each sound ricocheted through my head.

The microwave started and a full water

bottle was set on the end table. Beck leaned over the back of the couch and held out his hand. Two white pills sat in his palm.

I accepted them, popped them in my mouth, and took a few pulls from the ice water. I didn't care what they were, but since I'd had to scrounge for alcohol, the pills were probably just Motrin. "Thanks."

"You smell like a liquor store got into a fight with itself and lost."

"What the hell does that smell like?"

"Have you been in the same clothes since…"

"Since Kate left me?" My chest squeezed. "Yep."

The microwave dinged and he disappeared. A sex scene unfolded on the show. They were doing it in the back of a van.

I hadn't had sex with Kate in the back of a vehicle. I'd wanted to. Several times on the way to King's Creek, I'd been tempted to pull onto one of the side roads, find an approach, and make use of the tinted rear windows of my pickup. She wouldn't have had to undress. I'd crowd in the back seat behind her, tug her pants down, and take her from behind until we fogged up—

Beck found the remote and clicked the show off. A ham and cheese sandwich appeared on a plate in front of me. He'd warmed it enough to melt the cheese and soften the sourdough bread Kate liked.

"Did Dad send you?" I took a bite. It could've been dust between two slices of mud and I wouldn't have known it.

"You weren't answering your phone. I told him I'd check on you."

Because Dad was doing all the work I should be doing. And after all these years, he knew I wouldn't talk to him about my personal life anyway.

Beck sat on the ottoman in front of a high-back chair to my left. "After you're done eating, you're going to shower and change clothes."

I didn't want a shower. But I needed one. I ate the sandwich, one bite at a time.

Beck watched me. My stomach was both grateful and upset at the onslaught of food.

"Dad told me what happened," he said quietly.

I set the plate aside. "Yep."

"You're really upset."

I cut him a glare. "Why wouldn't I be?" He peered at me, and I pressed. "Wouldn't you be fucked up if Eva left you?"

"She did leave me, before we got married. I was fucked up, and you didn't bat an eye."

"What do you mean?"

"You sent me a message that said 'Sorry it didn't work out with Eva' and that was all."

I rubbed my aching temples. The pills couldn't kick in soon enough. "I did more." Hadn't I? I had made sure my brothers were taken care of, that they'd done their homework and eaten supper. I'd even set up a chore chart. Then I'd graduated and left home. On to my next role in life. Scion of the family company.

But I still cared if they were hurting. It'd been clear how much Beck had fallen for Eva. I had to have sent more than a bland message.

"Nope." He tented his fingers. "But I didn't expect anything from you. You've been a robot for so long I almost forgot that you must still have real feelings."

I scowled and winced. Feelings hadn't done me a damn bit of good in life.

"So when Dad said you weren't answering even his calls—and that you'd trashed your office—I realized how mistaken I was."

My stomach clenched around the sandwich I'd eaten. This might be my first hangover, but I wasn't going to throw up. I could only be so pathetic, and I'd tipped the scales too far already. This was why I never drank. Losing control had never done me any good, and no one cared anyway.

"You love her." He said it as if it was a little-known fact he'd never heard before.

"Why do you sound so surprised?"

"Robot."

I tossed out his old nickname for being the family ass-kisser when we were growing up. "Gooder."

"It's not too late, Aiden. If you love her, it's not too late."

"She's going to think I want to keep the fifty million and not her."

"Then prove you love her."

I kicked my feet up onto the coffee table that ran in front of the couch. I refused to let hope creep in. This was Kate we were talking about. She wasn't impulsive. She was measured. Even-keeled. She hadn't rushed into the divorce. She'd thought about it. Contemplated it. She wouldn't have had the papers drawn up if she was undecided.

"You don't know Kate," I said.

"Do you?" That earned him another glare, but he remained unmoved. "Look, I know we haven't been the closest since you left for college, but you've been stuck in your own little world for so many years, I think you've forgotten that the people around you need you." He leaned forward. "*You*. Not what you can do for them. You."

He meant to make me feel better, but he was forgetting that he was one of the people who'd needed what I could do for them. He didn't even realize it—in that, I'd been successful. His lucrative tech company? That would've been a dream, a side hustle at the most, if I hadn't taken up the reins at King Oil. Falling for Eva? Yes, he'd thought he was pulling a fast one when he'd made the fake marriage deal with her. But he wouldn't have had the chance had the public learned about the trust—and they would've, if I hadn't gotten Kate to marry me in time. Our neighbor would've gleefully sold his story to the press. Hell, Danny Cartwright would've given that story away for free. But Danny had gone to his grave oblivious. And Beck had been able to take his time and move forward with the right girl instead of wondering if every woman who talked to him had dollar signs dancing in her head.

So he could get on me about being in my own little world, but he reaped the benefits. They all had. Xander with his travels that didn't revolve around where the oil company sent him. Dawson got to stay at the ranch, which had helped him reconnect with Bristol. Even Dad, who'd had the luxury of dealing with his grief in his own way on his own time. I was the one who'd paid.

Only, Kate had suffered the price with me.

CHAPTER 4

iden

THE LINES of the mahogany conference table widened and narrowed in uneven waves along the surface. The table matched the mantel around the electric fireplace in the conference room. Did the mantel have the same grain lines as the table?

"Mr. King?"

Or had they picked a slab of mahogany that was more refined for mantels? Did they sell them as matching sets? Here's a meeting table, and if you happen to have a fireplace in your posh conference room, then do we have a table for you—

"Mr. King?"

"Aiden." Dad's voice cut through my pondering and I raised my gaze off the dark lines in the already dark wood.

Shit. I was in the middle of a meeting on next year's projected expenditures. A key meeting requiring my participation, and I'd spaced out. The monitor positioned above the fireplace was filled with faces of execs from our satellite offices in Wyoming, North Dakota, and the rest of Montana. In the conference room, Dad, Kendall, Phillip, and six more of our department heads waited on me.

"Right," I said as I scrambled to figure out what the hell to say.

Kendall swooped in for the save. "Why don't I compile the information and disseminate it? Watch for it in your inboxes tomorrow."

Dad jumped in with more instructions about the information he expected to reach his desk—information that needed to come from me, but I was too lost to even look at my files and figure out what to say.

It was my second day back after taking a full week off. I couldn't leave Dad and Kendall to clean up after me any longer. I'd lost my wife. I couldn't lose this job or I'd have nothing. I also couldn't cost anyone else their job. In order to do that, I had to be in my office, files in front of me, working like I always did.

"All right, everyone. Have a good weekend." Dad tapped twice on the table between us. He wanted me to stay behind.

Kendall gathered her tablet and phone and chatted with Phillip as they wandered out.

As the room cleared, Dad murmured, "Can I talk to you in your office?"

I dipped my head and avoided looking at anyone. Dad followed me up to our floor and into my office.

He closed the door behind us. "How's it going?"

I sat behind my desk. "Oh. You know." If pondering wood grains in office furniture during important meetings was okay, I'd reassure him I was fine.

I wasn't fine.

His concerned gaze brushed over me. My stubble was morphing into a full-fledged beard, my hair hadn't seen more than a finger comb in days, and I was wearing the wrinkled suit that I'd worn the day before my world had been upended. I was running out of laundry and dry cleaning hadn't occurred to me in the last week.

He sat in the chair across from me. "Have you talked to Kate lately?"

"We've messaged."

He cocked his head. "And?"

I let out a gusty breath. Discussing my impending divorce wasn't going to help me do my job. "And what, Dad? She wants to know when we should meet and sign the papers."

Dad's sigh was quiet but so was my office. It was as loud as a tornado. Guilt snaked through me. He didn't have time for this, for my lack of attention to tasks only I could do. He had to be swamped, both him and Kendall burning the midnight oil, sacrificing sleep and time together while I'd been useless on my couch, watching the whole damn series of *Shameless*.

Protecting Dad from overdoing it used to be enough motivation to keep me in the office, especially after his heart attack. But this divorce had blindsided me.

"Have you two actually talked?" he asked.

"I'm afraid we're past that point."

"You still have time."

I didn't respond. First Beck. Now Dad. But neither of them knew my wife.

"Where's she staying?"

I shrugged and stared at the black screen of my computer. Kendall had requested even visual notifications be silenced when IT set up my new monitor. "I dunno. Her parents' place maybe. A hotel."

"Have you asked her?"

"It's apparently none of my business," I said bitterly. Unlike me, Kate normally shared what was going on in her life. If she hadn't told me, she didn't want me to know.

Dad let out a long breath and pinched the bridge of his nose. "Goddammit, Aiden. You've mastered everything you've done in your life. You made state wrestling. Magna cum laude at college. King Oil wouldn't be where it is if you sucked at your job. You're here because you're the best. Direct some of that energy and determination to your marriage."

I ignored the part about my job. I was where I was because I was a King. I would've been fired years ago otherwise. I shifted my gaze to him and spoke slowly. "She had the papers already drawn up." Behind my back, which had been easy, since I was never home.

"Have you been faithful?"

I rocked forward so suddenly Dad flinched. "Of course I have." He couldn't step out of my life whenever it was convenient for him and then charge back in and assume the worst about me when it came to Kate.

"Does she know that?"

I'd never strayed. *Never.* "She should."

"All she knows is that you didn't tell her about something that she thinks was your sole motivation for marrying her. All she knows is that you didn't tell her she'd get half and so she assumes that's why you're still married. Does she know you didn't give her your mother's wedding ring?"

I winced. Those rings were Mama's. She'd never liked me abusing the entitlement I'd grown up with. So ironically, I'd bought a giant ring for Kate. One that she looked at as if it'd grow fangs and bite her. "I bought her a ring that's her own."

Dad's infuriating, steady gaze told me I

hadn't answered his question. "She's going to question everything. The late nights. The work trips. The hours you spend on your phone or your laptop around her."

"You do the same around Kendall."

He ticked a finger out. "One, Kendall works at the company. She knows what I do better than anyone." Another finger. "Two, I didn't have a trust hanging over my head with stipulations." A third finger went up as his gaze intensified. "Three, and this one is the most important, *we talk*. We talk about how we feel, we talk about work, and we talk about *us*."

I clenched my jaw. I lost on all three points. No wonder my marriage had been taken down by a little gossip.

"It's the talking, Aiden, that's the most important. When your mother died, I held it all in. I did what felt good and took the pain away. I filled a gaping hole with temporary company and kept it all to myself and it wasn't until you—" He rubbed his temples. "It wasn't until it looked like you married Kate for the money that I realized I'd been a piss-poor example of a man."

This was the first time Dad had acknowledged, to me at least, that his promiscuous behavior had been tied to grief, to not knowing how to deal with Mama being gone and having four kids to raise on his own. He'd had the luxury of getting away, of finding some solace in someone. I hadn't had that.

The sharpest edge of my resentment dulled. He'd been hurting, and I'd been angry at him for so long, so damn furious, that I hadn't been able to look at it directly. Instead, I'd focused elsewhere: single-minded determination to secure the fiscal future of all things King.

I was exhausted.

I'd resisted defending myself for so long that it was difficult to form the words on my tongue. "I didn't marry Kate for the money." It came out flat and lacking conviction, but it was better than saying nothing. Would he believe me?

Dad scooted to the edge of his seat and pressed his fingertips together like he was in a board meeting. The same move Beck had pulled. "If you want to stop the divorce, then you need to talk to your wife. But first, you need to think about what kind of husband you want to be, and if it's the kind of husband she'd want."

What kind of husband I wanted to be? I provided. I could give her anything she ever wanted. Except Kate wasn't a woman who gave a damn about things. If she did, she wouldn't have been daunted by the money.

She treasured the people in her life. Her family. Friends. Coworkers. Patrons at the library. I'd used her to land the family treasure and then had taken her for granted. I'd put off talking to her, convinced I'd do it later, that there'd be a better time that would somehow make my lies hurt less.

Later was here and she was gone.

I had succeeded in securing the trust and the company. Could I secure a future with Kate?

No, the question was, could I secure a future with Kate where she knew the real me?

Did I even know who the real me was?

Kate

IT WAS AN UNUSUALLY warm autumn day. I'd made it through two weeks of work, and I'd done it without telling my coworkers I was getting divorced. I hadn't been able to tell anyone since I hadn't confirmed with Aiden a time to meet and discuss the terms of the divorce so we could each sign.

It had been two weeks since I'd last seen him or talked to him. Our messages were short and infrequent.

The confusion in his gaze when I'd told

him I wanted a divorce haunted me. The way he'd shouted after me as I had left. He never raised his voice. Aiden was steady, restrained. Frustratingly so.

"Katie can do it," Jason taunted.

I tipped my head up, straightening in the lawn chair I reclined in on the porch Randall had built off the back door of the house. It took up a quarter of the small yard, but when it was nice out, my family used it like another living room. Jason circled his oldest boy, Caleb, on the brown lawn. We'd gotten a dusting of snow earlier in October but the last of it had melted two weeks ago.

The grass crunched as they circled. Caleb, a lanky twelve-year-old, would lash out with his hands, trying to capture his dad's legs for a takedown or get a collar grip on his neck. Jason would dance out of his way.

"Stalling," I called.

"Told ya," Jason said to Caleb. "She

knows what she's talking about. Who do you think Mattie and I practiced with?"

Caleb shot me a disbelieving look.

With Mattie, I wouldn't have called getting my face ground into the carpet practice. That had been his excuse when Mom had yelled at him to leave me alone. Jason had been serious about the sport and having someone similar in age and size—until he'd had a growth spurt—to work on takedowns with anytime of the day had been convenient.

Randall chuckled from the other side of the deck. His curly black hair was trimmed short with shoots of gray through it. "Caleb doesn't believe you." He gave me a sidelong look. "You should prove him wrong. Dust off those moves."

How long had it been since I'd messed around in the backyard with my brothers? I had been older than Caleb's twelve, but by the time I'd left for college, I had left all the roughhousing behind. During holidays, my nephews usually defaulted to wrestling until their mom or mine got after them. I'd always sat out. Then I'd married and missed more holidays than I cared to think about.

I stood and toed out of my canvas slip-ons. "Those moves were more impressive when I wasn't an adult facing off with a twelve-year-old."

"Aunt Katie?" Caleb straightened, forgetting his dad. He didn't think I'd follow through.

I shed my silver hoodie and tucked my Under Armour T-shirt into my black yoga pants. "If you can wrestle a grown woman, then you won't bat an eye when you face off with someone who dehydrated themselves into your weight class."

"Told ya," Jason repeated as he backed away, his hands held in surrender.

I windmilled my arms as I crossed to Caleb. Cool, dry grass crunched underfoot. Randall kept a healthy lawn. It'd be perfect to practice on in the summer if it weren't for the grass stains. All I'd be after this was gritty.

I adopted the same stance as Caleb, knees and arms bent, and circled him.

The screen door from the house slammed shut. "Holy crap," my other nephew, Corbin, cried. He was ten years old and just as stunned.

"Door." Randall's reprimand was absentminded. After all, he'd been saying it for over twenty years with three different doors. "The glass is going to shatter one of these days."

"Sorry, Grandpa." Corbin strode onto the lawn and waited by his dad. "Aunt Katie wrestles? I thought it was just Uncle Aiden."

"Aunt Katie wrestles." Jason's mouth quirked.

The screen door squeaked again. I didn't look over my shoulder, but Matt said, "Maybe if Katie wrestled Uncle Aiden more, she wouldn't be here."

I shot him a glare, and nearly flipped him off like we were kids again, but his grin was unrepentant. When Caleb lunged for me, I knew that had been Matt's intention:

throw me off. I had Matt's support with my divorce—but he was still my jackass brother.

I shuffled away from Caleb's scrawny arms, keeping just out of reach while looking for an opening like Randall had taught me.

Both of my brothers had rallied around me. Jason's wife, Sophie, had brought me a few pints of ice cream and given advice that was similar to Mom's. *Fuck him.* Matt's girlfriend had sent memes every day to make me laugh.

"Neither boy has seen you wrestle, Katie," Randall said as Caleb and I returned to facing off. Was the kid seriously advancing on me? "That means it's been over twelve years. Don't hurt yourself." His deep chuckle only told me he was doing the same thing as Matt: trying to psych me out.

Caleb was half my size and probably didn't wrestle nearly as dirty as his dad had. I could take him.

Billings hadn't had much for girls

wrestling when I was growing up. Mom would've gone head-to-head with the wrestling club if I'd wanted to officially hit the mats, but I had been an odd duck already. I couldn't be the girl who wrestled with the boys. It wasn't unusual now, my seven-year-old niece wrestled too, but I hadn't been a trailblazer.

Caleb reached for one of my legs halfheartedly. I'd have to make him take this seriously. Take *me* seriously.

I snaked my arms out, catching him behind one leg. Muscle memory kicked in and I executed a flawless single-leg takedown. His back hit the ground and he didn't have time for a sprawling defense before I was on him.

His training kicked in. He bridged and twisted, his slight weight straining against my hold. I'd have plenty of time to take it easy on him. First, he needed a lesson.

I rolled over him, using my size as an unfair advantage. After all, my only experience had been with my brothers and fairness didn't count when it came to siblings.

Jason hit the ground on his knees and slammed his hand on the ground. "That's a pin for Katie." He laughed.

I let Caleb up. He shot to his feet and dusted himself off. "That wasn't fair. She's bigger than me."

"But you're not going to underestimate me again, are you?"

Caleb puffed his long bangs out of his face. "I didn't."

I stood and clapped him on the shoulder. "You did too. You were thinking 'there's no way this old lady can take me down. I might hurt her.' "

Pink brushed across his cheeks. "Did not."

"Did too." I ran my hand around my waist to make sure my shirt hadn't gotten tugged out. "Again?"

His little-kid grin warmed my heart. "I ain't going soft on ya."

I loved spending time with my nephews.

I hadn't done enough of it beyond spectating at their matches and games, going to plays and music performances. The last two years, I'd slacked off. Facing the inevitable "Where's Aiden?" had caused more anxiety than it was worth. I'd avoided the family that had always had my back no matter how much I'd tried to be different from them.

Never again.

I grappled with Caleb. He was a strong kid, but he hadn't hit his growth spurt yet. My body remembered all the moves. How to breathe so I didn't get tired out. How to roll and twist in a way that wouldn't hurt him, but would give him enough experience to make it worthwhile.

"I'm next. I'm next." Corbin danced around us.

I took turns between the boys. I wouldn't be able to walk tomorrow after pulling half the muscles in my body. My workouts until now had been as pointless and lonely as my marriage. The gym in our house—Aiden's house—had all the amenities, everything but other people. It had seemed wasteful to join a gym when I had all the same equipment under my roof and twenty-four-seven access to any group fitness class I could stream. I had thought of taking up swimming just so I could justify the cost that I had no problem covering in order to be around other people.

I'd have to factor going to the gym into my budget and my time. Same with being with my family.

My distraction cost me. Corbin took after his dad and the little bugger tickled me during one round.

"You little shrimp," I gasped between giggles. Jason used to do the same thing when he got tired of practicing. "I'm going to make you pay."

"I'll save you, Corb!" Caleb jumped in and I had to summon all my rusty knowledge to keep from being pinned and tickled by both of them.

The screen door squeaked. Had Mom come out to watch? My niece Violet?

"Kids," Jason said. "That's enough." Why wasn't he egging them on? That was more like him.

They didn't listen. I barked out a laugh as Corbin tried to roll on top of me, as if his slight weight could pin me.

"Boys," Jason barked.

Caleb heaved off me first, hearing the warning tone in his dad's voice. Corbin tried to get in a last armpit tickle, but I hooked my arm around his neck and put him into an illegal headlock with his arm cocked and immobile in the air.

I was raking my knuckles over his scalp for an auntie noogie when the way Jason said, "Um, Katie?" made me stop.

I puffed my hair out of my face and twisted around. My heart hammered once. Twice. The guy standing next to Jason was the hottest, sexiest, most mouthwatering man I'd ever seen. Tall. Built. His long-sleeved Henley hugged his torso like it had been sculpted onto his biceps and abs. Powerful legs filled out worn blue jeans. What rocked me wasn't the unruly cowlick that hadn't been ruthlessly shellacked into place with hair gel, but the rugged scruff covering his strong, square jaw.

He was all things masculine. He oozed sex appeal. And he looked at me like he'd never seen a rumpled mess of an aunt wearing dried grass clippings and a shirt twisted around her stomach.

Air whooshed out of my lungs. "Aiden."

CHAPTER 5

iden

MY MIND STRUGGLED to register what I was seeing. Three red-faced and sweaty people, two kids and one adult, laughing in a carefree way I hadn't heard since before Mama died. My nephews peeled away, leaving Kate in the middle of the brown lawn. Her hair was a tangled flurry and her shirt had ridden up to reveal a patch of creamy skin above her yoga pants.

Her wide smile died and took the mischievous glint with it. I was tempted to back up, retrace my steps like I could rewind life, just to put that gleam back in her eyes. Sexy. Alive. Unreserved.

Kate was a mess. I'd never seen her in such a state. When we went to King's Creek to work cattle, she kept to the fringes and made coffee runs. She came out the cleanest out of all of us. But in a trailer park in Billings, in the middle of a lawn, after she'd been wrestling—and I'd been here long enough to see that she knew what she was doing—she was the dirtiest of us all. And I fucking loved it.

She stood and dusted herself off. Randall rose, towering over me like usual. He was older than Dad by several years, but age hadn't stooped his back.

"Jason," Randall said. "Why don't we go help your mom set the table." He clapped a big hand on my shoulder but I couldn't take my gaze off a stunning Kate. "You staying for a bite?"

I couldn't tell from his tone if he wanted me to. Randall would offer to be polite, but he'd boot me the hell out if Kate asked him to. "I just want to talk to Kate."

Kate glanced from me to her stepdad and gave a little nod. In less than a minute, I was alone with my wife. I stood on the porch and she didn't move from her spot on the grass.

"Hi," I said.

She pushed her hair off her face, but half of it fell over her eye again. "What's going on?"

"We should talk."

She crossed her arms. In typical Kate fashion, there wasn't an ounce of cleavage showing, but my gaze was drawn to her breasts anyway. It'd always been drawn to her breasts since the first time I'd seen her. I'd always been drawn to her tits, and when she was naked and underneath me it was hard to keep my brain powered up enough to keep from doing anything but staring at them.

"You had a chance to look at the papers?"

Fuck the papers. "Not yet."

She blinked and shoved her hair behind her ears. She didn't wear much makeup normally, but today she didn't have an ounce on. The natural beauty that made her stand out in a crowd kept me riveted.

"Then what's wrong?" she asked.

I took the steps down to the cement landing and kept going until I reached her, my athletic shoes crunching through the grass. "I know the timing looked bad, and no, I wasn't going to let that money go to the neighbors when Mama left it for us, but us—you and me—it wasn't about that."

If I'd expected her to fall into my arms, it wasn't working. Her gaze grew guarded. "You're going to have a hard time convincing me of that when fifty million's riding on the divorce. I told you I don't want it."

"I don't either. I'd rather have you."

She took a step back, creating more

distance between us. "You had four years to show me that you wanted to be with me. You did everything but be with me."

"I can change."

She worked her lower lip between her teeth and stared at the ground between us. What was she thinking?

"Please believe me, Kate." I didn't know what else to ask. I didn't know *how* else to ask. *Please look at me like you have been since I first saw you. The way* only *you ever do.*

I was so far out of my element. There was a reason I'd left my messy emotions in my childhood.

"And then what?" The question overflowed with challenge.

"What do you mean?"

"You're going to have the same job. Grams won't trust anyone else in the inner office. If we take the trust out of the equation, you're still married to your job, not me."

"I'll work on it." *I'll work on me.*

She tipped her head and gave me a

dubious look. This was a side of Kate I hadn't seen before. Just like the side that put her nephews in a headlock. How many other parts of her didn't I know? How many times had she been hiding her real feelings around me?

I thought I'd been the only one to do that.

"I'll work on it," I said with more authority.

She squinted into the neighbor's yard, where overgrown weeds encroached on an old warped metal swing set. She wouldn't look at me. "For fifty million?"

"Kate, it's not about the money." I stepped closer to her. I wanted to cup her face, capture her plump lips, and kiss her until she melted under me. But I kept my hands at my sides. "Can I have a chance to prove it?"

"We're going to keep circling back. Your job, the money. I…don't trust you anymore. I don't know if I ever should have."

"What do you mean?"

She gave me another look that I'd never seen before. One filled with disappointment aimed at me—and staggering insecurity.

Why the insecurity? Dad's hard words in my office trailed through my brain. The one time he'd gone full parent on me and he'd been right. If he hadn't talked to me, would I even get what she was asking now?

My brows drew together. "Do you think I've been with someone else?"

Before Kate, my dating life had been dismal. I'd gotten hit on enough, and if I'd wanted to get laid, it hadn't been hard. But by the time I was done with college, I'd gotten tired of the small talk. The shallow get-to-know-you phase that didn't dive too deep because neither of us wanted to waste time on someone who would prove temporary. I had been old enough when Mama died to know what it'd been like between her and Dad. They'd been best friends and I'd wanted the same.

I thought that was what I'd had with Kate, but after today, I was coming to the awful realization that I didn't know her very well. And it was my fault she didn't know me.

"I don't know what to think anymore." Bare vulnerability shone in her eyes. "Short of lipstick on your collar, you displayed all the signs."

My brain churned in confusion, but hadn't Dad asked the same question? "There's never been anyone else. *Never.*" I was faithful. I didn't want anyone else. It shouldn't need to be said.

She nodded, but disbelief lingered across her expression. I shouldn't have had to tell her I was faithful, but I clearly hadn't done enough to keep her from thinking it was a possibility. "Remember when Beck first brought Eva home and they had that engagement party?"

"Yeah?" My skin rippled with dread.

"You were on your phone the whole time until some girl you went to school with sat down to talk to you. You ignored me the entire night."

"I never ignore you."

She barked out a laugh. "You do. All the time. It's rude. It's disrespectful, and you know what? I don't have to put up with it anymore. I don't care if your excuse was work or a piece of ass, I'm done."

"My excuse was never a piece of ass. I don't just work at some company. It's my family's company. *I'm* the company. In a small city, surrounded by rural towns, I can't disconnect from it. I don't have that luxury. I can't ignore anyone, because they might be a contact I have to deal with in the future."

"But it's okay to ignore your wife?"

I snapped my mouth shut. That was what I'd done. I hadn't wanted to ignore her, but there was the trust between us. My work. As each brother married, I'd waited. Waited for Kate to learn what I had done. I hadn't cheated on her, but I wasn't much better than her father.

"Listen to yourself, Aiden. You came here to, what? Ask for me to come back? Only you're arguing about everything I'm saying. You're not even trying to understand." She edged around me. "Do you realize this is our first argument? We've been together for over four years and we're only now arguing. Our relationship wasn't healthy."

"We're talking now. We can work on us."

"I don't like how I am with you." She put her fingers to her lips like she wanted to stuff the words back in.

Silence fell between us as we both processed what she'd said.

The Kate I saw today wasn't the Kate I was married to. What she didn't know was that this Kate was the one I wanted. The one I thought I'd married. Yet I'd been too ignorant to notice she'd changed.

"I didn't realize you were so unhappy," I finally said. I should've. I should've gotten to know my wife well enough to know that her smile was a cover.

"I didn't either," she replied softly. "I think you are too."

Unhappy was better than fucking miserable. There wasn't a mental box big enough to shove that emotion into. "Where are you staying?"

"Here."

She could buy her own house and be moved in a day. We had the money. But then she'd be alone, and wasn't that what she'd just told me was part of the problem between us?

"For how long?"

"As long as it takes."

Shadows darted past the window. The kids were watching us. The adults were probably getting updates from them. The screen door banged open and Matt's daughter, Violet, ran out. She sprinted past Kate and jumped into my arms. I didn't see her often, but whenever I was around, she was my shadow, firing off a million questions.

"Uncle Aiden, guess what?" she asked

like she hadn't intruded on the most important conversation of my life.

"What?"

"Chicken butt." She chortled, her seven-year-old little face lighting up.

A chuckle I hadn't thought was in me escaped. I set her down. How had she grown twice as much as the last time I'd seen her? "I used to get my brothers with that all the time."

"Uncle Jason taught me." Her proud smile displayed two top teeth growing in. "Come inside. It's time to eat."

I wished I could take her hand and follow her in. But I'd only make a large family gathering awkward. Kate's family was here to support her, not me. "I can't stay, kiddo. Run on in."

She grinned and skipped inside.

When my gaze returned to Kate, my chest grew tight. Sadness filled her eyes. I was the cause.

I couldn't quit trying to make things right between us. "Can you give me some time? I don't want to rush this." I took a step closer. "It's too important to me."

You're too important to me. I had feared losing her, of being the villain in her fairy tale. My silence had done exactly that. I didn't know how to rectify that. Yet I had come here, knowing I had to try.

She inspected me like a bloodhound on the scent for a lie. Would she see the sincerity in my gaze? I didn't know what else to say. I fought for words, but they weren't there. All those years of not talking, of stuffing my emotions down, had left the well dry. Practice made perfect and I'd benched those skills long ago.

"Yeah, fine."

Relief almost made me sag. I'd take what I could get. "Okay." I had a chance, and that was all I was going to get today. "Bye, then."

She gave me a small smile. I turned toward the gate on the side of the house to get to my pickup parked on the street. But before I reached it, the screen door opened again. My mother-in-law came out with a plastic container. She held it out over the porch railing. "I made more than enough."

My stomach chose that moment to remind me I'd had little more than sandwiches and beer in the last two weeks. Other than when I went to Dawson's, I rarely had home-cooked food. Dad and I stocked the office, and I was hardly home in time for a meal. I accepted the food. Giving back the container would give me another excuse to stop by. "Thank you, Sharon."

"Mm-hmm." She turned away.

I caught Kate's perplexed expression before she smoothed it over. She did that a lot. Hid what she was really thinking. From me. Did she do that with everyone else? Were her parents and brothers the only people she was comfortable being Kate McDonough around? Around me, my family, and the rest of town, she was Kate King.

I should've seen it. I came across it often enough in the boardroom, being told what someone thought I wanted to hear. I hadn't expected to find it in my own house, with my wife. But now that I knew, I wouldn't forget. All those hours in the office were going to be good for something.

Kate

I WALKED OUT OF WORK, keys in my hand. The sun was sinking low. I'd only worked until five tonight, but the sun set early this time of year. I walked past my coworkers' cars to mine. Movement by the back end caught my attention and my heart leapt, then fell. After Aiden had appeared at my parents', I'd been looking for him everywhere over the last week.

Kendall gave me a tentative smile, looking young and sophisticated in a way I could never attain. Her hands were shoved into her long beige knit coat, which matched her wedge boots. Her hair was in a long, sleek ponytail. "I should've messaged you, but I wasn't sure how much you hated us."

"I don't hate you." I couldn't deny the reverberating disappointment that'd been a constant companion with my loneliness and heartbreak. "But I'm hurt."

"Want to grab a drink with me and talk?"

I didn't really. I missed chatting with Kendall. She'd become a friend I didn't get to see often enough, but the betrayal left behind after learning about the trust couldn't be ignored. Avoiding it wasn't going to do me any good though. "Sure. It's been a long day. Can we go somewhere quiet?"

The Kings weren't the only ones who could keep a secret. No one outside of my family knew about the divorce yet. But if I showed up at the Irish pub any more times this week, people were going to talk.

"We can grab a beer and burger down

the road. It won't be quiet, but less eavesdropping." Kendall didn't want anyone overhearing her business either.

"Meet you there."

I found parking easily enough on the street. Thursday nights could get busy but it was early yet.

The noise in the bar and grill was a low thrum as we were led to a table in the corner. I skipped the beer and ordered a burger and water. Kendall did the same.

"How did you know when I'd be done with work?" I asked when the server left.

Kendall flashed a small smile. "Aiden."

I bit the inside of my lip to keep from asking how he was doing. He'd asked for time. I hadn't bothered him. I dreaded hearing that after another week to think he was ready to sign the papers. I dreaded it as much as I anticipated his name flashing on my screen.

"He's eased back into work after that first week," she said.

"What do you mean?"

Her brows lifted. "He took a week off. Just walked out after…" She pursed her lips. "Walked out isn't accurate. Gentry 'suggested' he go home after he threw his computer screen across the office. Didn't you know about that?"

Why would I? "I haven't really talked to him in the last couple of weeks."

Sympathy filled her gaze. "I can't imagine how you must feel." She flattened her hands on the table. "We all feel terrible. I don't know if it'll help you to know that it wasn't like a big conspiracy to keep you in the dark. It was just…as individual couples, we all suspected that you didn't know since you never mentioned it. None of us wanted to be the one to spill the beans."

"I know it wasn't, ultimately. Aiden should've told me." I lifted a shoulder. "You're right. It felt like a conspiracy."

"I don't know what happened when Aiden learned about the trust. I know that he met you after, and I don't know what he was like before then, but he doesn't seem like the type to use people."

"He fosters relationships that might be good for business later." *Always an agenda. Just like Dad.* No, that wasn't fair. If Aiden hadn't cheated, then no, it wasn't like my dad. But I'd kept Dad in my life even after I had heard all the stories about him. He was my father. I didn't want another man who talked to me when it was convenient for him and didn't think about me otherwise.

Kendall leaned forward, her gaze earnest. "But the money, Kate. You and I didn't grow up like them. We know the struggle of a family that needs to support a lot of kids. Money doesn't affect them like it does us. It was the fact that the Cartwrights would get it when Danny was alive."

"It's still a lot of money. And he thought he'd lose half, but I don't want it."

Kendall's gaze turned confused and she chewed the inside of her cheek. "If that was the case, why hasn't he done anything with it? Why sit on it? He only needed to be married a year. It's been four, but he hasn't touched it. Even if he fears losing half, what is he going to do with it? Why hasn't he done it yet?"

Those were just some of the constant stream of questions I had that needed answers, but I wasn't sure I could trust his answers. "I don't know."

"He might've been afraid of losing you. Because then he'd have to tell you about all of it."

"I don't get why he thought I wouldn't find out."

Kendall was quiet for a moment before she said, "I'm sorry. We all are. It just turned out really shitty."

"Agreed." I didn't elaborate. My marriage had been shitty for a while. It had taken the talk with Taya to know why.

Our food arrived, and right as Kendall took a large bite, I blurted, "Did he really not work for a week?" To save Kendall from an awkward silence while she chewed, I continued, "I saw him last Friday and he looked…" Hot. Sexy. Like divorce suited him. "Good."

"Beck saw him the weekend after…" She winced. "Aiden was hungover. Liquid diet for days, if you know what I mean."

"Aiden doesn't really drink." He had a few beers when he got together with his brothers, and maybe one drink if he was schmoozing other execs.

"He did that weekend. A lot."

I scanned the restaurant. Happy couples dining together. A family with an older baby. The mom was trying to feed the little boy a french fry, but he wanted to wave it around like a baton. I shifted my gaze away before I started thinking about what I'd put on hold at Aiden's request.

How was I supposed to interpret the information about Aiden? Aiden didn't lose control. The only time Aiden lost control was when he was coming.

Heat washed through my body and I

squirmed. For my own sanity, I couldn't think about anything sexual with him.

"Anyway," Kendall continued, "Gentry moved some projects around to take the pressure off all of us and is running interference with Grams."

"Does she know?"

"We haven't told her. Neither of you need that right now."

"Thanks." A whole week off from work? And Aiden had just walked out? "Did he really throw a computer screen?"

"Right after you walked out. Gentry got it all cleaned up, but Aiden kept not coming in for work. Gentry couldn't remember the last time he'd seen him in sweats. He's taking it hard and, sorry if I'm out of line, but I don't think it's because of the money. When he's around you, he's…lighter." She fiddled with a fry. "I shouldn't say this, I've stepped in enough that's not my business, but Gentry says that when Aiden's around you and his brothers, he sees more of the kid he was before Sarah died. He said Aiden was a true mama's boy."

My lungs deflated. This trust mess had all started with Sarah's death. Why hadn't I connected the dots backward a little more? He'd lost his mother, and he rarely talked about her. But sometimes when we were in King's Creek, he'd get this faraway look that tugged at my heart. He'd shake himself out of it and look around like he hoped no one had seen him. I'd pretend like I'd just caught his gaze and smile, and I'd leave it at that.

"And the way Gentry dealt with it afterward"—Kendall waved her hand around as if she could conjure a glimpse of the past—"wasn't good. He was there for the boys physically, but not emotionally. He's talked before about how he was afraid it affected the guys. I mean, if Sarah hadn't made those trusts for each of the boys, they all might still be alone."

I nodded and dug into my food. For the rest of the conversation, I steered clear of my divorce, and if she noticed, she didn't make any attempts to return to it. After an hour and a half, we parted ways and I went to Mom and Randall's place.

I'd been staying with them for three weeks. They said it was fine, but I doubted they wanted their grown daughter crashing their time together. Both of them worked full-time and then there was me, invading their evenings and taking up bathroom time in the morning.

Finding my own place would be easy enough. I could go back to apartment life. Live in a place that would fit into the garage of our house. *His* house. My gut clenched. No doubt the apartment I found would have a bigger bedroom than the one I slept in now.

I pulled up in front of the trailer. The streetlight in front of my parents' place was out. The rest of the street was quiet. I enjoyed the quiet of the neighborhood and the bite of cold in the air that promised snow in the near future, taking my time going to the door. The talk with Kendall was on my mind, but I wanted to wait until I was in pajamas in bed before I thought about everything she'd told me. When it was dark, I could think clearly.

That was what I told myself.

Inside, I was taking off my coat in the entryway when Mom appeared around the corner, her hands clasped together.

I set my tote bag on the washing machine. "Sorry, Mom. I didn't think to let you know I wasn't going to be home in time for supper. I already ate."

"No problem. We ended up having company, so there won't be too many leftovers."

The street was lined with vehicles, but I hadn't paid attention. "Who?" I asked as I followed her to the dining room.

Aiden rose from the table. He was in his business clothes, but he'd shed his suit coat and tie. The top button of his shirt was undone. I forced my gaze to stay on his face instead of tracing down his wide shoulders and admiring how his defined chest tapered to his waist. If he turned around, all bets were off. His ass was unfair.

"I returned your mom's container, and she invited me to stay since you weren't home."

Mom grunted and picked the serving dishes off the table. Randall rose to help her. Stuffed pork chops. Damn. My burger had been good, but not miss-Mom's-stuffed-pork-chops good.

"I admit to being selfish," Mom said. "He eats my food like he can't afford the best in town."

The corner of his mouth twitched. "Yours *is* the best in town."

Mom rolled her eyes but turned her back before we could see her smile. Randall lifted his chin toward the hallway. "Go on and talk in your room or something. I'm afraid there's not much privacy anywhere else."

"And outside is too cold," Mom added.

Their backs were to us. Were they pushing me and Aiden together?

I shifted my gaze to Aiden. He hadn't taken his eyes off me. I could kick him out, but after my earlier talk, maybe Aiden and I needed a few more words. "You mind?" I asked.

His shoulders relaxed. "No."

I should've picked the office, but there was only one chair. The way Aiden sat in an office chair was sinful. He did that lean thing, with one elbow on the armrest. He'd been sitting like that when I'd dropped the papers off and I might lose my nerve if I saw it again. But having him tower over me while I asked him personal questions wasn't the answer either.

That left my bedroom. My tiny bedroom with the twin bed.

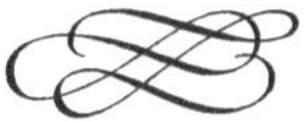

iden

KATE CLOSED the door behind us. We were shut into a tiny space with nothing but a bed to sit on.

She crossed her arms and sat on the edge of the mattress. "So you got Mom's stuffed pork chops, huh?"

I took the middle, leaving some space between us. "Just don't ask me to pick between her and Dawson for who's better."

She plucked at the edge of the black skirt she wore over black leggings. "I wasn't home because Kendall caught me after work."

I studied her face, trying to find a hint of how the talk went. "She asked if you had a regular schedule, but she didn't tell me she planned to jump you today."

Her smile was brief. "She didn't jump me. But she basically apologized on behalf of all your siblings and their spouses."

"Did it make you feel better?"

She thought for a moment. "Yes. It helped."

"Good. I mean it, Kate. I never wanted to hurt you."

She opened her mouth to say something, then shut it.

"Go ahead." I leaned closer and she tensed, but she didn't inch away and fall off the bed to get away from me. "You've been censoring yourself around me."

Her expression flickered. "Neither of us was as open as we should've been. How come you never talked to me about your mom?"

I went numb inside. I didn't talk about Mama to anyone. My brothers and I shared stories, mostly of the good times, and sometimes we shared our fury over how she'd been stolen from us. I never talked about how it had affected me. My throat thickened and I dropped my gaze to the floor. "It wouldn't help anything."

Kate scooted closer and laid her hand on my thigh. "You should. To someone. Your dad. Your brothers. A professional. It's had an effect on you."

"My *dad*." My laugh was cold and Kate lifted her hand from my thigh. Emotions I hadn't allowed out of a mental box for years piled up behind my sternum. I saw him every day, but I'd given up on talking to him years ago. "Dad kept our routine up, kept us moving forward, but he checked out mentally. It wasn't like I could go sleep around like he did when I wasn't even in high school yet. By the time I reached the age where I could, I had responsibilities. Obligations. It was all I could do to justify sports. And the way Dad acted was…" My breath gusted out. I hadn't told anyone how I'd felt about those years. I'd checked out too, just like he had.

I sagged toward Kate and rested my forehead on her shoulder. I needed the contact. And it was easier to get the words out without her gaze on me. "I did talk to Dad once, you know. Made some comment about how he'd acted." The day in his office before my wedding haunted me. I'd finally called him on his behavior and he'd listened, only I'd done it so he'd lay off me about Kate. A brash emotional outburst that hadn't cost me, but had hurt him.

Her arm draped around my back and I was in the familiar comfort of her hyacinth scent. "What happened?"

"He changed. Instantly. And it almost prevented the relationship with Kendall that gave me my dad back."

"That was his decision, not yours," she

said quietly. "And maybe that pause you gave him made him see what he could have with Kendall. He might've missed some meaningful, healthy relationships because he refused to commit and risk his heart again. But you gave him the time to think." Her chin brushed the top of my head.

I hadn't thought about it like that. All I knew was that I'd finally said something and it had bitten me in the ass. "I've never told you about Grandpa DB."

"None of you talk about him."

"He was like Grams on steroids. Old-fashioned. Hardheaded. Ruthless. Dad's parents left King's Creek and never looked back. They became birthday-card grandparents."

Kate's head tilted before she nodded. "Right. You only hear from them when you get birthday cards. Kind of like my dad."

"With Dad tied up with the company, Grams did what she could. She softened a little for Dawson. I guess she couldn't tell him to man up like Grandpa told me."

"He said that to you? After your mom had just died?"

"I had lost my shit with my brothers and stalked off. Morning chores hadn't been done yet. I was tired of ramrodding three depressed siblings every morning and afternoon, so I said fuck it and hid. Grandpa found me in the barn, sitting on a bucket in the corner, crying."

"And he told you to man up."

"Among other things."

You're not a baby like Dawson. You're old enough to know what's at stake. You're old enough to act like you have a little sense. Sitting here crying when two hundred cattle are relying on you for food? Goddamn it, kid. It's not like you have an oil company to run and hundreds of employees like your dad. You have chores and school. Do you think we're asking too much?

"That's awful." Her arms tightened and she did nothing but hold me. Her cool fire soothed the raging burn around my heart. "You were just a kid. Did he talk like that to your brothers too?"

I hadn't given him a reason to. I'd stood up, kicked the bucket over, and done my chores. I'd even done my brothers' share. Partly so I didn't have to return home so soon. But also so DB would leave them alone and they could have the time to grieve that I wasn't allowed to. "Not as severely. He was old-fashioned. The oldest carries the rest of the family. That's how it was done in his day."

"God, Aiden. I'm sorry."

So was I.

"Does your dad know DB said all that?"

"Grandpa died a couple years after that."

"But you can still talk to him—"

"He's happy now, Kate," I said softly. "He's healthy. I don't want him to stress about the past." His heart attack had scared the shit out of me, out of all of us. I'd been so angry that he'd been distant all those years and then he'd almost been gone for good.

"You're allowed to, you know."

I brushed the backs of my fingers down

her face. "You plan to talk to your dad about how upset you are with him that he doesn't talk to your brothers? Or how you wish he was more than a birthday-card dad?"

"I'll give you that. But there are other people you can talk to."

I didn't want to talk to anyone but her. Her face was an inch from mine. It'd be so easy to capture a kiss, but it was too soon. One small kiss would show me everything I was missing while she was no longer under the same roof as me. "You have to know that I loved you when I married you. I wasn't lying about that."

"Learning about the trust highlighted a lot that's wrong between us."

I caressed her jaw, unwilling to quit touching her. "You're giving me time. Can you give me a little more?"

I cupped her face in one hand as she gazed into my eyes.

I didn't hide myself. I resisted the urge to stuff away the feelings flowing through me into that handy mental box and I let her see inside. Let her see me again, and every turbulent emotion inside.

"It's not about the money?" Her voice was ragged, her anxiety about the foundation we'd just built evident.

"I'll give every damn cent away tomorrow if you tell me to. I just ask we make sure it goes to a worthy cause."

She nodded and swallowed. "I think we both need more time."

Relief soared strong in my chest. Instead of smiling, I blew past my resistance and planted a kiss on her. She jumped but didn't pull away, and I didn't push her further.

I broke away after a couple of seconds. "Have a good night, Kate."

I rose before I could sport an erection and ruin the progress I'd made with her. Before I walked out the door, she said, "Aiden?"

I looked back. Her hair shone golden under the weak light of the room. The multicolored knit sweater she wore cupped her breasts and flared over her rounded hips. Her soft beauty was captivating. Always had been.

"Violet asked me if you could come to her wrestling tournament. It's in a couple of weeks."

The corner of my mouth hitched. Violet had no idea how much I owed her. "I'd love to. Send me the details?"

Kate

BOISTEROUS LAUGHTER SURROUNDED ME. Mom had pulled out the leaf for the table and her card table for the kids. Thanksgiving at her house used to be one of my favorite days, but today my smile was fake and I sat with the group but stayed on the fringes of conversation.

My belly was stuffed. The aromas of turkey, stuffing, and all the fixings lingered in the air. We were at the part of our traditional day when the dishes had been cleaned and we'd lost all the football lovers to the TV, their shouts cutting through the laughter. Mattie would let out a swear word and Jason would whap him with his ball cap. Pie would be in an hour, when we could pile more food in our bellies.

I started the dishwasher and turned. My sister-in-law, Sophie, stood behind me. "It's a nice day. Want to go for a walk?"

The temperature had reached forty degrees today, but the sun was out and the wind down. It felt as good as a sixty-degree day. "That sounds nice."

We each got into our boots and jackets and stepped out. Air gusted around my face, but the sun eased the ache in my temples.

We started walking. The dusting of snow we'd gotten earlier in the week had left a few icy patches that were rapidly melting in the afternoon sunshine. Other than a few lighthearted comments about how nice it was out and how good the food had been, we didn't say much for the first couple of blocks.

Then Sophie glanced at me. "On a scale of one to ten, how bad does today suck for you?"

Sophie had been through a divorce. From what I understood, it had been a short, passionate romance that had burned out as dramatically as it'd started, and they'd both been young. Then she'd found Jason and fallen for his gruff exterior and teddy-bear insides.

"A five. Maybe a six," I answered.

She nodded as if she'd guessed my answer before she asked. "My first year alone was hard. I went from living with my parents, to being with Freddie all the time, to just me."

"I should be used to it." I'd been twenty-eight when I'd married Aiden. I'd had a dorm mate in college, a long-term boyfriend I'd considered staying with after college graduation, then a roommate when

I'd gotten my master's. I'd moved home and been single for a few years before meeting Aiden. "But on holidays, after returning to Billings and being around you guys, then around Aiden's family, this…sucks."

"You weren't really around us a lot though. Was it because of Aiden?"

"I wasn't ashamed of you guys." I snuck a peek at her.

Sophie met my gaze. "Sometimes it felt like it."

I hadn't been… Had I? "Maybe some part of me thought I had to be more a stoic King and less a rowdy McDonough."

Sophie chuckled. "Kate. You're a McDonough, but you're not rowdy."

"They're not exactly rowdy anymore, are they? We've all grown up."

"Except the next couple of hours when football is on, yeah."

I flashed her a smile, but I couldn't leave the conversation there. It would be simple to leave it at me being ashamed of them. But I'd lied to myself long enough. "Every minute of every day, Aiden works. Even when we go to King's Creek, he's got his computer, tablet, and phone. Many times he stays in the office." I tilted my face to the sun for a few moments. "It's hard. Everyone asks where Aiden is, and they're only asking because they care. But it didn't take long before I felt like I should have a sign that read *He doesn't want to be with me, okay?*"

"Ouch." She nudged me. "Sorry I was one of the ones asking."

"It's how I took it. I'd probably have felt lonelier if you hadn't asked. Messed up, isn't it?"

"That's people for you." We turned onto the walking path that ran along the main road by the trailer park. "I was never sure what he thought of us. Every time I got intimidated by him, I reminded myself that he'd played with cow shit growing up."

"He still plays in cow shit. And he really doesn't mean to be intimidating." He was wound so tightly that I feared none of us could unknot him.

"I thought he was an arrogant fuck the first time you brought him to meet us," Sophie announced.

I'd been seeing Aiden for a month, and he'd invited my entire family out to eat, reserving a room for us at the most expensive place in town. "He comes off that way."

"He has resting arrogant face."

"RAF?"

"He's, like, the opposite of Jason. Reserved, cultured, quiet. I can see how that would appeal to someone like you. Not quite opposites attract, but opposite of the men you grew up with. Except Randall."

Randall was as mellow as Aiden, but emotionally available. "I love my dad. But Aiden's nothing like him, so yeah. Part of the appeal." I dropped my focus to the uneven sidewalk. At first Aiden had seemed nothing like Brandt McDonough. Aiden was reliable, loyal, and honest. The honesty part was being tested, but I thought his claims about the trust were genuine. But was that wishful thinking? Aiden hadn't given off greedy vibes as long as I'd known him, but fifty million was a lot to shrug off. And our romance after he'd asked me out had been a light and airy whirlwind. In hindsight, it was exactly what I would expect from some generic rom-com if the hero had to marry some unwitting girl for a lot of money in a short amount of time.

The talk in my bedroom had been raw. And insightful. He was hurting, had been for years, and for so many reasons, he'd refused to talk about it. Until now. Was he protecting others' feelings, or himself?

As we'd talked, I'd gotten the sense that what was wrong between us wasn't about money, but about how he'd grown up. How he'd been treated. The way his worldview had been formed.

Fighting to keep the money in the family, that seemed like him. Reliable, loyal, and honest. Traits that had attracted me.

Part of the reason I'd jumped at the chance to marry him was because he'd seemed so unlike Dad. Then when I'd learned about the trust, he'd resembled him too much. Dad was also gone all the time. Restrictive with his affection. But I wasn't obligated to put up with it because he was family and I'd decided that scraps were better than nothing.

"I respect the hell out of you though," Sophie said.

"Why?"

"You didn't shy away from a millionaire CEO."

"CFO."

"The guy's family owns the damn company. Is there a difference?" She raised a brow and I had no argument. "You married that shit. Like, fuck yeah, Aiden King wants to marry my trailer-park ass."

Laughter escaped me. That wasn't exactly what had gone through my mind. I'd been too afraid to question it.

"Then," she continued, "you're like, my trailer-park ass deserves better and I'm not gonna take your money. The librarian is

dumping the prince. Baller, lady. Baller."
She whispered, "I don't know if the kids say
that anymore."

"Probably not." I hadn't talked much
about my divorce, and this was the first
chance Sophie and I had had to chat. She
didn't know the divorce was on pause.
"We've decided to take some time."

She stared at me. "You have the papers
all drawn up."

I avoided her gaze. "We've been talking.
About stuff that we've never spoken about
before."

We reached an intersection and
simultaneously turned right.

"Kate." Her brows were pinched. "I don't
want to interfere. It's just that my first
husband and I tried to work it out. A few
times. Each time I was so hopeful, but
really, all I did was put my happiness on
hold. I almost did it again, and I would've
missed my chance with Jason if I had." She
gave my arm a squeeze. "I'd love you two
working things out, but I also know you

haven't been the same since you've been with him."

I stopped. "What do you mean?" Aiden had said something similar the other night. That I hid what I was really feeling around him.

She stopped and scanned the neighborhood, but her expression was hesitant. "I mean…you're always dressed like you're ready to go to work. You wear makeup on the regular. Your clothes are nice, and I mean, mine would be too if I had your lifestyle, but you don't"—she twirled her hand around as if she was trying to conjure the right words—"let your hair down anymore. Even when Aiden's not around."

My brows pinched together. I hated that I knew exactly what she was talking about.

She leaned closer. "Has he ever held your hair while you puked?" My expression must've looked as horrified as I felt. "Exactly. You'd probably lock the bathroom door and die before you let him smell a body odor that wasn't Chanel No. 5 or some fancy shit like that."

"I'm not that bad," I muttered.

"You know what Jason did for me when I was pregnant with Caleb? Prenatal vitamins made me nauseous. And how I found out was driving to work after I took one with breakfast. Imagine getting off the interstate as you're vomiting into your shirt."

"Oh my gosh."

"And on the seat belt. Then you get out and the seat belt goes back in—"

"I get it."

"And then you have to get out of the car and it's leaking everywhere cuz you had a bowl of cereal—"

"Sophie."

She crossed her arms and hefted a challenging stare at me. "Jason cleaned it up. All of it. While I was inside crying, taking a shower, he ran the washer and cleaned every crevice of my car. So two questions—is Aiden the type of guy who'd do that for you, and would you let him? If the answer is no to either one, you might want to rethink what love really means."

"Love means cleaning puke?"

She rolled her eyes and her lips twitched. "I know Aiden's stupid rich and can pay for the car to get cleaned, or just buy you a new one, but you know what I mean." She hooked her arm in mine again and dragged me back toward my parents' house. "Just something to think about. There's nothing like being with someone who knows the good, the bad, and the smelly. Marriage can be really smelly." She wrinkled her nose. "Motherhood is smellier."

I laughed with her, but my mind whirled. I thought I'd been oblivious to my unhappiness, but the family I didn't spend nearly enough time with had seen it. That wasn't Aiden's fault.

Did you tell him that? Mom's simple question the day I'd served him papers.

I'd been hung up on the trust and how

little time he spent with me. I'd ruminated on how different or alike than my dad Aiden was. But the truth was I didn't know as much about my husband as I should by now. And I had some responsibility in this failing marriage too.

 iden

I WALKED into the gymnasium that Randall was using for the tournament. His club headquarters was in a room just off the gym, part of a larger community center. He'd started the wrestling club decades ago. Kate said that was how he'd met her mom. Sharon used to clean the center. After they married, she'd brought Jason in for his first lesson and the rest was history.

This weekend's tournament was smaller than most. Only two other clubs had come to town. Randall liked to supplement the season with shorter tournaments that meant the kids wrestled more and sat on the mat waiting to wrestle less.

I stood out in my work clothes, but I was used to that. Still, I should've brought something to change into. My suit jacket was in the pickup, but my steel-gray shirt and black slacks didn't mix with the jeans and sweatshirts of everyone else. Normally, I didn't waste energy on thinking about this stuff, but today I wanted to blend. I wanted to be Uncle Aiden and not the CFO.

A guy my age walked by me on the way to the door. He was holding a little girl around two years old in one arm, and a young boy that must've been part of the tournament held his other hand.

He did a double take. "Aiden?" He jerked like he was going to hold his hand out but they were both claimed. "Been a while."

His name came to me along with an image of him sixteen years ago. A muscular teen with determination in his eyes and headgear protecting his ears. "Craig, how've you been?"

He shrugged and tipped his head toward the kids that were staring at me, his smile rueful.

"Who dat?" the little girl asked.

"An old wrestling buddy of Daddy's," Craig answered. "You have a kid in the tournament?"

I couldn't identify the flip my stomach did. Most of my discussions outside of work centered on light chats about King Oil, and if they went deeper, then the person I was talking with knew I didn't have kids. "No. My niece is wrestling."

"Who's that?"

"Matt McDonough's daughter. You remember him? He was a few years ahead of us." Matt had been in a lower weight class, but whether he'd been eligible to wrestle or not based on his behavior had been more memorable than his time on the mat.

"Violet, right?" Craig barked out a laugh. "She's a bloodthirsty one. I told Mattie that she's going to show us what he could've done if he hadn't been suspended so often."

I chuckled. Matt's wild teen years had made him a laid-back adult, for the most part, and he'd be proud to hear that about his daughter's talent. "She's quite a girl."

"You might have time to catch her. I think she had one more match. Jason's youngest was on the mat when I left." Craig's little girl twisted in his arms and whined. He edged toward the door. "Been a long day for her. Maybe I'll see you here again?"

Tendrils of longing trailed through me. I'd gotten to know Craig as more than an opponent. The guy had wrestled out of Miles City, but we'd seen each other enough for him to feel like a friend, or the closest thing I'd had to a friend outside of my brothers. Seeing him surrounded by kids after enjoying a day of watching what they could do… Those were feelings best left unexamined. I had obligations Craig didn't. "See you."

The stands in the gym were half full. Mats were spread out on the gym floor, covering two-thirds of it. Kids sat on the side, cheering on their teammates, while refs circled the wrestling pairs. I spotted Violet's scrawny body folded over another little girl. Determination narrowed Violet's brown eyes. Her dirty-blond hair was braided and her singlet made her look even smaller than seven years old.

My nephew was done wrestling and he couldn't sit like the other kids. They stood just off the mat, shouting instructions at Violet, but her focus was unwavering. The ref prowled the mat, evaluating her performance.

I smelled the soft floral scent of Kate's favorite shampoo before she spoke. "I think she's going to win by a pin."

My gaze flicked to my wife and stuck.

Her hair was pulled back in a haphazard bun and she wore a dusty-blue ZooMontana sweatshirt that swallowed her body down to her thighs. The jeans she had on hugged her legs all the way to her ankles and on her feet were gray and pink athletic shoes. She looked like the first time I'd seen her. Vibrant. Refreshing. And more interested in the wrestling than the people.

"She's doing good."

Kate's lips curved. "She's on a rampage. She lost her first match and dissolved into tears."

"They all do. When they're this young, they leave it all out on the mat. The older ones just won't admit they feel like crying when they lose. How'd Corbin and Caleb do?"

"Corbin got a medal. Caleb's wrestling for school, so he and Sophie are in Lewistown."

I turned my attention to the kids on the mat. They were so little, but the basic skills were already there. If I'd gotten here earlier,

I could have seen how far my niece and nephew had come since I'd watched a tournament last year. If I could attend these more often, I would recognize kids and witness how much they'd grown.

But…work. More regrets that did me no good. "My meeting ran long."

"On a Saturday?"

My attention flicked back to Kate. Her steady gaze was on Violet, but the hard set to her mouth was new. "It was the best time to meet with the developers we hired to help us integrate centralized financial reporting." I uttered the words with the same emptiness all my excuses seemed to have lately. I had a lot of power at King Oil, but I couldn't control people. I had to be accommodating when it came to people and contractors. The days of being a dictator were over. But I felt the need to tack on, "Once it's fully implemented, it should cut down on the time required to gather data for future mergers and acquisitions."

Kate didn't reply, but that didn't stop me from hanging on the reaction that never happened. Was she upset? Was she glad I'd come, or did she wish I'd skipped?

The time ran out on Violet's period and we waited for the final decision. The ref lifted her little arm and a grin split her face. She didn't win by a pin, but she won. Kate drifted away to join her family, and I followed.

Jason caught my arm. "You mind helping us put everything away? Randall's getting a migraine, and he's too damn proud to say anything."

"No problem." I unbuttoned my cuffs and rolled my sleeves up. The tie was already gone. Damn thing had bugged me all day. I took my shoes off to walk over the mats.

Jason, Matt, and I rolled mats. Kate helped gather record sheets and stack chairs. Jason and Matt herded Randall out the door with instructions to get home before it was too bad to drive. Violet cartwheeled across the gym floor. Her winter coat hung open over her dark blue singlet.

I stacked rolled-up mats in the far corner of the club room. The feeling of being watched itched between my shoulders.

When I turned, Corbin was at the edge of the room. His skinny legs stuck out from his winter coat and his feet were tucked into wide black snow boots. "Hey, Uncle Aiden."

"Hey. Heard you did well."

He nodded, but his intense little gaze darted away.

"You don't feel like you did?"

He lifted a bony shoulder. "I would've gotten first if I'd won that match, but he got me on a sprawl. I couldn't get out."

I unbuttoned the top button of my shirt and beckoned him closer, onto the club room's mats. "Show me."

His face lit up and he shrugged out of his coat. Dumping it on the floor, he stepped out of his boots and tossed his wrestling shoes on the ground next to them. I dropped to my knees when he padded toward me and he did the same. He shoved his head toward the mat and I leaned over him, carefully putting my weight over him like his opponent would've.

"Okay, what'd you do?" I asked, my hands around his thin waist.

He grunted and his arm wrapped around my thigh. I rotated that foot like a clock and kept it out of his grasp. "Stop my foot," I instructed and eased some of my weight off him. My proportions were much larger than his opponent's, but the problem was clear. "You can't sweep behind me if I can move around and keep my leverage over you."

His hand clasped my shin, his grip straining.

"Okay, pause." I moved the foot of the leg he had ahold of side to side. "See how if you can stop me moving from that foot, you could sweep?"

"I'm trying." Frustration laced his voice. He'd had a hard day and those tears Kate and I talked about earlier would flow if he continued to struggle.

I straightened and moved the hand that was between my legs to right above the knee and positioned his other hand over my calf. "Now pull in opposite directions."

He did, and of course he couldn't budge me, but he got the point. I tapped the hand over my calf. "See how the more of my lower leg you have ahold of when you're keeping my calf from moving, the less ability I have to move?"

He nodded. His grip tightened and I patted his side. "Now chase my corner and get behind me." I eased myself over him and let him execute the move until he'd broken out of my hold. "There you go. Easy peasy."

He rolled his eyes but breaking out of his uncle's hold made pride shine on his face.

Kate's voice drifted through the open door from the gym. "Matt took off. I can lock up and bring the keys back to Randall. You and Corbin go get something to eat."

Kate and Jason entered the club room but stopped before they were on the mats.

Jason grinned at Corbin. "Getting tips from Aiden? Don't I know enough anymore?"

"Didn't he used to beat you?" Corbin said as he got his shoes and coat on.

I rose, enjoying the stretch after being on my knees for a few minutes. It'd be fun to work with Corbin longer. I missed this sport. I could've wrestled in college, but I hadn't needed to chase the scholarships. Sports would've taken my mind off my studies, and I'd known my future was with King Oil. I couldn't move into the CFO position right after college and have people think I didn't deserve to be there.

Jason smirked. "He only beat me a few times."

"Only when it counted," I added and Jason chuckled.

He looked at Kate. "You good?"

"Go. I'll lock up."

Jason and Corbin left. Kate smiled at their backs, then grinned at me. "Corbin is starstruck."

"Why?"

She folded her arms. "Because Jason talks about you all the time. He's always referencing ways you took him down." She shook her head. "Corbin's definitely not going to think wrestling with Auntie Katie is cool anymore."

I beckoned her to me with both hands. "I need to see what Auntie Katie knows."

Her eyes flared and pink dusted her cheeks. "What?"

"Come on, Kate. I should've known that Randall wouldn't let a kid under his roof not learn. Show me what you've got."

She made a choking sound. "I can't. We can't…"

I glanced at the door. "No one's around to witness you get destroyed."

Her eyes narrowed and her mouth formed a mutinous line. Damn. Kate had some pride when it came to her moves. I held my grin in and kept my expression challenging.

She toed off her shoes and took her sweater off. The plain pink shirt she wore underneath molded to her body and her breasts jiggled ever so slightly as she stalked toward me. Warmth flooded my groin. She was going to have an advantage before she reached me. I couldn't wrestle with half my blood pooling in my dick.

Each step closer made her cheeks flush deeper, but her eyes shone with determination. Kate liked a challenge.

Why hadn't I realized that?

I dropped into the stance I'd used for so many years facing off with opponents. But no matter what title or medal was on the line, I hadn't wanted to get my hands on them like I did Kate.

Kate

MY HEART SLAMMED in my ribs. I might have some moves I learned as a kid, but I had no real experience other than being a practice dummy for my brothers. Aiden might not have wrestled for over ten years, but he was far more skilled than me.

Yet I approached him, bent my knees, and circled him, looking for my opening. Anticipation stoked the mischievous gleam in his eyes. That look was the one I craved when we went to King's Creek. The look that melted years of stress off his shoulders. The look that suggested a long-repressed sense of humor that was dying to break out.

That look was hot.

Heat curled through my insides, but I concentrated on strategy. He'd lean and lunge, trying to fake me out. I knew better.

He could take me down any second; he was choosing not to.

"You're stalling," I accused.

The corner of his mouth hitched up. "Prove it."

I had no idea how to do that, but I lunged, going for a double-leg takedown. Throwing all my weight into my legs and heaving him over, I got one of his feet in the air and his other hip hit the mat. There was no way I should've been able to get him on the ground. He was six inches taller than me and solid muscle.

I didn't have time to think about it. Power rippled through his body and I moved quickly, taking advantage of the momentum to roll him onto his belly. Using my legs, I wheeled around to his side and over his back until I straddled him. Going for an underhook, I wedged an arm under one of his to wrench it behind his back and did the same to his other side. The next feat was to roll him over to get him flattened on the mat as much as I could.

I scrambled to his side, impeded with my arms anchored around his elbows, but I pushed anyway. He didn't move. I strained using my feet. Still couldn't budge him. I shifted my weight and shoved with all my might, muscles straining. Nothing.

A low vibration rippled through my body the same time a rumble reached my ears.

I frowned, eyeing the center of my husband's back. The rumble grew in strength. "Are you laughing?"

His body shook with the tremors. I huffed out a breath and sagged. My muscles screamed from the type of exertion I hadn't done for years.

His chuckles grew in strength. I'd put everything I had into those moves and he'd been messing with me the whole time.

Without thinking, I smacked his ass. The thwack echoed through the room, almost as satisfying as my husband's laughter. I swatted him two more times before I sank into a mermaid pose. "I was trying really hard."

He flipped to his side, a grin cracking his face and delight alive in his dark eyes. "I know you were, and you were doing really well. Good technique."

I adopted a playful scowl and shoved his shoulder, but I didn't want this moment to end. I could count on one hand the times I'd seen Aiden smile without restraint. He was devastating as the intense oil executive, but when he grinned and let me glimpse his sly sense of humor, his hold on my heart coiled tighter. "You were messing with me through all of it."

A wicked glint in his gaze was my only warning. He wrapped his arms around me and executed nearly the same move I'd tried on him, but from a different angle that would've been impossible if he weren't so much larger than me.

A squeak escaped as I was yanked down, pinned as effectively as a piece of paper superglued to the floor. I bridged, trying to get my back off the mat, but all it did was pull my shirt tighter across my chest as my shoulders protested his hold.

"You mean like this?" he asked, not even out of breath.

Then I was flipped over. His body was half over me, pinning my lower half to the mat while his arms wove under mine to immobilize me. My forehead kissed the mat thanks to his big hand on the back of my neck.

"Or like this?" His velvet voice was deceptively innocent.

And he rolled me, pressing with his knees as he moved me to my side. One of my arms was over my head, no thanks to anything I could do. I was helpless against his power. And frustrated because he didn't hold the pin for long. Each time he moved, I mourned the loss of his body heat.

His chest was pressed to my side. I'd seen Jason get out of this move before, but I couldn't roll through. Aiden sank low on his hips, allowing no wiggle room.

Again I was stuck due not only to his size, but also the impressive skill that hadn't waned as much as I'd have thought for a guy who hadn't wrestled beyond high school.

"Yes, just like that." I was more breathless than my level of exertion dictated.

He released me and spun around until he was over me, chest to chest. The smile was gone, and blazing heat filled his dark gaze.

He dropped his head so his voice was in my ear. "I never mess with you, Kate." A shiver coursed down my body and I unconsciously spread my legs to make room for his body. "Except for today." He lifted his head until his gaze captured mine. "But I think you've been holding out on me."

"I don't hold out…" The lie died on my tongue. The intensity of his stare captured me like a tractor beam. He was joking, but he wasn't.

I didn't necessarily hold out on him, but I wasn't my genuine self. I'd tried to make myself into Kate King, wife of King Oil CFO Aiden King. A successful and wealthy man from a well-respected family didn't need a dumpy spouse. I hadn't been Kate McDonough around him—ever. As soon as he'd asked me out, I'd started dressing better. Using more makeup than just a swipe of mascara and lip gloss. I acquiesced, I didn't argue, and I didn't ask for more.

"Don't you?" he murmured. He dipped his head and pressed a kiss along my jaw. "Then why didn't I know you could execute a flawless double-leg takedown on a much larger opponent?" Another kiss as his weight shifted and settled squarely over me. "Why didn't I know that you don't like backing down from a challenge, especially if it's from your husband?" The next kiss landed by my mouth and I squirmed against the growing erection pressing against my stomach. He feathered his mouth over mine. "What else don't I know about you?"

"Everything." I couldn't believe I'd said it. Uttered exactly how I felt. When had I done that around Aiden?

The coiled tension eked out of him. His gaze brushed over my face. "I want to know everything."

Did he though? "I grew up on bags of cheap cereal and mac and cheese. Off-brand toilet paper. The kind that left behind more than it took." My cheeks burned, but Sophie's pep talk rang in my brain. Aiden didn't flinch from the bathroom talk. He hadn't moved, and that hard length compressed between us branded itself into my belly, but he waited. "When Mom married Randall, it was the first time my brothers and I experienced brats and burgers on the grill."

"While my family was cooking up prime cuts every weekend?" No sarcasm laced his words. He was stating a fact.

"Randall moved us from a single-wide with a leaky roof and a mouse infestation to a double-wide. A nice double-wide, in a trailer park that didn't make the news because someone had been found shot or stabbed. But I still couldn't walk to the bus stop by myself because the guy on the corner gave everyone under the age of eighteen the creeps." That was a danger in many neighborhoods, but as a kid, it'd felt like a *me* problem because my family didn't have as much money as others.

"The point being that we grew up differently." Another plain statement.

"I woke up for school and Mom was plunging the clogged kitchen sink. She would be in her robe, a cigarette hanging out of her mouth. Or the car didn't start when it was twenty below zero because we had no garage and the extension cord to plug in the engine heater kept getting stolen. And when Matt called to get bailed out, Mom brought me along. A little life lesson for both me and Mattie. I knew the police station's front-desk folks on a first-name basis by the time I was thirteen."

Jason hadn't been better; he'd just never gotten caught.

His gaze roamed my face, leaving traces of heat that were all but tangible. "I bet you were a good girl because of that."

"Mom had it hard enough. I didn't hang out in a bad crowd, even if it meant I didn't have many friends." It was why I liked being involved in wrestling with Jason. I was part of a group, and while I wasn't the life of the party, all of Jason's teammates just kind of accepted my presence.

Maybe I hadn't changed that much for Aiden. I had defaulted to my people-pleasing ways, molding myself into what the people in my life needed.

"You aren't going to scare me away, Kate. But I get wanting to be good for your parents. Did I tell you about the time Mama cleaned my mouth out with soap?"

My scandalized gasp snuck out. "Aiden King swore around his mama?"

The corners of his eyes crinkled. "Once. She gave us a pass if we were dealing with cattle. But no cussing when it came to church, schoolwork, or each other." A small smile played over his lips. "Beck took a couple of my toy cars and busted one, then tried to lie about it."

I pictured two dark-haired little boys, one with an adorable cowlick, arguing over metal cars that cost a buck a piece. "What'd you say?"

Aiden's gaze grew distant. "I think I said something like 'you lying little fucker, you're always breaking my shit.' And when I told her I'd heard Dad say something similar, she almost went after him with the soap." His eyes twinkled. "But it was natural stuff, so the flavor wasn't awfully strong like the store-bought stuff."

I twirled my fingers into the cowlick that was breaking through the gel he'd put into it. "And Aiden King never swore around his mama again?"

His expression grew serious. "I'm just Aiden, Kate."

I cupped his face. This guy could melt me with one kiss. He'd sweep into bed and be gone before sunrise, but not until he'd rocked my world at least twice before he satisfied himself. Yet this moment was more intimate than all of those other times combined. "You're not *just* anything. Everyone around you strives to be better, work harder, be the best version of themselves."

His forehead creased. "I don't want to make people feel like that."

"Then let us in."

CHAPTER 8

iden

A QUICK KNOCK at my office door preceded Kendall poking her head in. "Got a minute?"

"Yes." I clicked out of the projected expense report that should've been done last week. No later than the weekend, but I'd been rolling around on a wrestling mat with Kate, not giving a damn about the pile of work I'd left waiting.

With a quick smile, she clicked the door shut behind her and sat across from me. As Dad's executive assistant, it wasn't unusual for her to confer with me separately, but I got the sense from her tight shoulders and the pinch around her eyes that this was more.

"Is Dad okay?" Around the office, I called him Gentry, or Mr. King, depending on who I was talking to. Between us, he was just Dad.

Surprise flared in her eyes. "Yeah, he's well." Her unrepentant grin eased my anxiety. "You know I won't let him be anything but stellar."

She was a bulldog when it came to him, and she had my undying appreciation. A high-stress job and a life of traveling for work—not to mention eating high-sodium, high-fat foods, and drinking a few more brandies than needed—had given him a mild heart attack shortly after he'd married her.

Kendall had woven in more virtual

meetings and online presentations and spun it so our investors thought we were being more environmentally conscious. Which was true. Technology didn't replace the effectiveness of networking in person, but it was a balance that Kendall had a good feel for. Dad and Kendall went on lunch break walks if the weather was nice, and she ate the way Dad was supposed to. When he wasn't constantly on the road or in the air, it was easier to take care of himself.

It was a good thing his heart attack had happened after he'd met her. He'd been too afraid to let someone get close to him for so long, but he was all in with her. And she with him, making her the only one who could've gotten him to the doctor and then sorted out the lifestyle changes afterward. My brothers couldn't have. I wouldn't have been able to. Dad didn't want me interfering in his life any more than I wanted him meddling in mine. I might've had more luck getting through to him that he needed to change his habits because of work, but that was the majority of our relationship. Work.

So if it wasn't Dad that was worrying her, it was work. Or me. "What's going on?"

"I've talked with Gentry again about approaching the board." Grams. She was the president, but the rest of the board followed her lead. She made sure of it. "We'd like to add more positions to the company, including at least two in the inner office. But really, we need at least three. In reality, a lot more, but I thought it'd be easier to start conservative."

I folded my hands on top of the desk but concentrated on not wringing them. Discussion about adding more people to the inner office didn't just stress Grams. "She's going to balk."

Kendall sighed. "I know. But I've gone through three other exploration and production companies that are similar in size and operation to King Oil. Compared to them, we are down a senior vice president, a VP for finance and treasury, and another one for operations." She tapped her tablet. "Actually, we're short on VPs for all major departments. Mrs. Chan could easily be promoted to marketing VP and we could hire a replacement for her old position. Gentry has trusted people in engineering and operations, but he shouldn't have to oversee them all. That's what a VP would do."

"That's five positions." I lifted a shoulder. "Four, since you function as more of a VP than an executive assistant."

"Exactly. We all function as something else. I'm Gentry's executive assistant and take a lot of a VP's duties. You're doing the job of CFO and finance and treasury VP. Mrs. Chan is in the same position, and what happens when our top engineers find other jobs that don't require such long hours?"

"They're paid for those hours." I hated to be the dick that pointed it out, but Grams would do the same. She had. Several times.

"They are compensated well. No one can accuse King Oil of crappy wages or benefits."

That topic had kept me up more nights than I could count. Job security. Compensation. I had cost enough employees their livelihood.

"But," she continued, "I have wage and benefit package comparisons too. We're not that much better. Ultimately, we can't keep going like this, Aiden. Emilia needs to understand that a company isn't any stronger than its employees and if they're burning out at alarming rates, the business will burn out."

What she said resonated more than it had in the past. I didn't approve of how Grams presided over the board as if the other members didn't have a say, how she maneuvered the votes to go how she wanted. But when it came to this topic, the topic of hiring another VP to work under me, I'd resisted. For good reason. And

Grams had backed me up without saying as much.

I wasn't a natural micromanager. I hadn't wanted to be. Until I'd experienced the hell that was having the buck stop at me when the person under me, the vice president that Kendall had wanted to hire, had majorly fucked up.

So I didn't push Grams when it came to the inner office. Between Dad's relationship with Kendall and my brothers nearly ignoring the stipulations of the trust, she'd been pushed more than she had in her whole life.

"All right," I said. "All we can do is approach her and lay out the data. Hope she sees the need."

Kendall leveled her turquoise gaze on me. "I need your voice too, Aiden."

Damn. Anxiety curled up my spine. I didn't want to oversee anyone. That just gave me more information that I might miss. I wouldn't suffer the repercussions. I was the boss's kid. Wasn't that what the headlines had said shortly after I started in this position?

"Let me know what you need." It wasn't exactly noncommittal. Grams might see reason and approve more positions, and that didn't have to be anyone under me.

"I need numbers," Kendall said. "How much would it cost to advertise for and hire qualified applicants, and for job retention. Emilia's going to see the cost and that a handful of us are already getting it done. I'd like you to put a price on how much it would cost the company if we lost you, or Gentry."

My brow furrowed. "We're not going anywhere."

"Not by choice."

My eye twitched at her statement.

"Don't mean to be morbid, but this isn't healthy. I love this job. So does Gentry. So do you. But there's more out there, and our balance is weighed too heavily on one side."

This topic had come up again because of my meltdown. Shame burned in my gut.

"I'm sorry about that week I was out." And this last weekend I'd taken too much time off. I couldn't regret it, but then it hadn't affected just me.

Her gaze softened. "It's not that, Aiden. You've been long overdue for a week off. When was the last time you took a vacation?"

I'd been with the company for nearly ten years. I'd busted through my bachelor's degree and fast-tracked a master's so I could get on staff and be useful.

"Exactly," she answered for me. "Between you and Gentry and me, we haven't used any of our leave. I doubt we could dig through our comp time in a month or two before we had to tap our vacation days. Did you even take a honeymoon?"

"Yes."

She cocked her head and her knowing gaze bored into me.

Right. She'd talked to Dad. "Kate and I

went to the French Riviera for a long weekend."

"A long weekend," she echoed. "And you probably still worked."

I lifted a shoulder. My mama had had a way of asking questions that would lead me to admitting to just what she'd planned to accuse me of. Kendall was on the same track.

I clicked my computer screen on. "I'll get you those numbers."

Kendall watched me for a heartbeat just like Dad would've. Not only was she my stepmom, but she was like an extension of Dad. A parental figure that was my age. "Thank you. But don't do it at the cost of taking care of yourself."

If I didn't do that, then I'd never get any work done.

~

Kate

.   .   .

I KEPT the engine running after I parked in front of the trailer.

My pulse rate kicked up and I clutched my phone. I needed to call Aiden. It'd been three days since our time wrestling, but his heat hadn't left me. The weight of his big body. His defined muscles. That kiss.

I was giving him time, but I hadn't considered that it might mean we'd stay together.

I pressed a hand to my fluttering stomach. This feeling rivaled the nerves I'd had on our first date. I'd been so nervous that I'd almost thrown up. My face had flushed so hard it'd looked like I was on day four of being sick with mono. I'd even taken my temperature to make sure I hadn't come down with something.

I blew out a breath and hit the button for my husband.

He answered immediately. "Kate."

"Hey, you mind if I stop by the house tomorrow and grab some of my belongings?"

"Anytime."

My eyelids drifted shut at the way he purred the answer. Did everything about the man have to turn me on? "Thanks. It's a last-minute conference. I mean, the conference isn't last-minute. Well, it's usually earlier in the year, and my boss was supposed to go, but her dad landed in the hospital. The admins said they could transfer her registration to me. Unfortunately, it's not that easy with the airlines, but the conference covers innovative uses of communications in the library. Between the cost and the massive amount our patrons use our electronic services, someone should get the information."

I wrinkled my nose and picked at the hem of my jacket. None of this mattered to him. Like before, I couldn't dam the rambling.

"When do you fly out?"

"It was supposed to be Friday morning, but I might have to take the red-eye from

Denver to Indianapolis. They're going to check tomorrow."

"You can use the jet."

The private plane King Oil used? Aiden's brothers also used it occasionally for personal reasons, and when Aiden and I had started dating, he'd flown me to New York for a meal that cost almost as much as my first semester of college. "No. It's all right."

"Consider it a donation. For the library."

It'd help the budget since they wouldn't have to buy a second set of tickets. "Are you sure?"

"What are the details?"

"Well, it'd be nice to get there Friday night for a networking meeting."

"Want to leave Thursday?"

I closed my eyes again, picturing him scribbling notes at his desk, his broad shoulders curved over a small square of paper. He didn't need to write a single detail down. His memory was a steel trap, but he wasn't a guy who could sit still for long. He did, out of pure discipline, but at home, he paced the house when he was in a long-distance meeting and he often dictated notes to himself when he mowed the lawn. "Yes, that's fine. I wouldn't be able to fly back until Sunday afternoon. I don't want to tie the plane up for that long."

"Do you want to leave Thursday afternoon, or in the evening?"

My eyes fluttered open. "Aiden, it's okay."

"Kate, whatever you need."

Was he talking about us, or the trip? "It's this Thursday. I don't want to make it inconvenient."

"When are you coming over?"

"I have Thursday off. I can just swing by on my way to the airport." Aiden would be at work and I wouldn't have to bug him any further.

"I'll double-check everything and send you a confirmation. It should take less than an hour."

The King Oil Gulfstream flight crew

would answer Aiden immediately. "I appreciate it. I'll let you go now."

"Kate—"

I waited for him to finish, but he didn't continue. "Aiden?"

"How was work?"

"Good." Had he ever asked me about work before? "Other than the conference rearrangement, it was pretty quiet. Normal."

"Lauren applied here."

"Lauren? From the library?" She was one of our regular patrons, and the staff was extremely protective of her. She wore stilettos and dressed for a Southern brunch when it was the middle of winter. Most days she tied a bandana around her military cut, and many times, she didn't shave her salt-and-pepper five o'clock shadow. She talked with a low rumble while wearing her reading glasses, peering at everyone over them as if she were working on the computer. I considered her more of a friend than a patron after all these years.

"The same. She applied for the entrance receptionist position. She put you as a reference but didn't list a number. Human Resources asked if it was okay to get your personal phone number."

"Yeah, that's fine."

"No need. I said you spoke highly of her. I gave her a reference."

He remembered me talking about Lauren? It'd been nothing more than commenting about the old war movies Lauren wanted to check out and maybe a running tally of how many online MS Office courses she'd completed during her allotted computer time.

"Do you think she'll get the job?" Lauren hadn't done reception work before. She'd mentioned once that she'd spent thirty years working a tow truck but wanted a job out of the elements to get her to her retirement years.

"I don't pull rank often, but I expect my reference will go further than the others."

He spoke so plainly my lips twitched. "I

hope that means she's not going to quit coming into the library."

"She won't be between the hours of eight and five Monday through Friday."

I chuckled. Aiden's sense of humor didn't make an appearance nearly enough. "Thank you for checking on the flight."

"The pilot just messaged. They aren't scheduled, so your trip is cleared."

That flight was more money than a lot of annual donations the library received.

I was about to ask him if I could stop by Wednesday night, perhaps late enough to catch him at home, when a phone rang.

A soft gust of breath came over the line. "I have to go."

Work beckoned. "Thanks again, Aiden."

As he disconnected to go back to work, I couldn't quit smiling.

CHAPTER 9

iden

I WHIPPED my pickup into a parking spot and hopped out. I yanked out my suitcase from the back seat and took off toward the terminal where the King Oil plane waited. It was supposed to have taken off twenty minutes ago, but I'd been hung up by a damn laptop. My travel computer had failed and I'd nearly pounded our IT guy's door off the hinges to get another one running with all the programs I needed.

I didn't take the time to use the wheels. With the suitcase in one hand and my tech bag in the other, I swept through the terminal and outside. The pilot waved from her seat in the cockpit. I lifted my chin, hating that I was holding up the show.

Luna probably didn't care. She was getting paid the same amount no matter what, and this delay was nothing compared to what her commercial pilot of a husband experienced in his job, but it was a matter of pride. I didn't abuse those who worked for me.

Mama had made sure I knew better than that.

Our longtime flight attendant's back was to me when I charged inside. Kate was in one of the quad seats that we sometimes used for meetings in the air. She was unloading a book from her tote bag, her hand stalling and her eyes going wide when she saw me.

A pair of dark-rimmed glasses sat on her face. She never wore her glasses.

Shirley spun, her grandmotherly eyes sparkling. "Oh, I'm sorry, Aiden. I didn't see you coming." I didn't recall her calling me Mr. King once, and I wouldn't change a thing. A private plane was better if it felt like I was flying with friends. To Shirley, all of us were like her kids. "What can I get you, hon?"

"All I need is a moment with Kate."

She gave me an indulgent grin. "I can do that. Just let me get the door closed and latched."

Kate watched me stalk toward her. Her book was still half in and out of the bag. She stuffed it back in. "Is something wrong?"

"No," I said as I dropped in the seat across from her. I'd left my suitcase by the entrance. Shirley was picky about where they were stored or I would've done it myself. I dropped the tech bag on the seat next to me. "I'm coming with."

I tensed as I waited for her reaction. I rarely overstepped like this with my wife. The trust money had been enough.

She blinked, her eyes wide. "Oh. I didn't realize that you had business in Indianapolis."

"I…sure."

Her eyes narrowed. "You don't?"

"I thought it'd be a good time to talk."

"I'll be in workshops, and the social Saturday night—" She blinked again and shook off an unvoiced thought. "It's for attendees only."

"That's fine." I tipped my head toward my tech bag. "I'll be working."

She adjusted her glasses like she wanted to take them off but didn't want a blurry world. They were cute, highlighting her wide hazel eyes. "And where will you stay?"

Disappointment pummeled my insides like a punching bag. After our time grappling on the mat, I'd hoped we'd moved further than that. But that was the point of hitchhiking on my own plane. To find out what was still broken between us and figure out how to fix it. It was my fault I'd thought a few minutes of honest discussion in a rec center would be enough.

"I'll get another room. I just want to be with you, Kate. If it's only during the flight while you read and I work, that's fine." My gaze flicked to the bedroom in the back, but I tamped down the overwhelming lust that surged through me. We'd never had private-plane sex. The bedroom was rarely used by me or Dad. Maybe Beck and Eva got their fair use out of it that didn't include sleeping. But I'd never broached the subject with Kate, afraid she'd be mortified that Shirley or Luna would realize what we were doing.

Her expression softened and she inched the book out of her tote.

The cover came into view and I couldn't stop myself from making a choking noise. A woman was splayed in a sultry pose in the middle of three stacked, shirtless men. The subject matter was evident…and not what I'd seen Kate read before. "Catching up on the classics?"

Her cheeks flamed. "A few of our patrons have complained that we only offer basic, vanilla romance, and a couple of others have asked about this author. So I thought I'd read a few different authors of this content so I can *do my job* and purchase and recommend material to patrons."

At home, books were stacked on Kate's nightstand and on the end table in the living room, and the room I'd made into her office was full of bookshelves. Seeing her read a romance wasn't unusual, and I'd never thought about it beyond trying to win her over with textbook romance before I had proposed.

But her flushed cheeks and obvious defensiveness was more than I could ignore. A flustered Kate was like my catnip. I sat forward and put my elbows on my knees. "I need you to clear something up for me."

"Okay?"

"What do they call it when it's more than three people having sex? Ménage à trois doesn't work."

Her blush deepened and she pushed her glasses up. "Um, this type of book is called reverse harem."

I repressed my smile, feeding on her discomfort. "One woman, many guys. I see. How does it happen? One at a time? All at once?" I tilted my head. "How would that work? Logistically?"

She blinked her owlish eyes. "Aiden King, are you playing dumb?"

My grin broke free. She tried to cover up an eye roll, but she giggled. I managed billions of dollars, but making my wife laugh right now was a bigger accomplishment.

I reclined in my seat. "Vanilla sex, huh?"

The blush returned but she sighed. "We often buy books off of curated lists. Usually, they tend to be by well-known authors, books from bestseller lists, authors or books that have won major awards, you know, something along those lines. There are a ton of romance categories and those readers tend to be prolific. They burn through our physical and online stock and then give us feedback on what they'd like to see. I noticed a theme emerging that the books were too tame."

"They want more Fifty Shades?"

"Yes and no. They want more variety than just the most popular of the most popular. They want more heat."

I dropped my voice a few notches. "Heat?"

Scarlet now, she scowled at me. "Heat."

I'd push for a definition, but I wasn't making just Kate squirm in her seat. If I kept talking to my wife about the sexual content of books, this flight would be the most painful I'd ever experienced. Add in the bedroom in the back that I doubted she'd want me to haul her into, and I was in hell.

Shirley saved me. "Everything's ready. Can I get you anything before takeoff?"

I kept my gaze on Kate and the extra sparkle in her eyes after our conversation.

"No, thank you, Shirley," Kate said.

Shirley hated doing nothing for an entire flight. I tried to have at least one task for her each time. "Did you have time to hit up the new bakery in town?"

The older woman beamed. "Oh, yes. I've been dying to go there and you gave me just the reason. I have a nice assortment of sweets and baked goods I think you'll both like."

"Thank you. Can't wait." Kate's gaze was on me as Shirley went to her jump seat and buckled in. I'd never cared what Shirley packed for snacks or meals. This was a first-time request for me. And I liked the way surprise lightened the brown in Kate's irises. I made sure to capture her gaze when I said, "I bet there'll be plenty of non-vanilla options. Enjoy your book."

I deliberately broke the connection and reached for my laptop bag. Messing with my wife was my new favorite hobby.

But as I fired up my laptop and Kate started reading her X-rated book, I realized that I'd messed with myself more. The joke was on me. I wasn't going to get a bit of work done while wondering if Kate was reading a sex scene and thinking of me.

THE CAR I'd hired to take us from the airport to the conference center pulled up to the hotel. Several work vehicles were pulling away, done for the day. Vans emblazoned with plumbing and electrical companies lined the street. Contractor and construction company vehicles. Taxis and Ubers dropping off and picking up.

The driver parked by the row of glass doors. I got out and helped him unload our bags. I took both mine and Kate's and let her lead the way into the hotel. The din of footsteps on the marble floor and at least twenty conversations around the lobby hit us.

Kate went to an open agent at the counter and I stepped to an empty spot next to her.

The woman behind the counter was dressed in black slacks and a crisp white shirt. Her name tag read *Cynthia*, and she grinned as she watched me muscle all the bags into a tidy pile. "How can I help you?"

"Hi, Cynthia. Can I get a room for the next three nights?" Preferably as close to Kate as possible? I glanced up. Seven levels. What were the odds I'd land on the same floor?

"I'm so sorry, sir. We don't have any vacancies."

None? It was December. A slow month for conferences and sporting events. Ah. "Construction?"

Her smile was sympathetic. "I'm sorry. I can help you find a room in a hotel nearby."

I hadn't expected to spend a lot of time with Kate while she was at her convention, but I'd at least hoped to be under the same roof. The roof might house a few hundred rooms, but I'd remained optimistic.

Kate's attention was on us. "No opening?"

I tucked my wallet back into my slacks. "No problem. I'll talk with Luna about the bedroom." Could I use it when the plane wasn't in use? I didn't care to sit in another hotel.

"On the plane?" Kate glanced at the young man helping her, then at the woman assisting me. Her gaze landed on me, full of resolve. "Just stay with me."

"This is your conference." I could fist-pump right now, but I hadn't meant to intrude this much on her weekend. She was technically working, after all.

"It's all right, Aiden."

I thanked Cynthia for her time, gathered my suitcase and Kate's, and shouldered my tech bag while she finished up.

On the way to the elevator, she handed me a key, hesitant. "There's two beds. Two queens."

Damn. "All right."

Still. Progress was progress. We were talking. She hadn't asked when we were going to sign the divorce papers. I was making progress whether I was back in her bed or not.

We were about to get into the elevator when a woman approached us. Her jeans could've been painted on and her top was cut low enough that most guys could guess her cup size.

"Kate? Hey!"

Kate's expression went from her usual curious fascination when we were in a new hotel to bland. "Hailey. Hi."

"Oh my gosh. You finally brought your husband to one of these."

Hailey extended her hand, her smile wide enough to devour me whole. Tension started at my shoulders and ran down my body, muscle by muscle. Why would Hailey care if I was here?

I was sifting through my memories for a Hailey that Kate might've mentioned when

Hailey said, "Yeah, my dad is in the wind energy business. Mertens Energy." She flashed me a self-deprecating look. "Hailey Mertens."

The amazing luck that had landed me in the same hotel room as my wife vanished. Mertens Energy was a vocal critic of the oil and gas industry. Dad and I had done a lot to keep out of Mertens Energy's spotlight, mainly from their owner and CEO, Gregory Mertens.

"Nice to meet you. I guess you already know me." I clasped her hand for a shake and she latched on like she was going to cuff me, her other hand slapping onto both of ours.

Hailey's giggle crossed the line into flirty. "My dad was just talking about King Oil the other day."

The elevator dinged and I wanted to run, but I had to extract my hand first without looking like her clammy touch was revolting. I couldn't undo all of the progress we'd made with Mertens Energy by being rude to his daughter.

The elevator doors closed and Kate pressed the button again. Grateful she'd skipped the first open elevator, some of my tension eased. "How is Gregory doing?" I asked politely.

Hailey shifted and it somehow brought her between me and Kate. "Dad's good. He's working on a new wind farm in your neck of the woods. You're in Billings, right?"

I nodded and heard the elevator ding. Kate's presence centered me. I'd finish this conversation, then take her out to a nice meal tonight.

"So, I've been dying to hear an oil company's take on the whole wind energy topic." She swung her hair until long, shiny locks landed over her shoulder. "I hear my dad's side all the time."

People streamed out of the elevator. No one else waited to get on. Just us.

I was asked about wind energy more than Hailey would expect. "Well—" Kate lifted her suitcase from my hand and disappeared inside the open elevator. My head whipped around. "Wait."

Kate ignored me and pressed the button for our floor. The doors started to close.

Shit. I jumped to put my hand between the doors and they popped back open. "You'll have to excuse me," I said as I ducked into the elevator with Kate.

Kate hit the button to close the door. Hailey was frowning, her lower lip sticking out in a pout. I gave her a nod, hoping she didn't tattle to her dad that the CFO of King Oil had ditched his baby girl mid-conversation. Gregory Mertens was the kind of guy who'd hold that against the whole company.

The doors closed us in. "Kate—"

She shook her head. "No." She stuck a finger toward the door. "That's exactly what I was talking about. Women like that corner you about 'business' "—she used air quotes—"and you think I should hang out in your shadow and be okay with it."

"It *was* business, Kate. You heard who her dad is."

Kate stepped close to me, four years of anger radiating from her blazing eyes. "Hailey doesn't give a shit about oil. She doesn't give one flying rat's ass about the wind-versus-oil debate. And I doubt she has half a fuck to give about her dad's company as long as he keeps giving her large sums of money for Christmas. Librarians aren't always pillars of morality, Aiden. Sometimes they're douchebags. Hailey likes the power she gets from making supposedly good men stray from their partners. That's what she lives for at these conferences."

I recoiled. "I wasn't going to do anything but talk shop. I didn't want to do even that."

"Then don't." Her voice cracked like a whip. The elevator lurched to a stop. We were at our floor.

I kept pace with Kate as she stomped to our room. I kept my voice to a hiss. "She's exactly the type of person who'll gladly wield bad PR against those guys who don't stray from their wives. Her dad's worse. Balancing that is just another game in business."

Kate lifted a shoulder. "If you want to play that game, go ahead. I'm done with it."

She stopped at our room and swiped her card, then slammed the door open and stormed in.

I stepped in and let the door slam shut behind me. I'd never seen her this pissed before. She toed off her athletic shoes and dumped her tote on the desk. Her body was tight, her movements short.

Was this how she'd felt every time I talked to another woman?

You think I should hang out in your shadow and be okay with it.

No, it wasn't talking to women. It was ignoring my wife while I did it.

It wasn't just about insecurity. It was about respect. It didn't matter the subject, I talked to other women while not talking to her. First, she thought I didn't love her. Now, she thought I didn't respect her.

No matter what, she was my wife and I should make sure everyone around me knew that she was the most important person in my world. That I cared about her more than what Gregory fucking Mertens thought of King Oil.

"I'm sorry."

She paused mid-ravage of her suitcase. The zipper wouldn't have survived much longer. Her mouth was set when she looked up at me. "Thanks."

"Seriously, Kate. I didn't realize, and I should've." I closed the distance between us and gripped her arms, brushing my thumbs over her long-sleeved shirt. "I relied on your support through those conversations so much that I never considered how it made you feel."

"I didn't support you though. No one wanted to talk to me. Not even you."

"I could give a fuck about the people I was talking to." Her pupils dilated at my harsh tone. "I meant it when I said that I'm usually sitting there wishing that it was over. I just wanted to be with you, and I was always grateful you were with me." I leaned into her, dangerously close to kissing her when a bed was only feet away. "Can I take you out tonight, before you get wrapped up in the conference?"

The anger drained out of her and she softened in my grip. "Where?"

"There's a haute cuisine—"

She wrinkled her nose and stepped away. "I hate those places." She grabbed a pair of slacks out of her suitcase and hung them up.

My brows shot up as I stood abandoned in the middle of the room. "Really?" She'd been in awe and gushed over the food every time I took her to a Michelin-starred restaurant. That'd been an act?

She noticed my confusion and sighed. "I mean, I like the experience. But half the time, I want to go to McDonald's and get a Big Mac or something because I'm starving afterward." She waved a hand around. "I hate the worry about what I'm going to wear and how to pronounce the entrees and trying to remember which fork to use first. It's tedious."

"So the entire time we dated, you were miserable? Our honeymoon?"

"It was nice," she said lightly. "But that's not how I want to live."

A Michelin-starred restaurant was only nice? The French Riviera was just nice? My sole goal during the months we'd dated and been engaged was to secure her wedding vows, to tie her to me. I'd wined and dined her and swept her off her feet…only to learn years later that she'd rather have had her feet on the floor in comfortable shoes and Golden Arches over her head.

I'd planned a campaign to romance a wife, and I'd assumed I'd done a good enough job.

"What do you want?" Had I ever asked her that, not just in relation to food or eating out, but about anything? Or had I been too afraid I wouldn't be able to give it to her?

Pushing her glasses up, she thought. "I'd rather order in a burger and sit in my pajamas and eat while watching a show."

She spoke like she'd done that before, but *we* hadn't done that before. This was what my wife wanted. Just to be with me. To be comfortable with me. Did I know how to give that to her?

Kate

THE FINAL WORKSHOP of the day dragged on. I was taking notes on ways to market the library's services to those who needed them the most and trying to keep my mind off the last two nights.

I'd managed to avoid Hailey since her blatant flirtation with my husband. She'd latched on to a young assistant library director from Massachusetts with a wife and kid number two on the way. Poor guy looked like he wanted to vomit each time Hailey appeared at his side.

Finally, the speaker wrapped up and I scribbled down her contact information for my boss. My friend and old college buddy Bisa leaned over. "Is that your hubby who's dropping jaws every morning in the gym?"

I didn't bother to downplay his effect on people. I was more susceptible than anyone. "That's him."

Bisa chuckled. "I swear there were twice as many women in the gym this morning versus Friday morning."

"Only one reason I don't work out with him." Aiden pounded himself to the ground in the gym. When he worked out, his focus was as complete as with any other task. He might not notice my boob sweat and the low mph on my treadmill, but I noticed it enough for the both of us.

She nudged me with her elbow. "You get to do all the other fun stuff with him."

I smiled, but my body reminded me that I had not done any fun stuff with Aiden for weeks. I hadn't thought I was a woman with a high sex drive until I'd quit getting it on a regular basis. A portion of my body's blood kept my nether region stoked and flared every time Aiden was in view.

Workshop attendees drifted past us as I packed my notes away.

"Do you want to grab a bite before the social tonight?" Bisa asked. "Oh, you probably have plans with Aiden."

"No, he's working." Except for Thursday night. We'd each ordered a burger from room service. I'd eaten in bed, in my Harry Potter pajama pants and a college T-shirt. Aiden had done the same in flannel pants I rarely saw him wear. He'd had his phone and his tablet to work, but he'd been next to me, albeit in his own bed. After that night, he'd set up shop at the desk in the room.

I could invite him out with us, but I couldn't ask him to pretend we were living under the same roof for one of my oldest friends. I wasn't sure I could do it and not die slowly from anxiety. Sleeping next to him for two nights in separate beds had left me achy and needy.

I messaged Aiden that I was meeting a friend to eat and wouldn't be back to the room. I didn't want him waiting for me, but I refused to cancel on Bisa so I could go and watch him work. Last night had been nice. But ditching a friend to do it meant I hadn't learned anything from our divorce situation.

Bisa and I went to the same restaurant Aiden and I had ordered the burgers from. The meal didn't last long enough. Not only did I want more time to catch up with Bisa one-on-one, but I was dreading tonight. I shouldn't be. Social nights with Bisa were my favorites. And tonight's social was dress-as-a-book-character night. She and I had gone to a party like this in college and we'd dressed as compatible characters. We were doing it again tonight. It was tradition.

Aiden hardly saw me in my glasses. He'd never seen me dress up. Halloween was just another work night for him. No kids ventured out to our house, but I'd been ready with a bowl of candy and my Mary Poppins costume anyway. By the time Aiden was done at the office, I'd been changed and in bed.

I shouldn't be anxious. My husband should know me at my worst and my best, but since the day of the open house when he'd asked me out, I'd striven to be at my best around him. Unrealistic, but that was where we were. Why I'd filed for divorce when I'd learned about the trust.

I let myself into the room. The blinds were open, but only residual street light filtered in. Aiden was at the desk, still in his flannel pants and a tight white T-shirt that shouted better than a neon sign *Look how cut these shoulders are.* He hadn't done anything with his hair since he'd showered. The cowlick curved higher at his hairline. My palms itched to run through it.

He glanced at me and his eyes warmed. "How was your day?"

All I wanted to do was cross to him, drape myself over his lap, and get lost in one of his lingering kisses. I couldn't afford to confuse chemistry with a strong relationship at this moment. "Good. Bisa and I went to many of the same workshops."

"She still in Idaho?"

"Same place. We talk about getting together all the time, but the drive across Montana to Billings eats up most of a day."

"You can always fly there."

"Yeah, I suppose," I said as I dug through my suitcase. I'd kept my costume under all of my underclothes. It should've been hanging up, but then I would've had to explain, and after I'd ripped his head off about Hailey, I'd been raw.

Had I ever thought of going anywhere by myself since I'd been married? When I was single, I'd traveled as much as my pocketbook would allow. A week in

Cozumel. A weekend in Regina, Canada. Going alone didn't bother me.

Going alone when I was married did.

I rose with an armful of blue tulle and caught Aiden staring at me.

He was doing that thing with the office chair. His body was hitched to the side, an arm draped over the back. A move that was devastating in his dress shirt and suit jacket. But with a T-shirt that left nothing to the imagination—well, I didn't have to imagine.

Concern welled in his dark eyes. "What's wrong? Why wouldn't you visit Bisa?"

Sometimes he surprised me with how astute he was—about me. Not about anything else. "It just never worked out."

"You enjoy traveling. I would've gone with."

How did I explain? "When I was single, I made sure it didn't limit me. I wasn't going to be one of those spinster women who sat home with a bunch of cats and read books. After I was married…I didn't want to travel with someone who didn't want to be with me."

He unhooked his arm and rose, towering over me. "I want to be with you, Kate."

And I wanted him to understand. When we were together, he was rarely with me. The few minutes on the plane before we'd taken off was what I wanted. I didn't demand his entire day. I knew work was important to him. I just wanted to be important too. "We're working on it, Aiden. That's enough for now."

His expression remained pensive until his gaze dropped to the bundle in my arms. His brows drew together. "Are you going to wear that?" He peered closer. "Is that a blue wig?"

"It's, um, dress-as-a-book-character night, and Bisa and I have this thing. She's a children's librarian, and…" I blew out a breath and looked at the getup I held. "We go as Thing One and Thing Two. Yeah, so, we do the costume with blue tulle and red-

and-white-striped leggings. More comfortable than red footie pajamas, and…" I stopped before I started describing how I hated using a public restroom when I had to unzip the red pajama-style costume and strip down just to pee.

The corner of his mouth hooked upward first, then the rest as I was rewarded with a breathtaking grin. "She's coming to grab you, right? So I can see the both of you together?"

I scowled. "No. I was going to meet her."

"Then I want a picture."

"No."

"Kate." He crowded into me, and god, did I love when he did that. "I'd really love to see a photo of you two together having fun."

Sincerity filled his words. He wasn't doing it to laugh at me. He'd never done that. I might've pointed out some of Aiden's faults on this trip, but he had a lot of good qualities. A lot of reasons why I'd fallen in love with him. "All right. I'll message her and ask if she can come up."

"I just need to know one more thing." He dipped his head down by my ear until his hot breath whispered over my ear. "Are you Thing One or Thing Two?"

ate

THE TRAILER WAS QUIET TONIGHT, like it was most nights. The only sound was the tinkling of dishes as I loaded the dishwasher and the TV.

The quiet nights at home as an adult unsettled me, without my brothers tearing the walls down with their wrestling and without Mom or Randall chewing them out for whatever stupid prank they played that brought the police to our house.

When I was younger, I couldn't wait to leave for college. To go out in the world and prove that I was better than everyone I'd grown up around. Not just my family and how the outside world viewed us, but the kids I'd gone to school with who'd ignored me and forgotten who I was as soon as I was out of sight. The teachers who'd overlooked me because I did well enough, but wasn't in sports and therefore wasn't worth extra effort. My hometown had felt so limiting to a girl who'd had big dreams and plans to be someone.

Looking back on it, the hubris was shocking. Why would I be the center of everyone's world? Yet all I'd really yearned for was to be the center of *someone's* world. Mom and Randall had been busy with my brothers. My dad was a trucker and he called to meet for a meal whenever his route took him through town, but he didn't come here otherwise. My friends from school had other, better friends and we'd drifted apart. The teachers had stellar students they could push harder and worse students who needed extra attention. My college sweetheart hadn't felt strongly enough about me to change his career plans and I'd felt the same. We'd gone our separate ways, like me and Bisa, except I didn't keep in touch with Gabriel.

What I'd been missing growing up, I found through my work. Patrons needed me. I was not only good at my job, I was useful. People appreciated me. I had a purpose, and it kept me busy enough to mask what I was missing at home.

After a long weekend with Aiden, I realized why I'd really left him.

More importantly, I realized why I wanted things to work out between us. Why I wanted to believe that his heart was in this relationship as much as his pride. When his full attention was on me, I believed I could be the center of his world. I believed he loved me, and because of the loss he'd suffered so young, he didn't know how to show it.

Bisa had swung by the night of the costume party so Aiden could see us together, rocking our red bodysuits and blue wigs. With Bisa present, I hadn't expected to see another grin, but humor had danced in his eyes before he'd kissed my forehead, earning a nose full of fake blue hair, and said, "Have fun, Thing Two."

My lips curved at the memory until I was grinning to myself. I switched the dishwasher on and dug out some plastic containers. I packed Mom's leftover meatloaf for tomorrow's lunch.

Randall dozed in his recliner as the last of a crime drama played. Mom was in her corner of the couch, bent over the crossword puzzle from a newspaper she'd gotten at work. I set my lunch on top of the bags I'd packed for each of them. Part of my payment for living here was to clean up after meals and I included packing their lunches. It was the least I could do. Randall had landed a day shift at the refinery years ago, but it exhausted him as much as switching shifts. And while Mom had worked her way to supervisor for hotel housekeeping, she had to clean just as many rooms as she had before, between employees calling in sick or being no-shows.

Mom popped her head up. "Damn, I forgot to grab milk."

"I can get it on my way home tomorrow."

She scooted forward in her seat, shaking her head. "No, Randall's a bear if he doesn't have milk for his morning coffee."

"I'll go get some. Sit down."

"Are you sure?"

"Yeah." The bustle of the grocery store sounded better than my small silent room. "Need anything else?"

"Maybe some more Folgers?" Her mouth quirked. "I did that once. Made a special trip for milk and then the next morning we found out we were out of coffee."

Randall was a mellow man—unless he

was undercaffeinated. He and Mom had an arrangement. He thought coffee magically made itself every morning and Mom made it her personal mission to keep him stocked. But then she never had to worry about a snowy sidewalk or driveway. Randall woke before her and moved snow, often opening the garage door and starting her car so it was warm for her.

I grew up witnessing those trade-offs. I'd gone into my marriage assuming we'd have them. But my attempts had fallen flat when he hadn't reciprocated. He'd let me use the jet. Maybe I just had to recognize the times he did try instead of shoving him into a rectangular container like I'd just packed the meatloaf in.

I grabbed my keys and stuffed a patterned stocking hat over my hair. I'd gone to the gym and showered after work, but it was just the grocery store. I didn't need makeup or the contacts I'd taken out as soon as I'd gotten home. My gray sweatpants and purple fleece athletic top were fine. A couple of months ago, I would've changed back into my work clothes thanks to self-imposed expectations that had no grounding in reality.

The drive was fast. I parked at the end of the lot under a streetlight. A few extra steps would make up for the chocolate that wouldn't fail to land in my basket before I checked out.

I ran through the store, grabbed the milk and coffee, and saved my sweet tooth for a jumbo muffin that I'd eat for breakfast. As I was walking to my car, I narrowed my eyes.

Was my tire flat?

The closer I got, the more certain I grew. Yep. It was flat. I could limp it to a pump, fill it, and get home, but then it'd deflate overnight. Randall would insist on putting on the spare after the car had been sitting out in the cold all night.

I dug out my phone—and stopped. Who was I going to call?

Aiden?

He'd flown me to Indianapolis and back. Was it fair for him to keep bailing me out?

Mom and Randall?

No, I didn't want to disrupt their evening in the middle of a workweek.

Jason?

He worked at the refinery too, and I never knew what shift he was on. Sophie would know how to change a tire, but she did shift work too at the hospital.

I would do it my damn self.

Randall had made sure my brothers and I knew how to do the basics. But changing a tire was easier on a wheel that'd been taken off and put on three other times. Wrestling lug nuts off after an impact wrench tightened them had to be harder.

I tossed my items in the passenger seat and dug out the manual. I managed to find the tire-change kit under my back seat. The metal of the jack sapped heat through my thin gloves. I hadn't made it to the tire yet and my fingers were getting numb.

My breath puffed around me as I

squatted, placed the lug nut wrench, and strained.

Nothing budged.

Was I going the right way? Righty-tighty, lefty-loosey.

I tried again and had to stop and flex my fingers. I placed the wrench over a different lug nut. Same effect.

Shit.

All I needed to do was get on the spare and I could bring the car in tomorrow. I didn't work until noon.

I tried every single nut and none of them made me optimistic. I dropped the tools and looked around. The flat was on the opposite side as the store. My efforts were blocked by my car and no one paid me any mind.

I slid into the car, started it, and took out my phone. With numb fingers, I called Aiden.

He answered on the first ring, his deep voice warming me more than the heat pumping out of the vents. "Kate."

"I have a flat and I can't get the tire off."

"Where are you?"

I rattled off the grocery store and finished with "Sorry to bother you."

"It's not a problem. I'll be right there." He hung up.

I waited in the driver's seat until the headlights of his pickup flashed over me. He parked on the side with the flat and hopped out at the same time I climbed out.

God, he looked good. It was winter, but his coat was probably draped over the back seat. He shrugged out of his suit coat and my mouth went dry. His pewter dress shirt shone under the parking lot light. He loosened his tie and tore it off all the way, tossing it with his suit jacket into the back seat. It shouldn't be possible for the flex of his muscles to be visible in the dark.

He scrutinized the tire as he wedged his hands into a black pair of gloves, his dark gaze sweeping over the tools I left out. "Did you try the portable air compressor?"

I bit the inside of my lip. "No, sorry. I

totally forgot about it." He'd given me one after we started dating and I'd never had to use it. It was tucked away in the winter kit in my trunk.

His gaze popped up. "No reason to be sorry. Do you want to wait in the pickup?"

The pickup that smelled like him? Almond and anise over a clean soap smell? Simple and uncomplicated, like I had thought he was. Three nights in a hotel room had been hell on my hormones. My car was warm enough. "I can help."

The corner of his mouth lifted. Not many would realize it was his smile. "Sure. Pop the trunk?"

I did and he dug out the portable air compressor. He plugged one end in the car and stretched around to hook on the nozzle.

The rhythmic cycling of the tiny motor filled the parking lot, but it was getting late and not many people were milling around. None of them bothered more than a glance toward us. All they saw was a damsel in distress and a hot knight who'd ridden in on his mighty steed.

"Were you at work?" I asked.

"No reason to be anywhere else," he said simply.

I chewed my lower lip to redirect the sting of pain his comment caused. He hadn't meant it as a barb about how I'd left him, but then again, I hadn't been enough to lure him away from work when we had been together either.

A few more minutes passed with us staring at the still-flat tire.

"I don't think it's going to hold air," he said. "I'll put the spare on."

He squatted down and I couldn't look away. His shirt pulled tight over his shoulders. His black belt held it tucked in and added a border over his tight ass. Powerful thighs twisted and turned as he set the compressor aside and undid the lug nuts one by one. The small grunt he let out before he loosened each nut made me feel slightly better about my inability to do the same.

The light scruff on his jaw gave him a dangerous look that my inner wanton craved. He could wear all the suits he wanted, but it didn't change that he'd grown up in the dirt, chasing cattle and his brothers. He'd polished those rough edges and I wanted to scrape them back up.

He put on the spare within minutes and cleaned up the mess before I could help. I continued to stare as he leaned in the car to tuck the tools under the back seat. What an ass.

When he bent to lift the flat, I stepped forward. "I can do that. You'll get dirty. Dirtier."

He glanced down and shrugged. "It's just a suit."

That cost more than my monthly paycheck.

He hefted the tire and carried it one-handed to the trunk and tossed it in.

Dusting his gloves off, he crossed to me. "Where are you going to take it?"

"Uh…" I'd had plenty of time to think this through, but I'd spent the last several minutes ogling my husband.

"I can follow you and give you a ride home."

"Sure. I think I'll go to that place on Central Avenue."

Aiden nodded his head once. "I'll call them in the morning."

"I should do it." I lifted my hands. I'd started the week reverting back to the starry-eyed ingenue after one weekend away with Aiden. But nothing had really changed other than we hadn't had sex.

One of the first things he'd said tonight was that I hadn't been enough to drag him away from the office.

Hurt flashed in his eyes and those soft lips of his pressed into a line. "Whatever works for you."

None of this worked for me. He'd swooped in and saved me, but he'd also devastated me at the same time.

Aiden

KATE HAD SAVED me from one of the most unproductive nights at the office. Her call had startled me out of the hundredth trance I'd found myself in.

She pulled into the parking lot of the tire shop. I idled behind the car as she ran around to grab her purse and a bag of groceries. She scrambled inside my pickup, using the running board and oh-shit handle to pull herself inside.

"Want to grab a bite to eat?" I asked as soon as she shut the door.

She blinked at me, her wide hazel eyes swirling with the millions of thoughts that streamed through her mind. When I'd started dating her, I realized I had to up my game. She was intoxicatingly intelligent. I could talk work without losing her, didn't matter if it was about King Oil or the ranch.

Regret infused her gaze. "I already ate."

"Want to join me anyway?" *Please say yes.* Since I'd heard her voice on the other end of the line, I hadn't wanted to be anywhere but at her side.

"Where are you going?"

"What about that Thai place we like?"

The corner of her mouth tipped up. "The place where I can't resist their spring rolls no matter how full I am?"

And I was after the moan she made whenever she bit into one. "Yes."

"All right. I'll let Mom know. I was picking up milk for her."

"As long as Randall gets his morning coffee."

Her gaze darted up to mine. "Yeah. You remember?"

"Yes." She shouldn't have to ask. Her family was important to her and I had paid attention to the details, the parts of her life she shared and talked about. I hadn't done enough with the knowledge, and I got that now. I pulled away from the tire place. "How are Sharon and Randall?"

"Counting down the days to retirement." And like I'd hoped, the floodgates opened and I relaxed into the cadence of her speech. "Randall retires in three years. He's not going to miss it, but if he doesn't find a hobby, he's going to drive Mom crazy if they both have to sit on top of each other all day. But he won't be able to take on more coaching. I think his days with the wrestling club are numbered. He just feels like he's letting them down if he steps away. He loves coaching, but it takes a lot out of him. He says the boys these days have more energy since they're not running wild through the neighborhood. He's so tired when he gets home. Then there's Mom. She talks about how she's going to have her desk packed a month before retirement. But she's going to be lost without hearing all the updates about her employees. She's like a surrogate grandma."

She didn't continue and I glanced over. The streetlights flickered over her face and she'd drawn her plump lower lip between her teeth. She wasn't wearing makeup and the sweatpants she had on weren't ones she wore often. She was cute in them. Whenever her coat moved high enough, I got a nice glimpse of her round ass.

Usually when she stopped on a dime like this, I stayed quiet and she continued. Not tonight.

"And then what?"

"Oh, nothing. It's just more rambling."

"I don't mind." Kate's voice worked better than any over-the-counter medicine I could buy for the stress headaches that'd been popping up for years. I hadn't gotten them until I'd started at King Oil. After I'd fucked up and taken on more work to keep mistakes from happening again, they'd gotten worse.

"We're here."

Damn. I parked and got out. She slid out and charged inside.

Once we were settled at a booth, I set my phone on the table. The screen flashed on. Full of notifications. Dad had insisted I shut off all the bells, dings, and vibrating alerts. Then he'd checked all my devices to be sure I had complied.

Nothing's that urgent, Aiden. We're in the oil business, not the ambulance business.

I hated to admit that I didn't miss a single one of those sounds. But I kept the visual notifications, and dread piled on my shoulders whenever I saw the screen. Emails. Messages in at least four apps. Missed calls.

The server came over and dropped off menus and water. Neither Kate nor I looked at them.

"How's work?" I asked. Another notification lit my screen and I suppressed my groan. I had a survey from a special advisory and consulting company I was supposed to finish by tomorrow. Something about what the focus of the company's future was from a CFO's point of view.

This CFO wanted a quiet meal with his wife.

Kate's gaze dropped to my phone and she waited a beat, like she was seeing if I was going to tend to business. When I didn't, she said, "Work's good."

Was she purposely not elaborating? She loved her job.

She fiddled with the edge of the menu she wasn't reading. The dark purple shirt she wore molded over her breasts and it took an obscene amount of effort to drag my gaze up. The ball on the top of her winter hat jiggled with each movement of her head. She hadn't taken it off.

"Aren't you hot?"

"Hmm?" She prodded her hat. "No. Well, yeah, but I showered earlier. Didn't think I'd be seeing anyone for a quick milk run."

"You look fine, take it off."

"No, thanks. My hat head would be criminal."

"Kate, I've seen you worse."

She tilted her head, her eyes solemn. "Have you though?" Before I could ask what she meant, she slid out of the booth. "I'll be right back." She headed for the restrooms.

What had she meant? I'd seen her in the morning. Most mornings. Some mornings. I woke earlier than her to work out and get to the office. On the weekends, she… I was at the home office a lot. But I'd seen her in boots covered in mud and cow manure and with dirt on her face. Though then she'd rushed through the bathroom first while I hung out with my brothers.

I scowled and picked up my phone. I could knock out that survey quickly.

I didn't know how much time had gone by when Kate slid in across from me.

"This'll just be a minute," I said.

The server arrived. Kate ordered her spring rolls and I sensed their attention on me.

"Do you mind?" I asked Kate.

She ordered my pad thai. Another page

on the survey popped up. Goddammit. Couldn't I get one night to myself?

I could've carved out tonight if I hadn't taken a week off for my meltdown. Kate took out her phone and tapped at the screen. I wished she'd talk. I could multitask, but she'd said nothing to me since she'd returned.

She'd taken her hat off and finger-combed her hair. The section that had been pressed down by the hat was still flattened, giving her a sexy, rumpled look. A fresh-out-of-bed look that I longed to see again. I kept the phone centered so she outlined everything else in my line of sight. Just sitting near her soothed the flurry in my mind. Kate was the calm in my storm. Without her, I was only pretending to keep my shit together.

My food cooled, but this damn survey... They'd surveyed oil companies all over the northern US and Canada. If I was the only CFO who didn't respond, it wouldn't look good as to what King Oil took seriously as future concentrations. I could just see our name called out on the report sent out to investors. But the questions required more of an essay for an answer than a short response and Kate was almost done eating.

I had to apologize. "I'm really—"

"Oh, that's my ride." She laid a twenty on the table by her plate.

The survey was forgotten and the apology froze on my tongue. "What ride?" Why was she paying?

"You're busy." She slipped out and grabbed her winter coat.

She was heading to the door before I'd gotten up and left my untouched meal behind.

"Kate."

She was out the door.

The twenty wasn't enough to cover our meal and tip, but I'd make it right after I talked her into staying. "Kate. Don't leave."

She paused with her hand on the door. "Aiden." My name came out in tired exasperation. Like she was physically exhausted because of me. "You need to find a reason."

I lifted my shoulders and shook my head. A reason for what? But the defeat in her eyes left me tongue-tied. I'd messed up and didn't know how.

She opened the door and asked the driver to wait a minute, then turned to me. Wind ruffled her hair. My hands itched to bury themselves in her silky strands.

She stuffed her hat on her head. "Between the trust and your work, I don't know what to think about us. You asked for more time, but for what?" She lifted her chin toward the restaurant. "So I can watch you on your phone for the next fifty years? So you can work so hard you have a heart attack like your dad? Tonight, you said you had no reason not to be working." She stepped closer and cupped my face, her hands warm despite the cold weather. "You need to find your reason."

She released me and put distance

between us. "Can you unlock the pickup so I can grab the groceries?"

I didn't respond but went to the pickup and retrieved them for her. She managed not to touch my fingers as I handed the bag to her.

"Everyone depends on me. *Everyone* at the company depends on me." I should've kept my mouth shut. She should be my priority and I'd just admitted that I worked so hard for everyone else.

"Do you think what they need out of you is to never see you?"

"It's how I can best serve them."

"And what about yourself, Aiden? What do you want?"

The answer came easy. "You."

Sadness darkened her eyes more than the night sky. "You have a funny way of showing it. Good night, Aiden."

And she was gone. I had to go in and leave more money for the food. Take my entree to go. I wasn't hungry.

For once, I had been honest with my

feelings, and it had done no good. Too little too late.

I'd asked her for more time and then wasted what she'd given me, just like I had the last four years.

ate

LIGHT STREAMED through large picture windows. The ceiling was arched, lending an openness to the space that would've been smothered with regular-height ceilings. The apartment's open floor plan did the same. A spacious island and ample counter space were inviting, and each of the two bedrooms was large and square.

For a moment, I was alone in the living area. I closed my eyes. Traffic buzzed outside those massive windows. The muffled echoes of slammed doors resonated through the walls. Voices carried down the hall.

No matter how beautiful, it was still an apartment. Way more sizable than the hole I'd lived in after I'd gotten my master's and landed the job at the library. But an apartment all the same.

The manager of the complex exited the farthest bedroom he'd sworn would make a plush office when he'd learned I didn't have kids. Another office. Yay. He'd stepped away and taken a call. I'd let reality sink in and rob my good mood with it.

"Sorry about that," he said sheepishly. Kurt was a nice guy. He hadn't given off any creepy vibes. And I'd been watching for them, since I was a single woman looking for a place to live where I wouldn't be the only one with access to the front door.

"No problem. It's nice."

He strode through the room, his stockinged feet sinking into the high-quality carpet. "The third-floor units really are the best. We can utilize the area around us better without running into another unit."

I agreed. But there were still three other units around me. One next to me, one across the hall, and one playing heavy bass music under me.

I missed my house.

Kurt was oblivious to the noise. For an apartment, it was minor. The place I'd lived in when I'd met Aiden had been party central for anyone around drinking age. My neighbors had been nice guys, but they'd loved company and drinking until my alarm clock went off in the morning.

Kurt dug into a folder he carried with a clipboard. "The application process is all online nowadays, but I'm old school." He flashed a congenial smile. "I've printed off the application so you can read all the fine print."

And so I had a sheaf of paper floating around that'd keep me from forgetting this apartment was available for half my salary. Kurt was nice, but he was still a salesman of sorts.

It was a fine place though. The building had an elevator and was close to the gym I was considering joining, though I couldn't yet bring myself to do more than purchase daily passes.

Foolish optimism, or abject denial. I couldn't decide.

He pulled out a three-page document that was stapled together. "We do ask for references."

I held in my groan. What was I going to do, have Aiden tell him that I was a decent roommate? That I paid for my half of the grocery bills? I stuffed the panic down. It hadn't been that long since I'd lived in an apartment.

"Another reason why I print out the application," he continued. "It's a lot of information we don't have at our fingertips if we've lived in one place for a while."

Astute Kurt. I'd given him my maiden

name when I'd called. No reason to do differently until I was actually signing legal documents. But my trepidation at looking at new places must've shone like a lighthouse beacon. Add in the lack of enthusiasm over the beautiful apartment and he'd figured my situation out. I accepted the papers from him.

He folded his hands in front of him. "Any questions? Would you like to see another unit?"

"No, I'll think on this."

He rubbed his temples, one of the many nervous tics he had. "These do tend to move fast—when they're open."

A kind, and anxious, fellow. Still a salesman. "I understand."

Beaming, he stuck his hand out. "It was nice to meet you, Ms. McDonough."

"Thank you, Kurt." I'd told him to call me Kate. Mostly because hearing my maiden name only reminded me that I'd been too chicken to give him my real name.

I parted ways with Kurt, relief melting

off my shoulders the farther I got from the massive apartment building. Tossing the papers in the back seat, I slid behind the driver's seat and heaved out a long breath.

This was the first apartment I'd looked at since I'd left my house, and I'd hated the experience.

Aiden had asked me for time, but we weren't much different than his cattle: going through the chutes and coming out the other side in a pen that looked exactly the same. Except Aiden and I weren't even going through the motions anymore. He hadn't called me since I'd ditched him at the Thai place.

My phone buzzed. No one called me except for Aiden, but when I glanced at the phone, it read *Dad*.

"Hey, Katie-bear." My nickname had survived the divorce. My brothers shunned most things related to our father, but Katie-bear had stuck. "I'm coming through tomorrow, late morning. You free?"

Dad's visits were normally bittersweet. I

was happy he called me, then the guilt set in. A little resentment that he only hit me up when he was coming through town for his job. Today I expected a bigger hit of bitterness, but it didn't come. Tomorrow he'd be saving me from a day of figuring out how to stay out of Mom and Randall's way. They didn't get much time together when they weren't exhausted. They didn't need a mopey daughter to deal with.

"Sure. Tell me when and where."

"I'll know better when I stop tonight. I'll message you. Love you, Katie-bear."

I hung up, a smile playing over my lips. It faded seconds later. I could feel bad about how Dad only called when his route took him through town, how he was another man in my life with hurtful priorities. But this time it was about my brothers. Dad never called them. He'd send a Christmas card to Jason and Matt, include some money for the kids. The effort of facing their wrath and answering for his behavior kept him from two-way communication.

I'd seen what that kind of behavior had done to my brothers. How they'd acted out as kids. The anger they still carried as adults.

I'd seen the effects from the perspective of a child and an adult. I'd observed it and acknowledged it on an unconscious level, until now.

Before the wedding, Aiden and I had discussed having kids. I'd wanted a family. I'd been bearing down on thirty, I'd been getting married, and I'd felt it was my time. He'd asked me to wait for a while. Work and all that. I'd waited. More unconscious acknowledgment. We weren't going to have kids. We were never going to have kids.

Work and all that.

I didn't want my kids to feel like my brothers did. If I stayed with Aiden, would he change his mind? If he didn't, then what?

THE BUSTLE OF THE CAFÉ, and the constant stream of vehicles and semis outside the five-foot-tall picture windows, made it easier to tell my dad about the last month of my life.

"I'm really sorry to hear that, kiddo." Dad took a long pull from his black-as-tar coffee and pulled his teeth back like the cup was half filled with vodka. He'd quit drinking shortly after he and Mom had split, and no coffee was safe around him. If they figured out a way to give it via IV, he'd be first in line.

"It is what it is." The good thing about spilling my story to him was that he never got overly emotional. If he wasn't going to ooze sympathy and give me a hug, then I wouldn't cry while telling him.

His smile was small, crinkling extra lines around his eyes that hadn't been there the last time I'd seen them, along with the additional gray at his temples and the widening thin patch of sandy-blond hair on top of his head. "Just like your mom." I shot him a questioning look and he elaborated. "You aren't going to put up with anyone's bullshit."

I wished that were true, but pride sang through me anyway. Was this why I couldn't cut Dad out of my life entirely? His scraps of affection made me feel special. I hadn't wanted to marry a guy like my dad. But I'd married one who made me feel the same way. A guy who put his life and everything in it first, but when he turned that focus on me? Addicting.

Our food arrived and Dad dug into his omelet and hash browns. I used a fork on my jumbo double chocolate muffin. I'd backed off this type of breakfast, the kind that was actually a piece of cake in disguise, but since leaving Aiden, I had it at least once a week. Maybe two. Or three.

I finished before Dad did and dug out my phone. "I recorded some of the kids' wrestling matches. Want to see?"

"I hate to rush off." Dad pushed his plate away and dug a couple of twenties out of his wallet. "But I gotta be in Bismarck by tonight. Send them to me and tell the boys I'll catch them next time?"

I never told my brothers anything of the sort, and I wouldn't wonder if he'd watch the videos. Wrestling was Randall's thing and Dad probably harbored some bitterness of his own. "Sure. I might stay and finish my Diet Coke."

Another short visit with Dad. I always hoped for more. Like I had with my marriage. For four years. Was Dad why I had accepted similar neglect from my husband?

"Tell your mom and Randall hi." Dad leaned down to kiss me and the aroma of cheap vanilla air freshener washed over me. Truck stops and vanilla-tree air fresheners would always remind me of Dad. And I was afraid that was all I would have of him.

He rushed out the door to his semi parked at the far end of the lot, loaded with mattresses to deliver later tonight. How many more of these last-minute lunches was I going to sit through? How many more was I *willing* to sit through?

My glass was refilled and I watched out the window as everyone came and went. What else should I do with my day? These were the weekends that made me miss working Saturdays and Sundays. I'd been at the library long enough that I only worked one weekend every six weeks unless I picked up a shift for someone. I would've, but no one took time off in the winter. The boys didn't have a wrestling tournament and I had nothing to do but hunt for apartments.

I moved ice around in my glass with the straw, searching my brain for errands to run. The obvious one was finding a place of my own, but my stomach clenched and my throat grew thick whenever I thought of apartment hunting.

"Katie?"

My head popped up at the familiar voice. My gaze landed on a guy my age. His face had rounded out since our college years, but his blue eyes were as kind as they'd always been and his grin was aimed at me. "Gabriel?"

He laughed and held his arms out. "Been a while, right?"

I rose and wrapped my arms around him. My college sweetheart. We could've been more than that, but we hadn't gotten beyond the sweetheart stage to madly in love.

What would it have been like if we had? Would we have found jobs in the same city? Would I have two kids by now and my own wrestling tournaments to prepare for?

Longing tugged at my heart. When I pictured two kids running around, Aiden was in the background. It was why I'd quit imagining what it would be like to have kids with Aiden.

Gabriel let me go, still grinning. "Small world, eh?"

"What are you doing in town?" I gestured to where Dad had been sitting. "Have a seat." Gabriel looked around, his gaze curious. I waved off his unspoken question. "I met my dad for lunch but he had to take off."

He slid into the seat across from me. "How is your dad? How are you?" He chuckled. "First question first. I had a conference in town. I'm heading back to Helena tonight. You live here though? I heard you got married." His eyes dipped to the hand my wedding ring should've been on.

My smile started to die before I caught it. "I did, and I work at the library. Dad is doing well. Caffeinated and chews through audiobooks on his long hauls."

"That's great, Katie." His head bobbed and his eyes once again dipped to my bare wedding ring finger. If it wasn't too obvious, I'd curl my arm into my stomach and hide it. "Were the rumors true? You married Aiden King?"

"Yes." I wiggled my hand. Did I commit to a lie? It wasn't a lie. I was still married. Technically. "I don't wear the ring. It's…"

Talking to Gabriel had always been easy. He was an enthusiastic rambler like me, but he was also an active participant in the conversation. And he listened. "It made me self-conscious."

"Ah. The Oil King got you a rock."

"A boulder."

He chuckled. "I admit to being disappointed when I heard you were off the market, but I'm happy for you. After you, I came close to marrying once, but I chose my job again."

"There's nothing wrong with loving your work." *Unless you use it to stay away from those you love.*

The waitress stopped by, digging in her waist pouch for a pen. "Can I get you anything?"

Gabriel lifted his brows at me. "You have to go soon?"

I shook my head. Talking to Gabriel would be the perfect distraction in my day. He ordered a bowl of chili and salad. My Diet Coke was topped off.

"So, you two have kids?" His lips curved into a rueful smile. "Sorry. Small-town nosy. I slip into it when I'm talking to someone I know."

Resignation spread through me. I was a married woman in my thirties; it wasn't an uncommon question. Most people who asked were looking for a familiar thread of conversation and grasped at the same questions they'd heard adults around them asking their whole life. I didn't take it personally, but I avoided the topic as often as I could. Sucked that it came on the heels of my question to myself yesterday. "No kids. You?"

He shook his head. "Maybe someday. I haven't ruled it out."

We chatted through his meal and three more refills of my drink. He asked about my family and work. Bisa. Trips I'd taken since I graduated. We laughed over college memories. Gabriel was nothing more than a friend, we had a history together, but the way he knew me was comfortable.

Reassuring. Our conversation was back and forth and he didn't look at his phone.

Would Aiden and I ever reach this point? Gabriel and I were like this even after we'd broken up. Aiden hadn't called once since I walked out on him.

The chances of our marriage surviving seemed slimmer than ever.

Aiden

THE WINTRY COUNTRYSIDE PASSED by the window as I drove to Xander's new place. Brittle brown grass stuck out of the snow. Green spiky bushes and ponderosa trees dotted the hills. Fence lines cut off ranchland from the road, running in clean lines between sections and quarters.

I turned down the long road that led into the driveway of Xander and Savvy's house. Given that my brother and his wife were millionaires, most people would assume their house was ostentatious, sucking resources down just for the right look. But their house was no different than other new builds around Billings. Savvy had gone with a two-level prefab, recycled-steel-sided home in brick red with locally sourced rock accents—she and Xander had roamed their land, digging their own boulders out of the dirt.

Most of the interior was finished, and the two world travelers wanted to spend the winter in their home. Xander had left much of the basement unfinished to give himself something to do while Savvy ran her consulting business.

I parked by the garage doors. The door in front of me opened, and Xander waved from the steps that led to the door to the house.

I got out and tipped my head at Savvy's hybrid car. "How's that handle in the snow?"

Xander chuckled. "She's determined to

prove that it has enough power to survive out here, but I'll keep my four-wheel drive just in case."

I followed him inside. A brand-new house, yet it welcomed a person better than the one I'd lived in for years. Warmth surrounded me and the soft smells of lavender and vanilla laced the air. The walls, though, they weren't much different than mine. The photographs that hung all over the house were Xander's own work. Pictures of the mountain he'd camped in outside Kosovo, brilliant blue water in Sri Lanka, sweeping fields in the Philippines, it all made the place uniquely theirs.

When Kate had moved in, she'd added to my sparse decor. Mama's photos were displayed, some of Xander's, and a few from amateur photographers in the area. The landscapes lining the walls of my house weren't much different than Xander's, but the atmosphere in each house was worlds apart. I couldn't put my finger on why.

"I'm going to get those pretty jeans of

yours dirty," Xander said as he led me to the basement.

"You mean when I show you how the hard work is really done?" The joke came easy. Xander and I hadn't hung out much since I'd left home. He'd avoided the family, only coming home for weddings and the occasional spring cattle work, sometimes the fall. He and Savvy had moved to Billings, but this was the first time he'd been around for any length of time.

I had an inbox full of work, but when he'd messaged asking if I could help this weekend, I'd traded a long day working for some brother time. I could work tonight.

"Want a beer?" Xander's voice echoed throughout the open basement. Windows let in what light the thick clouds allowed through. Small plastic domes lined tables. Each of them had something green growing inside.

Xander pointed to them. "If you get hungry, pick a lettuce."

"No kidding?" I wandered over. My

boots thumped over the gray flooring. Linoleum. I couldn't believe Savvy would use a material that people remodeled to get *out* of their homes, but she'd rattled off details about linseed oil, ease of manufacturing, and using it as fuel when it was no longer useful.

Xander turned into a nice-sized square room. "This is going to be my office. I wanted to finish it with my bare hands." He gave me a sheepish smile. "I thought that being surrounded by my own creative work would get the juices going on below-zero days."

I lifted a brow.

His lips twitched. "Shut up. Dick." He went to a stack of rectangular planks. "Cork flooring. It should be easy enough to install."

Between the two of us, we knocked out the floor in a few hours. Days like this made me hate the office, days when I could move and feel alive instead of like a mountain of paperwork would suffocate me. I lived for going to King's Creek and helping Dawson. A few times a year wasn't enough.

Xander grabbed a couple of beers from the downstairs fridge and we sprawled on the floor of his office.

"Gonna stay and help me with the trim?" he asked.

"Is it stained already?"

His grin was unrepentant. He had more work than just the flooring that he wanted my help with. "About that. There's space in the garage to stain it. Just like the floor, it won't take long with both of us."

I took a long drink.

"Unless you have to go back to work." He sounded resigned.

"There's always work." I didn't say I had to go. I didn't want to go back to the office, or to my quiet house. My stress headache was returning.

"Tell me to butt the hell out—because I know how Grams is—but why won't she let you hire on?"

Grams earned a lot of the blame we put

on her, but she wasn't the sole backer of this decision. Not for the VP of finance. The other positions were just her thinking small, thinking it was like the old days when companies backstabbed each other instead of collaborating. She thought more higher-ups meant more opportunities for subterfuge.

"Money. Trust. Loss of control. It's Grams; take your pick," I answered.

He set his beer down. "All right, then. How's Kate?"

I clenched my jaw. I'd rather talk about the company even after I'd just been thinking how nice it was to ignore it for a bit. "Fine. Living with her parents."

"Are you two…"

"For a guy who left home and made himself unreachable for over ten years to avoid talking about his life, you're really damn nosy."

"Maybe I learned that avoiding the issue made everything worse and cost me a lot of years with people I usually like to hang around when they're not being touchy assholes."

Touchy asshole. Astute description. "I asked her for time."

"You don't want to divorce?"

I glared at him. First Dad. Now Xander. "No. Why would I?"

"None of us really knew if you married for the trust or not."

"None of you?"

His gaze was steady. I ground my teeth together and stared at the off-white wall across from me. Dad and my brothers didn't think I'd married my wife because I loved her, and I hadn't thought I needed to justify myself. Maybe a little part of me thought my actions should speak for themselves, like they had with the rest of my life. And…they had.

"I love her," I finally said. "That's why I married her. It's as simple as that." Simple, but impossibly complicated.

His gaze bored into me for a few

moments before he said, "Did she give you time?"

I thought back to that night I'd bared a part of me to Kate in her old bedroom. "Yes."

"So what are you doing with it?"

I scrubbed my face with my hands. "I fucked it up." We had talked. We'd taken a trip together. Then I'd done what I always had and she'd left. "How am I supposed to change when I don't know what else I can do?"

"Have you talked to Dad?"

"Nope."

"Dawson? Beck?"

I shook my head.

"Anyone?"

I meant to be sarcastic, but I couldn't summon the energy. "Think that's my problem?"

Xander snorted. I shot him a dirty look, but his expression turned somber. "Maybe that's where you need to start."

"I tried."

"You gotta keep doing it. I also wouldn't waste that time she gave you. I saw her with another guy."

Fury spread through my body like a brush fire, only to be cooled by despair an instant later. Another guy? She wouldn't move on that quickly.

Would she? "Maybe it was a coworker."

"It was the truck stop with the restaurant."

The relief was so instant, I almost put my hand on my heart to make sure it resumed beating. "She meets her dad there."

"Does her dad look like he's our age?"

Damn. Her dad was older than ours. She wouldn't be that far from the library for lunch with a coworker.

Xander interpreted my silence as a no. "I was filling up and she was by the window, and I don't know, man. She was different."

"How so?" I couldn't brace myself against what he had to say. It was like my bruised pride opened up for the beating.

"She was laughing and talking and gesturing with her hands. She's so reserved around us, like she wants to engage more than she does. Do we intimidate her?"

"No. I do." I drained my beer. Had she moved on? Did I think we had more time while she was living the life she'd been missing out on? Like lunch in the middle of the day, at a place where she could get the greasy diner burgers and crispy fries she loved. When was the last time I'd met her for lunch?

Xander rose in one swift move. "Well, she's not here, but I am. Practice talking to me. Removing the stick from your ass is going to be hard, but I've got some ideas."

But doing something with my hands was better than listening to the litany of my own faults I could recite in my sleep.

As I went up the stairs and through his house to the garage, my gaze caught on a picture of Savvy laughing in a meadow, her arms spread wide and her hair streaming behind her. Beside it was another casual photo of both Savvy and Xander in front of a small cabin. Several more photos of them with their friends surrounded it.

That was it. The difference between his decor and mine.

Other than a wedding photo over our mantel, there were no other pictures of me and my wife.

CHAPTER 12

ate

IT WAS dark out by the time I parked in the driveway of my old house. The magnetic pull this place had on me would lure me inside to stay if I let it. When Aiden had first brought me here, I'd thought it was the most magnificent house I'd seen. Simple, but majestic. It blended with the rugged beauty of the hills and buttes around Billings. The deep blue of the siding on the peaks above the door and the garage paralleled the Yellowstone River that ran a ways behind the house.

I missed my home.

If only I was coming here for any other reason than to talk about our divorce. Aiden hadn't called. He'd messaged. *Can you come talk tonight?*

I hadn't heard from him for days and now he wanted to talk? It wasn't a good sign. Good thing I'd been in my bedroom in the trailer. The tears had been instant and plentiful.

There was a tap on the window. I screeched and jumped.

Aiden held his hands up. "It's just me." His eyes crinkled at the corner with his almost smile. "Sorry. The stars are out, so I came out to wait for you."

Aiden was taking time to admire the stars? It was after eight, but that was early for him to be home.

I got out and he shut the door behind

me. His breath puffed around him, mingling with mine. He wasn't wearing more than the Princeton hoodie that Beck had gotten for him and blue jeans. His feet were bare on the frigid concrete.

His gaze raked down my body, making the winter coat I wore feel invisible. The light from the house cast shadows over his face, but not enough to hide the heat in his eyes. Warmth spread through my body in all the right places. I scurried away.

No calls, no messages for days. I was imagining the heat. My attraction to him clouded my judgment and I needed to be at full capacity when we talked.

The front door was unlocked. I left my winter coat on a hook and stepped out of my ankle boots. He followed me in and up the stairs.

I wanted to sink into the couch, find a show, and enjoy the peace. The library was quiet, but the reference desk required constant energy and brain power. Some days I didn't get more than a few minutes to myself at the desk. I didn't mind, but eight hours of it could be taxing. The feel of my house sank into me, soothing my bones. It wasn't a cluttered house, full of memory-laden knickknacks. I would've liked to do more, but Aiden had seemed to prefer the starkness.

A blanket and pillow rested on an armrest of the couch. Had he been sleeping out here?

I didn't sit. I couldn't.

"What did you want to talk about?" I whirled around and stumbled back. He was close, towering over me in a way I loved too much.

"Why were you out with a guy the other day?"

"Gabriel? How did you…"

"Xander saw you."

The truck stop was on the same side of town where Xander lived and Billings wasn't a big city. It wasn't a surprise he fueled up there. How had that looked to him? Gabriel and I had laughed a lot while we were together. To Xander, I'd probably looked like I was having the time of my life. "I had just finished lunch with Dad and then Gabriel happened to stop in. He's an old…friend."

"I don't recall a Gabriel."

I sighed. "It's not like you told me about all your exes."

"I don't have any exes." At my doubtful look, he added, "Not long-term ones."

I crossed to the island. Our divorce papers were in a haphazard stack. Aiden never left less than tidy piles. "Well, I had a long-term boyfriend in college. That was Gabriel."

"How long?" Aiden tracked me.

I flipped through the papers. They lay like they'd been tossed. Had he even read them? "How long what?"

"Did you date him?"

I thought back to those days. College

seemed so long ago. Gabriel and I had been young, idealistic. We were going to save the world with nothing but our brains and our ambition. "Not quite two years. But he got a job offer in California and I'd already been accepted to the master's program at Montana State. It was an amicable breakup."

His expression darkened. "And suddenly you ran across him?"

"Yeah, Aiden. Coincidentally, we were in the same diner—in the busiest gas station in town. He was here for a conference."

"And he's single?"

Aiden's rapid-fire questions were unlike him. Normally, I'd find the way he latched on to the topic of Gabriel fascinating. Aiden King, jealous? But Aiden had asked for more time and he was doing nothing but working. "Yep," I said, popping the *p*.

His jaw worked. "How convenient."

My patience hit the wall and tipped it over. He wasn't jealous. He was just pissed I had the audacity to not sit around and wait on him. I knew how that would end.

I wasn't interested in Gabriel, but I had a point to make.

"You know what was also convenient? How he listened to me. I talked about library science and he didn't tune me out. Did you know that someone can have a conversation with me and not check their phone? Not be on a computer? Not have their mind drift off to work? I talked to him, and get this—he talked back." I lifted my hands like *who knew*. "He remembered things about our relationship, and then he listened. He. Paid. Attention."

Several emotions cascaded through Aiden's fathomless eyes. Raw jealousy. Unfiltered hatred. Primal aggression.

I took a step back. My reserved and collected husband was ready to go nuclear.

He prowled closer. I couldn't back up. The hard slab of the island pressed into my ass.

"He paid attention? Does he know your

favorite color is eggplant, but you can't stand the vegetable? You think its texture is like eating wadded-up wet toilet paper. You like cats—and dogs—you fucking love animals, but you're afraid that if you take one in, you'll empty out all the pounds and shelters in town." He was inches away from me, his gaze only growing more intense. "You love flowers but you hate cleaning up the mess they leave behind when they die. When you walk through a cloud of cigarette smoke and everyone else complains, you don't because it makes you think of your mom, and even though you live in the same town, you still miss her. You like our big bedroom and the king-size bed because you like feeling that you can twirl around like you're in *The Sound of Music*. And the decorations on the walls drove you nuts when you moved in because they weren't important. They were meaningless. And after a small house with limited space, you wanted to fill the walls with pictures. That's why you chose Mama's pictures. Because you knew I wouldn't say no."

My mouth gaped. By now he was pressed against me, a wall of big, determined man.

"Do you think I don't pay attention to you when you talk about work? That I don't know the names of every single one of your coworkers and their quirks that drive you nuts, like how the new circulation-desk part-timer snorts all the time when his allergies are acting up? Or the reasons you think they're the best group you've ever worked with? You love how they write down every day on the calendar and your favorite is National Muffin Day because you fucking love muffins. I know who your favorite regulars are, that you get attached to the homeless who spend their days there. The ones you cried for when the drugs won in the end. The ones you worry about that move on to other towns and you don't know if they've found the help they need. I know which interns you thought would go far and the ones you wished would just go. I know that your two favorite times of the year are going to work cattle, but it's not the working cattle part, it's being with everyone. It's being with me. I know you have a love-hate relationship with the big diamond ring I bought you."

He crowded closer until I laid my hands on his hard chest.

"You thought I was ignoring you when I talked to other women? The whole time I was talking to them, I was wishing they'd just fucking leave so I could spend some quiet time with my wife. Time I don't get enough of and it's all my fault."

"I…" Had no clue what to say.

"Want me to keep going? I can do this all night. I know you, Kate." He hitched my ass onto the island. Papers scattered under me and behind me, but I couldn't take my eyes off his. "I might not know the parts of yourself you've purposely hidden from me, but I fucking know you."

His lips crushed mine. My resistance was gone. All the things he'd said ruined me. He paid attention. To me. All this time I'd thought he was ignoring me, or avoiding me, but he'd listened. His hands were everywhere. Dragging my leggings under my ass. I wiggled enough to help him. I had to be closer to him, to feel his hot skin on mine.

My ass pressed against the cool countertop, but I widened my legs. He wedged in closer and thrust his tongue in my mouth. I was greedy for everything he had to give.

When he slipped his hand between us to unzip his jeans, I shamelessly rubbed myself against him. He flipped his hand around and stroked through my wet heat, stopping on my clit. I groaned. Behind his hand, his erection was wedged between us.

His hold tightened around me, but he managed to position his cock and thrust. I cried out against his mouth. Nothing but pleasure. A painful emptiness that only he could fill. He was impossibly hard, filling me until I knew nothing but him. Both his hands were behind my ass now. There was no thrusting, no pistoning. He could barely work himself in and out, we were as close as two people could get.

All I knew was him, stroking me higher. I'd been without him too long. I didn't need more than a couple of pumps before I was cresting my peak. I fisted my hands in his hoodie and moaned into him. Needy whimpers left me, swallowed by him.

My body went rigid, and molten lava filled me until it erupted. I broke the kiss to yell his name.

He grunted, slamming into me harder and harder, forcing me higher and higher. I drew my knees up and let him work me until his body tightened and he threw his head back. His arms were around me and he held me in place as he emptied inside of me.

Aftershocks undulated throughout my body and I squeezed every last bit of pleasure out of them. I was supporting his weight, but he kept me from sprawling across the countertop.

Aiden raised his head. He peeled a hand off my ass and cupped my chin. "I'm going to take you to the bedroom, strip you down, and fuck you properly."

A tiny tendril of logic rose up, but I quashed it. My body thrummed from only a couple of minutes with him and I wanted more. "Okay."

He lifted me and I had to reach back and swat off the papers stuck to my ass. I tried not to think about what we'd just done. It wasn't the sex. It was that we'd had sex on the divorce papers.

~

Aiden

. . .

KATE CLUNG TO ME, her legs around my waist as I carried her through the living room, down the hall, and to our bedroom. I left the light off in the room. Ambient light from the kitchen was enough. For now. I wasn't going to do anything to scare Kate away—unless devouring her whole made her run.

I laid her on the bed and stood back to strip myself of every stitch of clothing I was wearing. She propped herself on her arms and watched me undress. I loved it and might've slowed down a microsecond to savor the look in her eyes. Greedy. Insatiable. She wanted more of what we'd done on the counter.

Before this, I'd had sex with Kate like I had romanced her. Textbook slow and tender. I'd work to make her feel desired, cherished, and to bring her to no less than two and usually three orgasms. I loved it. She loved it.

But we both wanted more. I got that now. She'd accused me of holding back and

I had. I'd done so because it was either necessary to stay quiet, or pointless to speak up.

Nothing about Kate was pointless.

Slow and sensual vanilla sex was no longer good enough. If I couldn't get across in words yet how phenomenally important she was to me, then I'd show her how desperately I needed her with my body. And then maybe soon, I could do it in other ways.

"This is going to be fast and rough again." My voice was gruff.

Her breath caught and shining eyes met mine. "Promise?"

"The next time you're in the office, I'm taking you over my desk and I don't care if it's the middle of the fucking day."

She drew in a deep breath. It would've lifted her spectacular breasts if her sweater were off. I'd rectify that. I kicked out of my pants and prowled across the bed to her. My dick was hard like I hadn't just had the most powerful release of my life. I'd been without my wife for too long. There'd been no one but her since I was told I had to get married within months.

There really hadn't been anyone before her either. I could have gotten laid whenever I wanted, but I hadn't chased it. I'd been too busy and there'd been no one worth letting the work pile up for. There'd have been small talk and dating and the *more* that partners inevitably expected. Like Kate said about fancy restaurants and dressing up—tedious.

I stopped my progress to lift her sweater over her head. "Do you know how often I've fantasized about fucking you on my desk, Kate?"

"You have?"

"I was late for a meeting once. Had a hard-on I couldn't get control of."

Wonder dominated her gaze. "For me?"

"All the damn time." I snapped the latch to her bra and her breasts fell free. Thank fuck for front-latching bras. The straps fell down her arms and she lifted her hands and tossed it aside. "Do you fantasize about me?"

"All the time," she said in that breathy voice I craved.

I pressed her backward with my body until we were stretched out in the middle of the bed. I wedged her knees apart with mine. Her wet center opened for me, making a perfect, cock-teasing cradle.

I kissed the corner of her mouth and worked my way down her chin, her neck. Her breasts with her peaked nipples were my first target. "Tell me one."

"Th-the plane."

I smiled around a tight peak, my hand massaging her other breast. Licking across her nipple, I enjoyed her shiver. "The bedroom or the quad seats?"

"Anywhere. I want to be in the mile-high club. With you." She arched her back as I switched to the other side. "Do private planes count?"

"We'll make it count." I brushed my

fingers down her side, over her hip, then down her slit.

Another shiver, this time mixed with a moan. "Aiden."

"You're so fucking wet." I kept moving down her body, using my lips and tongue the entire way. "I love getting in bed and asking if you're still awake, and when I touch you, you're already soaked."

I didn't need the light to know her face was on fire. By the time I was done, she'd flush down to her belly button. "You're really good at sex."

"I'm going to be really bad in all the best ways." Then I quit talking and put my mouth to use.

My tongue swiped over her clit and she let out a long groan. I didn't have to hitch her leg up to get more access. She bent her legs and ground her heels into the mattress.

Her knees were going to be up to her fucking shoulders by the time I was done.

Gripping her hips and pulling her to me,

I feasted. Her knees hitched higher and she buried her hands in my hair.

"Oh, god, Aiden."

The early ripples of another climax were already beginning. Her arms crushed her boobs together as she gripped my hair. Her body was coiled tight, but pliant where it counted the most. Hair swirled around her head. This was the most wanton my wife had ever looked. Open. Demanding. If I tried to pull away—which I had zero plans of doing—she'd yank me back to her.

I didn't have to use my fingers to get her to come on my tongue, but I inserted one anyway. This wasn't going to be another run-of-the-mill orgasm. I stroked in, then out, then added a second, matching the rhythm of my mouth. We might've been vanilla, but I knew what she liked.

Her moans were steady. Muscles tensed around me as she tried to rotate and rock her hips, but I held her tight.

I closed my mouth around her nub and attacked.

"Oh my god!" She bucked once and released my head like she was trying to steady herself but the rocking wouldn't quit. "Oh my god—Aiden!"

It was the longest orgasm I'd ever wrung out of her. She hollered my name and it echoed through the house. My neighbors were over a mile away, but they could've heard it.

When she collapsed on the mattress, I raised my head but kept my fingers in her clenching, spasming body. I gave them two slow pumps and her entire body shuddered.

"I don't think I can take any more," she gasped.

"You can, love." I withdrew my fingers, and to be wicked, I swiped upward, teasing her clit. She barked out a cry and I grinned. "Just let me do all the work."

I was on my knees, shoving her thighs wide and using my hands to hold her open. The tip of my erection glistened and twitched, more than a little excited. I'd been terrified these days were over. But each time we did this, each time I could show her how we fit together, how it was meant to be, would secure our future together.

I took more time sliding inside than before. Inch by inch, I stretched her. Her eyelids fluttered and she looked down at our connection. "I love when you're inside me."

A force pumped through my cock, demanding I take her hard and fast. "It's the only place I want to be."

That was the God's honest truth. I had responsibilities. Obligations. People across the country relying on me. But if I could choose, this was where I would be every chance I got. Lost in my wife's body.

I powered in until I was buried. I could lean over her, take it slow, coax another orgasm out of her. The usual.

I loved our usual, but tonight wasn't the night for it.

I slid out and pounded back in. She gasped and gripped the comforter.

"Hang on," I said through gritted teeth. I

thrust, over and over. Her mewls and her gasps and the way she grappled for the headboard to meet each thrust fueled me. She was propane and I was a lit match.

My hands around her legs, I kept up the erotic assault. I shoved one of her legs higher and changed my angle. I knew what worked for her, but it was time to find out what else got her off. I *knew* what got me off—Kate's lush body. Seeing her lose control when I used only my tongue or did nothing but stroke in and out drove me crazy.

The force of my thrusts moved us across the bed. Her hands were splayed against the headboard, providing enough force to keep me from ramming her head against the wood.

"Fuck, Kate. I fucking love your tits." The creamy globes bounced and jiggled. I couldn't take my gaze off them. Had I ever told her how much I loved her body?

A flood of heat washed over our connection and she rocked her hips harder.

Yes. She was nearing another climax.

"Come for me, Kate. Show me how much you like this."

Searing pressure built at the base of my spine. I was ready to blow, but I couldn't, not until Kate got off again.

The noises coming from her were too jumbled to be words. The top of her head was dangerously close to the headboard. I was not going to give my wife a concussion.

I jerked out and she let out a shout at the loss.

Flipping her over, I didn't give her time to balance on her hands and knees before I placed myself and slammed inside. I stayed on my knees but draped myself over her back, one arm around her and gripping a warm, molten breast, the other stopping when I could lay a fingertip on her clit.

The force of my pounding was enough movement for her clit. My chest covered her back and I growled in her ear. "Give it to me, Kate."

Her whimper was close to a cry, but she

bowed and kicked her hips higher into me. The walls of her body squeezed me until my eyes damn near rolled back into my head.

I would not come until she did.

She lasted another second before she dropped her chest to the bed and cried out through another climax. Wet heat wicked over me until I threw my head back and roared her name. I lost count of how many times I slammed into her at my crest. At some point, I'd gripped her hips to keep her still while I emptied into a furnace so intense I had a hard time remembering my damn name.

I dropped down but rolled to the side to keep from crushing her. "You all right?" I panted.

"No," she said, her voice muffled by the blanket. "I'm not all right in all the best ways."

My breath eked out. Good. I hadn't fucked up. With this at least. I wrestled enough of the blanket over to cover her. I was hot enough I could be steaming. She'd taken everything from me, but I'd give her more. I'd give her more all night long.

"Get a little rest," I murmured and brushed her hair away from her face. "But, Kate?" Drowsy hazel eyes met mine. "I'm nowhere near done tonight."

CHAPTER 13

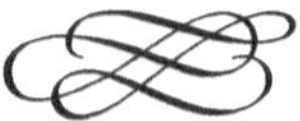

RHYTHMIC POUNDING woke me before my brain could register where I was.

My bed. In my bedroom.

I sighed and let the comfort of our California king bed with its primo mattress sink into my bones. I'd slept like a stone last night. No horns. No arguing neighbors. Nothing but the heat of my husband's body around me. A marching band could have gone by the window, and as long as I was in Aiden's arms, I would have slept soundly.

Grasping for my phone, I squinted at the window. What was the time? The room-darkening blinds were drawn, but light shone around the edges. It wasn't as early as I'd thought. Aiden had been rising before the ass crack of dawn longer than I'd known him, probably his entire life, but it was late by his standards.

I peered at the time. After eight.

Early by my standards for a Saturday.

I sat up. The blanket dropped from my chest and goose bumps spread over my body. I was naked. Another reason why eight a.m. felt more like four a.m., Aiden had kept me up until the middle of the night.

I'd known he had stamina, but I hadn't *known* he had stamina.

How could he have held back that much? And if he hadn't been getting what he wanted, why hadn't he strayed?

I flung the blankets aside. Rigid control.

Aiden was loyal to a fault, and he kept a tight rein on all extraneous bodily functions that didn't serve his goal. His primary goal was work, not sex.

Until last night.

And lord help me, I'd loved it. Aiden had gone out of his way in bed to make me feel treasured. I hadn't trusted the feeling, but that hadn't been his goal. If his goal last night had been to make me feel like an insatiable sex goddess who said yes to anything he asked, mission accomplished.

Sex like that would've made it impossible to draw up divorce papers.

I bit my lower lip. So now what?

It was too early to think about where we went now, or what to do with the divorce papers that might have bodily fluids on them.

I climbed out of bed and went to the walk-in closet. Dang, I missed this house. I could twirl inside this space with my arms open and my fingertips would barely graze the clothes hanging up.

I reached for a sweater I wore to work once in a while. It was beige cashmere, soft as a cloud, and fitted in a way that flattered my body type. Then what do I put on? Slacks? Do I go blow out my hair?

No. I had no plans today. If I'd woken up in the trailer, I'd have thrown on an old college hoodie with some leggings and fluffy socks. I'd kept some of my lesser-used loungewear here. After finding some, I finger-combed my hair and walked out of the bedroom.

Thankfully, our last round of sex had been in the shower.

The treadmill shut off. He'd do his strength training next, then come upstairs to chug a protein shake before he took a shower. Maybe I'd bring it down to him and do some shameless husband watching. He often worked out without his shirt.

I whipped his shake up. The bag of his strawberry mango powder was nearly empty. Did he know where to order it? I rolled my eyes. He'd been downing that shake since before me. He could take care of it.

But would I order the next bag? Or would he?

Would I move back in?

I concentrated on the single-serving blender and tried to forget the mounting questions.

I wasn't sure I'd like the answers.

I snagged a bottle of OJ and a banana for me. A muffin would be really good, but the exact opposite of the protein shake. I'd rarely brought a jumbo muffin into the house for a breakfast treat.

Despite that, he knew I loved muffins.

I carried the food downstairs. Weights clunked louder the closer I got.

There was a loud thunk, followed by a little grunt. As I rounded the corner, I spotted him. He jumped up from the bench and swung his arms back and forth as he sidestepped to the open center.

Stretch time.

He had an earbud in, but he caught my

gaze in the wall-to-wall mirrors that I usually avoided. His gaze dropped to the shake and appreciation filled his eyes.

"Thanks," he mouthed.

He must be listening to music. I suspected half the reason he worked out the way he did was because he loved a country song with a strong beat, and gym time was the only time he gave himself to indulge.

He swung an arm over his head and all the accessory muscles along his torso popped out. Behind him in the glass was me in loungewear and an armful of food. I couldn't bring myself to care.

I perched on the edge of the weight bench and munched on my banana. A wick of heat traced down my spine.

He was watching me eat the banana. I took a lingering bite but couldn't hold the come-hither face and broke into giggles.

His lips twitched and he dropped to stretch his legs.

I drained my juice. He popped up, took the bud out of his ear, and set it on the stand by the door that held the case with his other one.

I handed his shake to him and he gulped it down, standing over me. Tingles of awareness spread through my body. There was no way I was ready to have more sex. It had to be humanly impossible. Multiple orgasms only went so far. Right?

But as Aiden set his empty shake cup down and aimed his intense gaze at me, my lips parted. I wouldn't know how many orgasms were possible in twenty-four hours if I didn't try.

He dropped to his knees in front of me and growled, "Lie back."

Aiden

AFTER OUR SECOND shower together in less than twelve hours, I found Kate in the kitchen. She was preparing a brunch with the meager foodstuffs she could find. I'd been shit at getting groceries. Kate liked to shop herself instead of using delivery or pickup, and I'd happily let her.

I had my computer set up at the table, but out of the corner of my eyes, I tracked her progress through the kitchen. Especially when her ass was sticking out of the pull-out freezer. She found frozen sausage that Dawson had gotten when he'd traded a quarter of beef for a portion of pork. Then I got another look at her round ass when she dug out the waffle maker. Belgian waffles were a weakness of mine.

Most good food was a weakness of mine, but after Dad's health scare, I kept a strict diet. I sat behind a desk too long every damn day for it not to be.

The rich smell of waffles filled the air along with the sizzle of sausage and eggs. My stomach rumbled as if I hadn't eaten in a week.

But then Kate and I had worked up quite an appetite.

I was a dude. Most people would assume my thoughts revolved around sex and when I could get it next. But for me, sex was in the same category as my diet. If I let myself think about it, and if I indulged in it too often, I wouldn't get anywhere. Before Kate, it had been easier. Thoughts of getting off with a nameless and faceless woman could be controlled, confined, until the time I wanted to spare half a night to find someone who'd give me a better release than what I got in the shower.

After Kate, I'd had to develop strong mental muscles to keep from leaving my office at nine thirty a.m. because I knew Kate would be awake and didn't work until noon.

Staring at my computer on a Saturday morning, after experiencing the best night of my life, justifying why I hadn't done just that was difficult at best.

"All done." Kate set the frying pan by the sink and carried two platters to the table. One was piled with waffles and the other had the protein that would save me from inhaling the waffles.

I pushed my computer aside and popped up to get us plates and some water.

She sat next to me and we dug in.

"It's good."

She beamed. "Thanks. Mom's waffle recipe."

"How many did she have to make to feed your brothers?"

"I think she had to make at least five for Randall," she said with a smirk.

I chuckled and we ate in silence. Questions that had been pinging around my head wouldn't leave me alone.

When she finished and took her plate to the sink, I couldn't hold back. "What about us now?" Her shoulders stiffened before she turned around. I continued. "I'm not going to be dense and think last night"—my gaze heated—"or this morning, reversed the past."

She walked back to the table and I turned my entire chair. I sat at the head and she was on my right. I angled to be closer to her. She did the same with hers.

"I don't think it's a good idea to move back in yet."

Hurt ripped through my chest and gutted me. I'd laid everything out with her. Tried to show her how much she meant. I'd told her I didn't want to be dense, but damn. I hadn't done enough and I was paying for it now.

She grabbed my hand. "It's not you, Aiden," she said softly. I met her warm hazel gaze and clung to the sincerity in her eyes. "This is for me. Because of me. The last four years, I've been in this stasis and I don't like it. I was too timid to speak my mind with you, tell you how I was feeling. I stayed away from my family and friends to keep from speaking out loud the thoughts I'd tried to ignore. I did more of what I'd done in high school and tried to be what I thought I should be."

"I'm sorry."

"It's not your fault."

"But it is. You aren't comfortable around me."

Her lips curved. "Last night helped a lot."

I dropped my voice. "I can do more of that."

She squeezed my hand. "You'd better." Her humor faded. "But until I can prove to myself that I won't get intimidated by everything that comes with your name, or being your wife, I should stay with Mom and Randall. Just a little longer."

"Is being my wife the issue?"

She eased closer until she was off her chair and crawling onto my lap. "No, it's not. It's absolutely not." She brushed her hand through my hair. I groaned from the bliss. Why didn't she do that more often?

"I was almost twenty-nine when we married," she continued, running her hand through my hair again. My eyelids drooped shut. Her touch was heaven. "I should've been set in my identity, not some insecure little girl. But after we married I just…" She lifted a shoulder. "Wasn't really Katie McDonough."

"You weren't happy." Why hadn't I recognized this?

"I wasn't *not* happy. I've been in a stasis since our honeymoon, but *I'm* the one that put me there." She pushed another hand through my hair. "I like being able to do this."

"If that patch of hair didn't stick straight up, I wouldn't have to gel it."

The corner of her mouth tipped up. "It's cute." I arched a brow and she chuckled, her butt wiggling on my lap. "It makes you seem human."

"My brothers call me a robot." Their constant jabs about how much I worked and how little I poured my heart out to them got old. I wanted to leave the rest of my thoughts unspoken, but after worrying that she'd moved on, I couldn't backtrack with her, or myself. "I'm the oldest. I've always had the most responsibilities. The highest expectations from Mama and Dad.

Sometimes I feel like I raised my brothers, but they'd tell me Dad was around more than I know. He had to be…after I left for college."

"And it makes it hard to be a brother when you feel like you're not quite their brother, but not their parent."

I nodded. I wouldn't have been able to describe it like that, but she'd summed my feelings up perfectly.

"You loosen up around them a lot more than they realize."

I should get better about that too. But first, my wife. "Dawson invited me out for Christmas. Want to come with me?"

She dropped her hands to my shoulders. "Do you think it's appropriate?"

"There's nothing wrong with my family knowing we're working on our relationship." I rubbed her thighs through her soft pajama pants. "Bristol would like to see you, and I know how much you enjoy King's Creek."

"I enjoy King's Creek because of you."

"Because I loosen up." Jesus, what had I been like at home if being a dusty mess and smelling like horse sweat and cattle made me more approachable to my wife?

"Yes. And because you wear your cowboy boots." She leaned in to whisper in my ear, her breasts rubbing against my chest. "When you put your cowboy hat on, it drives me crazy."

I dug my fingers into her hips and pulled her closer. "Then next time I put my cowboy hat on, I want you to show me exactly how crazy it makes you."

Her smile held more than a hint of wickedness and I captured her mouth. Despite my growing erection, I didn't take it further. I was content to hold my wife and make out at the kitchen table. All my notifications were silent and it was easy to tell myself that I didn't have twelve hours of work looming ahead of me. Just like having Kate on my lap, meeting her tongue stroke for stroke made it easy to tell myself that divorce wasn't still an option.

ate

Sunlight shone through the driver's side of the window, highlighting Aiden's strong profile. He wore jeans and the same Princeton sweatshirt from the night we'd reconnected with explosive results. Our winter jackets were tossed into the back seat with our luggage and we were on our way to King's Creek.

Aiden and I had met up a few times a week for the last couple of weeks. We'd met for lunch one day. He'd invited me to his office too, but I hadn't gone. All I could think about was his promise to take me over his desk. As much as I wanted that, I wasn't brave enough to go knowing it might happen. And that Phillip would know what we were doing. And his dad. So maybe that'd have to stay a fantasy for a while.

My hands flew as I finished telling him my story. I'd been talking nearly nonstop since we'd left the house, but now that I knew he was not only listening, but enjoying my rambling, I was unfiltered.

"So then Mom says, 'Hey, there's this package for you.' " I paused to wait for his reaction.

He knew damn well what package I was talking about. He slanted a look at me, mischief in his eyes.

"*Yeah*," I said. "I didn't recall ordering anything but I didn't think twice about opening it right at the table in front of her and Randall."

Aiden broke into a grin. "Oh, no."

"Oh, yes, Aiden." I cut off a giggle. "Oh. Yes. And I see there are books inside, but the thing is, they were packed upside down. So I pull them out."

His deep chuckle vibrated through the cab.

"Randall almost chokes. And I turn the book around to see what's wrong and there's a woman with her legs around a guy. The one in my other hand is a woman in a negligee surrounded by four men."

"I tried to pick authors you might not have read." He tried to swallow his smile and failed. "For research purposes only."

My insides warmed. Not only had it been a thoughtful touch, it'd been personal. It wasn't the trendiest perfume in the one-percent crowd. Or a gaudy diamond ring. He'd taken the time to think about what I'd actually like. "To make it worse—"

"It gets worse?"

I nod. "Mom says, 'When you're done, can I read those?'"

"Sharon reads reverse harem?"

"She does now."

"Randall's going to thank me."

"That's gross, Aiden. I've heard them once already and almost suffocated myself with my pillow trying to muffle the noise."

He laughed, then his smile faded. "Are you sure it's okay you're not spending today with your parents?"

"Mattie and Jason are each doing a quiet Christmas Eve and going to their in-laws', or in Mattie's case, not-yet-in-laws." Mom and I had talked before I'd left. I wasn't sure if I should ask Aiden now or wait to see how the holiday went. Tomorrow was Christmas Eve and we planned to drive home Christmas night. I worked the day after. I'd ask now. This weekend wasn't meant to be a test. "But, um, Mom and Randall want to do a meal on New Year's. You're invited."

Surprise lifted his brows. "Yes. Sure."

Was I glowing? He hadn't hesitated.

So far, I'd been doing good on working on myself and how I responded to Aiden. When he had to work, which was still all the time, I made other plans that weren't picking up extra shifts or sitting at home. I helped Jason with the boys while Sophie was at work. I went to Violet's school recitals. Aiden had been invited, but he'd been working ahead to prepare for the time off he was taking today and tomorrow, and Christmas of course. Except, he'd do some work each day, but he was trying to strike more of a balance.

I put my elbow by the window. Between commentary on my coworkers' lives, my interactions with patrons, and thoughts on new books I'd read for work and for fun, I had plenty to ramble about.

But I didn't want to ramble more. The shift in the dynamics of our relationship had unearthed more than a few questions and I was committed to asking them. "Why don't you talk?"

He frowned. "What do you mean?"

"I can fill this entire trip with work stories alone. But you never do."

"Your work stories are interesting. Mine aren't."

I loved my job. The library staff. The patrons. I couldn't quit talking about them, and Aiden was my trusted source for all things normally confidential. With Aiden I assumed I was on a need-to-know basis and I didn't need to know. No doubt he had confidentiality requirements that extended to the billions of dollars he managed.

Your work stories are interesting. Mine aren't.

I worried my lower lip for a moment before I broached the new questions that had popped into my head. "Do you like your job?"

"Work is work," he said automatically.

I sucked my lower lip between my teeth again. His tone was neutral. Robotic.

Had his brothers used the term because Aiden had gotten so adept at shutting off his emotions in a job he didn't care for that it spilled over into his personal life?

"I thought you wanted to work at the company."

He lifted a shoulder without moving his hands off the wheel. "It was expected."

A horrible realization sank into my gut as solidly as a rock in a wading pool. "If it wasn't expected, you wouldn't have worked at the company?"

His mouth tightened so briefly that I might've missed it if I hadn't been scrutinizing him for all this new information. "It's a family company."

"Did your dad tell you that you had to work there when you were done with college? Your grams?" I could see Emilia doing that.

"Yeah, Grams and DB were pretty clear about their expectations for me. Beck talked about starting his own company even in high school. Xander obviously wasn't going to be an office jockey. And Dawson loves ranching, so we all knew he'd be running the cow-calf operation as soon as he was able."

"And you're the oldest," she finished. "But you wouldn't have chosen the company?"

"I didn't have to. It chose me," he said with zero emotion.

I tried a different tactic. "If you could've gone to school for anything, what would it have been?"

"I never thought about it, since it never mattered."

I switched my gaze to stare out the windshield. The snowy landscape on each side of the interstate was sparse and stretched as far as the eye could see. Brown grass stuck out in tufts, almost as plentiful as the snow.

Sadness filled my heart. Randall and Mom had worked to give my brothers and me the option of college if we wanted it. They couldn't have afforded to pay the full amount, but they'd put away as much as they could. My brothers had each chosen technical programs and I'd gone to a university. After that, I'd chiseled away at my student loans until I was married. Then Aiden had taken care of the entire amount with one hammer blow.

I hadn't taken it for granted that I could continue my education after high school graduation. What I *had* taken for granted, and only realized now, was that I'd been able to choose whatever program I wanted. I'd envisioned myself as a kind librarian with an ever-ready smile, like the ones that had helped and nurtured me while growing up.

Aiden hadn't chosen his career. He might hate his job and none of us would know. That…sucked. He made an obscene wage, but it had been at the cost of the rest of his life. He gave King Oil his everything, but it gave him little in return.

Aiden

. . .

I CLICKED through finance reports from our sites in North Dakota. A few sites around Williston were still moving oil, but several were shut down until the price of a barrel rose. It wasn't ideal, but that was the current climate.

It was early Christmas Eve and Kate was the only one sleeping. Bristol and Dawson had woken shortly after me and gone out to do chores. I was finishing work so I didn't have to be torn tonight for the meal.

Our arrival hadn't been as awkward as I'd anticipated. Dawson and Bristol had greeted Kate like normal and then they'd sat us down and showed us their growing plans for the sobriety ranch Cartwright Cattle would soon become. Bristol wanted it done right, so she and Dawson were taking their time, adding ideas and striking thoughts throughout the winter. Next month, they'd start researching companies to make Bristol's dream into a reality.

Upstairs, the bedroom door opened and a few seconds later another door closed. Kate was in the bathroom. My gaze drifted up the stairs and followed the railing that divided the bedroom area from the living room and kitchen space.

I clicked to another report. Tried to concentrate. My gaze rose to the second level. She'd be naked by now.

The entirety of our relationship, we'd never had sex in this house. I hadn't wanted to make Kate feel uncomfortable at the thought of fucking under Dawson's roof. Or having sex while one or two of my brothers, and maybe even Dad, slept nearby.

I sucked in a breath and adjusted my thickening dick. Sitting in jeans with an erection didn't make it easier to forget about my naked wife. I forced my eyes back to the report. Which site was this again?

Dawson and Bristol were still outside. If they came in and heard us, it'd serve them right. Dawson might rethink the robot bullshit. I flipped the lid shut on my laptop and bounded up the stairs.

The shower was running. I gripped the doorknob but it didn't turn. Damn. That was what growing up with one bathroom did to a girl.

I ran down to the office, found a paper clip, and straightened it as I sprinted up the stairs. It took two seconds to pop the lock and I was inside. The double shower curtain hid my nude wife.

Kate's soft humming stopped. "Hello?"

"It's me." I locked the door behind me.

"Oh. I'm almost done."

"I'm not," I growled as I ripped my sweater over my head. I'd picked the beige cowl-neck one that Kate liked, but she'd have to wait to see me in it.

She peeked out the door of the shower, her gaze landing on the hard-on I'd just freed from my pants. I kicked out of them, took my socks off, and stalked across the bathroom.

Her eyes went wide.

I answered her unspoken concern. "They're still out doing chores."

She flicked her gaze behind me like she was checking it was just us, then she pulled back the shower curtain wider to let me in.

I crowded her against the wall and the warm water spray hit my shoulder. I didn't want her anxious or mortified at the thought of getting busted, so I would make this fast.

Soap suds drifted down her shoulders onto her breasts. I flicked the bubbles away. "You missed a spot."

She puffed her chest out and her nipples grazed my skin. "Want to help me finish?"

I gave her a slow grin as I kneeled. She planted her hands on the wall as I hooked a leg over my shoulder.

It didn't take long with me tonguing her clit to get her wet and more than ready. She fought to keep her whimpers and moans quiet, but I could feel them vibrate through her ripe body.

I rose, sliding my hands up her slippery

body. Stealing an extra second, I got my footing just right so we didn't slide around like we were ice dancing. I gripped her hips and she let out a startled gasp as I lifted her. She automatically wrapped her legs around my waist and positioned her wet center over my straining erection.

I thrust up, and as soon as I pushed in, she flexed and lowered herself.

My groan was not quiet. I couldn't get enough of my wife. We didn't have sex every time we got together, but we'd managed it a few times since that first night. The way her body gripped mine and made my eyes cross, I'd think we hadn't had sex for a year or two.

"You feel so fucking good. This isn't going to take long." I crushed my mouth over hers and pressed her back against the wall. I licked into her as I thrust, steadily increasing my pace.

She was riding me the best she could while plastered against a shower wall. I tried to loosen my hold on her legs to wedge a hand between us, but my feet started slipping.

The tight fist of her body would push me over far sooner than her, and I wasn't finishing before her, not even for a quickie. I broke our kiss. "Touch yourself."

Her gaze jerked up to mine, her pupils dilated. I pumped in and out, waiting for her to make her decision. I'd never asked before and she'd never done it.

Timidly, she broke her hold around my shoulders and slipped her hand between our bodies.

Goddamn, that was hot. Another groan that wasn't quiet.

Her knuckles brushed against me as I thrust. I could feel the tiny circles she was making, the friction growing the heat between us.

Her moans were coming faster, growing louder. I captured her mouth, but my grunts weren't muted like I'd hoped. The force of my pumps increased along with the motion of her hips. Our teeth bumped and she giggled, but then gasped as the tip of my cock grazed the perfect spot inside of her.

I tried to shush her but it came out more a chuckle. We tried to kiss again, but she was so close. Her body tightened, the vise of her legs biting into my sides.

She crested, her orgasm rippling over my most sensitive skin, and as she cleared the top, she opened her mouth to cry out, then jerked like she'd just remembered we were trying—and failing—to be quiet. Her head thunked the wall, but her body was still spasming in climax. Another giggle cut through a moan. Then she tried to suppress the moan and laughed again.

I grinned, then my own orgasm hit. I clenched my teeth, but damn, blistering ecstasy mixed with my wife's laughter spurred my own.

"Shh," she admonished, her smile wide.

"You shush. You were louder." I chuckled and gasped as humor-laced aftershocks cascaded through my body.

"Oh my gosh. Good thing we tried this when they were gone," she whispered.

I helped her unhook her legs. Before I stepped out, I touched her lips in a firm kiss. "I'll let you finish."

I snagged a towel as I got out and replaced it with a new one for her. I dried off and redressed. My hair routine the days I worked from home was becoming a halfhearted finger comb.

By the time I got downstairs, Dawson was rummaging through the fridge. Kate was going to die inside when I told her Dawson had returned at some point during our sex session. He glanced at me, lingered on my wet hair, quirked a brow, then lifted his gaze to the bathroom. As if on cue, the shower clicked off.

He shook his head. "And to think Bristol put me off last night because you two were here and she was afraid you'd know we were doing it."

"She afraid you're too noisy?"

He turned his attention back to the

contents of the fridge and scratched the side of his head with his middle finger. I chuckled and practically bounced to the table.

He leaned back out of the fridge and pondered me the entire way.

I readied my computer but couldn't ignore him. "You're wasting energy."

He let the doors swing shut but didn't take his gaze off me.

My brother wasn't going to ruin my morning, yet his attention wasn't negative. It was… I couldn't identify it. "What?"

"Nothing. It's just nice seeing you like this."

"It's nice to feel like this." The confession came easily.

He left it at that and opened the french doors of the fridge again. "Damn." He disappeared behind the panels like he was going to climb inside. "How could I run out of butter? It's a travesty."

"I'll run and get some."

"Nah. I can get it."

"Dawson, you're doing all the cooking. I can run to town." I'd see if Kate wanted to come. "I just need to warm up the pickup."

I could start my pickup with my phone. I hit the button and frowned when I got a failed message. I tried again. Same thing.

"Something wrong?" Dawson drifted over, his hands stuffed in his jeans. His hair stuck up in hunks. He must use the same finger-comb method I did, only I hadn't worn a stocking hat all morning.

"The pickup's not starting."

We both got in our boots and coats and went outside. I tried to start the pickup. Nothing. "Battery's dead. The farm store open?"

Dawson ducked his head. "Until noon, I think."

"Can I borrow your ride?"

He didn't say yes, but a slow grin spread across his face and his eyes sparkled even though clouds packed the sky. I narrowed my eyes and his smile grew.

"The thing is, Aiden, I might need my pickup."

Like hell. He could use Bristol's. She hadn't upgraded her old beater, but it purred like a two-ton kitten after a few days at the shop.

"When Beck and Xander come to town and need wheels, they use the other pickup."

The only other pickup was… "You asshole."

ate

MY WINTER BOOTS hit the snow-packed parking lot and I let go of the door and the seat. This old pickup of Beck's was something. I hadn't ever ridden in it before, but I'd seen the others drive it around. A ride like this would've been right up my brothers' alley when they were teens. It had been easy to picture each King boy driving around in this as a teen, except for Aiden. Until now.

He wore his nice sweater and his good jeans with his North Face coat, but he had on cowboy boots and handled the big pickup like it was nothing.

My gaze lifted to the KC lights lining the top. Hadn't those gone out of style years ago? Way before my husband and his brothers' time.

A wall of heat closed in behind me. I'd almost needed my husband's help getting into the monster-truck wannabe.

"That was a climb." It wasn't much larger than a big farm pickup, but I wasn't over six feet tall like Aiden. I'd needed three points of contact to get in and out.

"It's something," he said grimly, but I didn't miss the humor underlying those words.

If I wasn't mistaken, Aiden didn't mind driving this. He probably wanted to hit the pastures like his brothers had. I'd heard them talk about whipping through the mud with it. How would it do in the snow?

He gripped my hand and led me inside the small grocery store that was one block off Main Street. Inside, we made sure to grab the butter first so we didn't buy fifty bucks' worth of groceries and forget what we'd come here for. Christmas music poured through the overhead speakers and the end of every aisle offered something green and red, whether it was chocolates or stocking stuffers.

Aiden and I had decided not to exchange presents this year. Still, he'd gotten me those books and all the laughs that had come with unpacking them.

I passed the muffins and sheer curiosity had me guessing the flavors. My attention was jerked away when a woman said my husband's name.

He gave my hand a reassuring squeeze. "Hey, Poppy."

I glanced over and the good day I was having took a downturn. I recognized the woman. She was the same one that had dominated Aiden's attention with inane chatter about high school and compliments about his job during Beck and Eva's engagement party. I'd sat on the other side of Aiden like one of those fish that suction to a bigger fish and just kind of watch the world go by while the predator fish ignores it.

"You're in town for Christmas?" Her grin could be on a toothpaste ad. I had worked hard at reining in my jealousy. I might not say "fuck them" like Mom, but I reminded myself I wasn't better or worse than someone like Poppy.

It was the lack of respect. Ultimately, how my husband treated me was between us. But Poppy didn't respect me. Years later, she pretended I didn't exist again.

Poppy didn't wait for him to answer. "Ohmigosh, it's so good to see you again. I was thinking about you the other day. Remember when it used to be Drive Your Tractor to School Day and you and your brothers all brought a different tractor? It was hilarious, but you guys were always *so* funny. I was just talking to the old wrestling coach the other day and your name came up."

Aiden pulled me close to him.

Did I ditch Aiden and go pay for our things? I couldn't tolerate Poppy any longer. Aiden wasn't ignoring me, but I didn't have to withstand these situations. The kind that wouldn't be helped by a snarky comment, or being a straight-up bitch. I'd look bad and I'd feel bad.

She took a step closer. "I think it's so—"

"Sorry, Poppy." Aiden clung to me. I blinked at him. Did I have the same startled expression as Poppy? "Kate and I were just grabbing something for Dawson and we have another errand to do before stores close. I hate to take you away from your family." His smile was one I'd seen him use a million times when talking to non-friends or family. Superficial and meant to placate. "I know how much I treasure getting alone time with mine. These trips to King's Creek are pretty special to me and Kate. You've met my wife, right? Poppy, this is Kate."

Poppy's gaze flicked to me, her lips turned down. "I don't think so."

He was brushing her off? And with such ease, like he'd done it a million times before. Had he been practicing? Or had he said what he'd been dying to tell others for so long when they dominated his time? Had all he needed was permission not to be "on" as the CFO twenty-four seven?

I adopted the same grin as Aiden. "I think we met at Beck's engagement party."

Her brow crinkled like she was struggling to, one, remember me and, two, recall that Aiden was married.

Aiden's brow furrowed in a way that was similar to his smile. Mild. Fake. "Were you there?" He shook his head and chuckled ruefully. "Sorry. I only remember being swamped with work and wishing I could just be alone with my wife."

Poppy blinked several times. She hadn't been the only one to latch on to Aiden that night, but she'd been the most persistent. I didn't like insulting people, but in this case, I'd forgive it. If Poppy hadn't been acting like she would steal him out from under me, then she'd only be mildly confused at his statement.

Aiden tipped his head, nothing but a pleasant gleam in his eye. "Merry Christmas, Poppy." He towed me away toward the checkout line.

The older cashier beamed at our approach. She chatted with Aiden about Dawson and Bristol's wedding and she'd heard it was nice. Unlike Poppy, she didn't demand all his attention, and she spoke to me as much as him.

We finished up. Aiden lifted the bag and wrapped his hand around mine until we reached the pickup. He opened the door and helped me inside. Once he swung into the driver's seat like it wasn't five feet off the ground, I said, "Thank you."

He leaned closer to me and dropped his

voice. "I bet she doesn't give a damn about wind energy either."

"Not one bit." I grinned as he fired up the engine. The loud rumbling echoed across the parking lot. All the pickup needed to do was backfire and we'd tick all the redneck boxes. "Did you have any fallout from brushing Hailey off?"

His jaw ticked and he took a moment to reply. "Her father stepped up his company's attacks against King Oil to make themselves look better."

And he hadn't wanted to tell me. "I'm sorry."

"Don't be. I talked to Dad about why I think it's gotten worse. We met with our PR team. They made sure a lot of our work with wind and solar development is more readily available on our websites, with factoids released regularly on all social media channels."

"Nice passive counterattack."

He slid a sly gaze toward me as he turned onto the highway out of town.

"We're also concentrating our factoids on our support of developing new wind technologies that are more efficient and less damaging to the environment than the big wind turbines."

"Subtle."

"But effective," he agreed. "It's actually been a real boon for our PR."

He parked at the farm store and we ran inside. There were no run-ins like with Poppy. He found the battery he needed and then we were on the road again.

I relaxed in my seat and marinated in the efforts Aiden had gone to for me. Not just him, Gentry too. The sting of being the only one clueless about the trust was fading as the rest of Aiden's family treated me as well as they had before.

We approached Dawson's pastureland but the dirt road Aiden turned onto wasn't the one that would take us up to his brother's place.

At an approach, he pulled in. "I'll open the gate. Want to drive through?"

Curiosity hounded me, but I didn't ask what we were doing. Aiden and spontaneous didn't usually go together. I scrambled over to the driver's seat. I had to sit on the edge to reach the gas pedal. Aiden swung the gate open, looking at odds with the landscape in his nice sweater and jeans, his winter coat hanging open. His boots were buried in the few inches of snow that hadn't gotten blown away. He looked like a city guy in the middle of nowhere, but he'd been born and raised on this land.

I pulled the pickup through, a thrill running through me as the engine roared with only minor pressure on the gas.

I put it in park and scooted back to my seat. Aiden closed the gate and hopped back in.

"Buckle up." Anticipation ran through his expression.

I looked at him, then out the window at the snow-covered landscape. We were at the top of a small hill where the snow wasn't as deep. It wasn't mud, but with this ride, it'd still be fun to tear through it.

I buckled myself in. "Are you going to—"

"Yep."

The pickup lurched and we were off. Laughter spilled out of me. Despite the seat belts, we were jostled around. I gripped the dashboard and the handle on the door as Aiden spun and floored the pickup around the hilltop. At one point, he hit an icy patch between two hills that must've been left over from a freeze-thaw cycle a couple of months ago and the pickup swung around.

His laugh mingled with mine. Then he floored it back up the hill and we bounded to the top. He put it in park. We were both breathing faster even though the pickup had done all the work.

"Wanna try it?" he asked.

My mouth dropped open. "Can I?" I'd never been irresponsible behind the wheel. Ever.

This was different. We were contained.

The hills in this pasture rolled gently and there were no cattle here during the winter. Dawson didn't move cattle out here until the spring.

"Just stick to the high points. The snow gathers in the low areas. If you get stuck, I'll gladly take the fall, but if you can prevent Dawson and the others from giving me eternal shit, I'd appreciate it."

I grinned and clicked out of my seat belt.

"And, Kate." His voice had dropped to the growl I was getting to know really well. He hooked his arm over the steering wheel to face me. I met his dark gaze. "When you're done, I plan on having you again."

"Out here?" In broad daylight?

"We're so far out, not even cattle can see us."

"Then let me in the driver's seat so we can get to the fun stuff."

Aiden

No matter how often I experienced it, I couldn't believe how different Christmas morning was as an adult. Dawson put his most requested french toast bake in the oven on a timer, then he and Bristol went out to do chores. I joined him for a couple of hours, then came back and cleaned up.

I was working at the table by the time he and Bristol returned. Kate was curled up on the couch, reading. She'd fashioned a book cover out of a paper bag to hide any illicit images. She'd gotten the idea from a craft project the library had offered teens for their own books and textbooks.

Bristol and Dawson were still in their bedroom, so I peered over my computer. "Chicken." When she looked at me, I lifted my chin to indicate her book.

A faint blush dusted her cheeks, and her lips quirked. She slipped the cover off to reveal a shadowy image with a frightened-looking woman. "It's a thriller I borrowed from Sophie and I wanted to protect the outside. I don't just use them when my husband sends me books with naughty things on the front."

"Your husband might have to do that again."

Dawson's bedroom door opened and he popped his head out. "You okay with a change in plans? More like a change in company. Grams."

We were all over twenty-nine and the trusts had been taken care of. I'd had the least trouble with Grams compared to anyone else, except maybe Xander, since he'd made sure to be unreachable. Bristol had taken the worst of it, so bad that I think Grams was even remorseful.

I glanced at Kate. Confusion creased her forehead. She had no idea why it'd be an issue. I hadn't told her about all of the drama.

More like I'd told her and left pertinent facts out.

"As long as you and Bristol are fine with it, it doesn't matter to us," I said.

Dawson nodded and disappeared into his room, shutting the door.

I caught Kate's eye as she was about to go back to her book. "I need to tell you about what it was really like for my brothers with Grams before they turned twenty-nine."

Her mouth formed an O and she winced. "Right. The money would've gone to Danny and Bristol." Her expression blanked and her gaze dropped to the page. "No wonder she immediately liked me."

"She likes you for more than that." This was Grams though. "I mean, she wasn't going to scare you off, but she likes you as much as she likes any of the rest of us in her cold, calculating way."

"You take after her."

I recoiled. "What?" I loved Grams, but at times, it seemed like I loved Grams because I'd grown up being told she was my grandmother, and grandkids loved their grandmothers. Not because she'd done anything to endear us to her. The months after Mama died, she'd softened for Dawson for a few weeks, but she'd told me to suck it up and help Dad with chores.

"That wasn't meant to be an insult." She closed her book and set it down. She was at my side in seconds. She sat on the chair adjacent to me. "I meant that I think she holds her emotions so close, in such a tight ball, that we forget she's a human with feelings."

I couldn't help but remember Dawson telling us how Grams had collapsed after she confronted Bristol. Grams had been holding her emotions in until they'd exploded and hurt everyone, even herself. I'd equated Grams with steel until that point.

Didn't mean she was soft and cuddly now. "I don't want to be like that."

"The Aiden I've been spending the holiday with isn't." She rubbed my thigh under the table. "But that doesn't change that I loved you anyway."

"I love you, Kate. Don't ever doubt it."

Dawson's door opened and he and Bristol came out chatting about the prime rib meal he planned to cook for an early supper.

Kate pulled away, probably to ask them how she could help.

But before she got up, she said, "I don't doubt it, Aiden. Not anymore."

Aiden

KENDALL PEERED out the front window. "I hope the wind doesn't pick up."

Dad walked up behind her and wrapped a hand around her waist. "There's no new snow. The roads should be decent."

He and Kendall had arrived a few hours ago with Grams. She'd ridden with them and surprised the rest of us. Grams usually liked to drive her own vehicle out. That meant bringing her own escape route. Dawson had snapped a picture and sent one to Beck and Xander.

As Grams had walked up the porch, Dad hovering behind her like he was ready to be a safety net because that was what a good son-in-law did, it struck me. Grams looked old. My indomitable grandmother with the cool gaze and bedrock of grit had a hunch to her shoulders I hadn't seen before. Her silver bob was combed and sprayed in place like always, but the lines of her face seemed deeper, harsher. Like it wasn't just that she battled against the natural progression of age and had lost, but that she'd stepped aside and given way.

Now Grams was at the table with Dawson. They were poring over plans for Sarah's Recovery Ranch. Bristol meandered back and forth between the table and the living area where I sat with Kate. Bristol and Grams weren't close, but their relationship was a few steps better than merely tolerating each other.

"I'd like to see it," Grams said, her tone suggesting that they should go see the land now.

Dawson lifted his gaze to Bristol and she nodded. "Anyone else want to go?" he asked.

Grams probably wanted to be nosy. She hadn't stepped foot on any Cartwright land for over forty years.

When Dad saw that Kate and I weren't moving to go, he answered for all of us. "You guys go on. It'll be easier to take one vehicle."

The three of them went through the back door.

Dad wandered over to us and dropped into a recliner, propping his elbows on his knees. "I'm not going to take up your holiday by talking work, but Kendall and I are trying to lay the groundwork for our meeting with the board next month."

Kate's questioning gaze landed on me.

A couple of months ago, I'd have told Dad that was fine and moved on, expecting the meeting to play out like they normally did, with Grams unwilling to change. I wouldn't have elaborated with Kate in the room either. She'd have asked questions I hadn't been willing to answer.

I couldn't act the same way I had before she'd asked for a divorce. "Kendall wants to ask the board to approve several more positions in the inner office," I explained.

Dad nodded. "We should have an inner floor, not just an office. We're getting stretched too thin."

Kate frowned. "Emilia still doesn't think you need more help? Wouldn't the data speak for itself?"

Kendall leaned against the chair, rubbing her hand up and down Dad's shoulder. Seeing them like this, I marveled at how they kept their hands off each other at the office. Outside of work, they were an affectionate couple. "Our work ethic seems to speak louder. Three of us are doing the job of six, but it's just not sustainable."

"Three new positions that correlate with the growth of the company shouldn't be too much to ask." I couldn't be noncommittal, nor could I be neutral. But it was difficult being supportive when I didn't want another VP under me again.

Kendall grimaced. "We think we should ask for five. We need them. If you can get me that information, Aiden, we might have a chance."

I nodded. Dad didn't take his gaze off me. If we were alone, I'd get a lecture. The only people who knew why I didn't have a VP under me were Dad and Grams. Kendall probably knew too, since I doubted Dad kept anything from her, but she hadn't been around when I'd fucked up.

"It'd help to get that information before the board meeting," Dad said evenly.

I'd been stalling. If I had to reprioritize work, gathering that data moved lower. "I'll get it."

Dad's stare was unwavering. "For all the positions."

Kendall's hand on Dad's shoulder stilled, her gaze bouncing between us like she sensed the tension rising. It wouldn't be hard.

My jaw was tight and the beginning of a stress headache beat at my temples. "Are you asking as my boss, or as your assistant's husband?"

"I'm asking because it hasn't escaped my notice that the battle to get more help in the office is a one-sided effort and it's not us against Emilia. It's been me and Kendall against Emilia. You haven't committed to growing the company. It's like you're afraid of change as much as your grams."

"I'm not afraid of change, Dad," I gritted out. "I just don't need someone under me to add more work."

"It wouldn't be more work if you hired someone you trusted."

"I trusted the last guy and look how that turned out." Guilt gnawed at my chest.

"You can't control the economy. Sebastian made the best decision he could with the information he had."

"We have decades of elections and politics to research before we make the kinds of decisions he made to ramp up production. It wasn't a surprise that state and country leadership would change. It's not as if we didn't have local, state, and national polls to evaluate before the election." My heart rate climbed. Dad appeared as calm as if we were talking about how the roads had been on his drive here.

"Exactly. And that was why he was fired."

"*I* should've been fired." I jerked my gaze around the room. Everyone was staring at me. I'd never admitted it out loud, but I'd known it at the time. Dad had probably known it and refrained from pointing out the obvious. As the CEO, he'd taken the worst press. The dam had broken, so I kept going. "I was his boss. I should've verified his work before I signed off on it."

Dad pressed his fingertips together and I flashed back to my office when he'd had to tell me to suck it up and win my wife back. He'd been right then, but I'd had a front-row seat to the fiasco Sebastian had caused. I'd seen what Dad had to go through to restore the company's reputation. I wasn't risking it again.

"By that logic," Dad said with frustrating calmness, "I should've been fired several times since I started. My first years as CEO, I should've been fired a few times a *year*. Mistakes are part of the job. If the people under us can't do their job, they're reprimanded or fired. But that doesn't mean we just don't hire anyone else and continue to take on their work."

That was only part of the problem. Sebastian had overinflated production estimates and approved the hiring of hundreds more employees. When demand had dropped like a brick, he'd had to turn around and order a massive layoff less than a year later. Not only had it been PR hell, but we'd had families on national news, telling their stories of how they'd uprooted their life to move to Montana or North Dakota and then been abandoned with no job.

The media had been out for blood, and Sebastian had been the sacrifice. It would've mollified the public more if I'd been fired. I was higher up the chain than Sebastian, but I was also the son of the CEO and the grandson of the board president. Grams and Dad had steered the company through it while I'd crunched numbers trying to minimize the damage.

It had been a bad look. I'd kept my job. Dad had traveled the world, suffering dog and pony shows to keep King Oil in good standing with our investors, suppliers, and purchasers. I'd doubled down—tripled down—on my work. I'd been a perfectionist before, but to avoid becoming a micromanager, I micromanaged myself.

"Regardless," I said tightly. "If that's one of the benefits, then I need to earn it."

Dad pinched the bridge of his nose. "Aiden. You don't have to work yourself into the ground. Trust our team to find someone who can do a good job."

"It doesn't matter. It's not what Grams wants and I don't know if challenging her right now is the best."

"What do you mean?" Kendall asked, confusion marring her features.

"She's not well."

Kendall frowned. "She seems fine."

"She's not fine. When she was coming up the stairs, it looked like a stiff wind could knock her over."

"We can't tiptoe around this because of her health," Dad said. "If she can't head up the board, then she shouldn't be in the position."

"That's harsh."

"It's business and if she insists on being in it, then she should be able to do the job." He spread his hands like he was seeking our understanding. "The thing is, we can talk to her about our concerns about her health and how we're worried she can't handle the position and she'll dig her heels in harder to prove us wrong, and it'll be to the detriment of the company. You've heard all the reasons why she and DB changed the company name to my last name. It needed rebranding to distance it from her and DB."

I hated that he was right. Why couldn't this be easy? "I'm not against asking for more positions, but I should be able to say whether or not I need a VP."

"At least an assistant?" Kendall's tone bordered on pleading. "Surely you have minor tasks that you would be willing to trust someone with."

Kate's gaze burned into me. She'd soaked up this conversation and was processing it but hadn't said anything. What did she think?

Grams would see the gap in equitable positions and assume I was in agreement with her. Worse, she'd try to support me.

The reaction Dad was afraid of would happen regardless. But they were determined, and in the end, I'd been ordered by my boss. "I'll get you the information."

Dad's dark gaze ripped through my placating promise. His jaw worked. Was he going to call me on it? Were we going to burn more of Christmas and argue about the subject and then grow awkwardly silent when Grams returned?

"Okay," was all he said. He sucked in a deep breath and looked around. "Think Dawson will get angry if I check on that prime rib? The smell is making my stomach growl."

"We won't do anything more than peek." Kendall followed him into the kitchen.

I glowered at the carpet. Kate hadn't said a word the entire time. Had Dad made a point to discuss this situation around her? He was a crafty bastard, and Kendall was just as cunning.

Kate would have questions. She'd want

explanations. If only my reasons sounded as strong now as they had before she'd asked for a divorce.

~

Kate

OUR AGREEMENT not to exchange presents hadn't stopped Aiden from calling in a favor with Dawson. In the back seat was a box with half a dozen homemade jumbo double chocolate chip muffins.

Those things were going to ruin me. I just knew it. My brother-in-law baked as well as he cooked. I'd never be able to eat another jumbo store-bought muffin without tallying all the ways it didn't live up to Dawson's.

"That was really nice of you both." I'd thanked Aiden five times already. It wasn't that long ago I'd been wishing for sweet gestures from him and now I was the one falling behind.

"I know how much you like them."

"I never eat them in front of you."

"Every time you see one, your eyes have sex with it."

I sputtered out a laugh. "Do not—yeah, I totally do."

He chuckled but kept his eyes glued to the road. Light from the headlights swept across the highway. The wind hadn't died down and snow snakes blew across the road. The weather had stayed cold enough and traffic was too light to melt enough snow to stick to the surface. Still, I was always glad when Aiden drove during these conditions. Bad roads never rattled him.

The conversation from earlier kept replaying in my head. It wouldn't quit. I'd gleaned enough to figure out the gist of what had happened, but Aiden hadn't elaborated.

Disappointment settled into my belly. I could ask him. He'd probably tell me.

Except that wasn't the type of relationship I wanted. I didn't want to beg for information. For years, I'd justified his silence with excuses about how things that dealt with his job weren't my business. But the subject they'd talked about had seemed to directly impact our relationship. It was my business and we should discuss it. Before I made my decision to move back in.

"The thing with Grams…"

My gaze shot to Aiden. Was he broaching the topic?

He worked his jaw before he continued. "A year after I started as CFO, the vice president of finance worked on a project with one of our sites in an area with a boom. Remember the surge in northwestern North Dakota and northeastern Montana almost ten years ago?"

I'd been on the other side of Montana in college, but the boom had been national news. Towns had been doubling in size as oil field workers and their families had moved to the area. Man camps had sprung up wherever someone could set up trailers and the bare necessities for facilities. Apartment buildings had flown up as if they were made of Legos. Once small towns with little more than a few franchises had become homes to giant department stores, chain restaurants, and strings of hotels that were immediately booked upon opening. All those workers' families had needed places to stay and housing couldn't keep up.

As well, the steep increase in major crime had outpaced the growth of local law enforcement. They'd called it the Wild West. Women had told stories about how parking lots of places they'd frequented their entire life became their worst nightmare seconds after dark.

Then the boom had crested. More stories about layoffs, ghost towns, and abandoned man camps had filled the news. King Oil had been featured several times. That hadn't been out of the ordinary. They were a Montana company, the state's pride and joy.

I vaguely recalled some other stories involving King Oil just as I was finishing my master's program. Reports of how layoffs had affected the workers involved. Disgruntled accusations that the repercussions hadn't reached the top tiers of the company.

Going to college in Montana meant I'd been insulated from it. Media in the state wasn't going to hunt a family they considered royalty, local boys who had done well, who had provided many of the residents with jobs at oil fields and the refinery. Montana was blue collar through and through, and they didn't forget that Gentry and Aiden had gotten their start wearing cowboy boots and raising cattle.

National news was different, and I'd had the luxury to ignore it. Aiden wouldn't have been able to. He would've taken it personally. He would've internalized the stress and his feelings and done everything in his power to make sure it never happened again.

"I remember the stories," I said. "Sebastian was fired?"

Aiden nodded. "He reviewed his plans with me, and I signed off. The buck stopped at me."

"For the record, I agree with Gentry. But I know you don't see it that way."

He shook his head. His rigid profile broke my heart. "I was brand new to the position. Sebastian was experienced, but he was arrogant and he made a major mistake. He didn't listen to the financial managers at the sites. Their data was in the report, along with Sebastian's reasoning why we should move forward with building more wells and hiring the personnel to do so. I should've caught it."

He was opening up about what felt like a personal failure, but it wasn't bringing him relief. He looked the same as he always did. Tense. His jawline hard, like he could cleave diamonds with it. Like he didn't realize the wall he'd constructed around his emotions was as formidable as the Hoover Dam. He'd taken DB's words to heart all those years ago, like the obedient oldest child he was.

Did Gentry know? Had he only added pressure, not understanding what Grams's and DB's words had done? All Gentry knew was that Aiden had taken the blame and was making up for it well beyond what his penance should be. Gentry didn't understand what motivated his son, and Sarah wasn't around to tell Aiden that he was only human and it was okay to mess up. That she was proud of him no matter what.

All Aiden had were the words "man up" when he'd been a grieving thirteen-year-old.

He had isolated himself, cut himself off from support. He wouldn't listen to anyone who told him to back off of being a perfectionist. None of us had known what was driving him—an unbalanced sense of responsibility because he'd been taught not to ask for help.

He'd let all those families down. He was the reason they'd moved and found themselves in a new state with no job. He was the reason some of them had ended up stranded, divorced, or homeless.

Other than defending his resolution to always be better, no matter the cost, he didn't have anyone to talk to.

Had he ever?

He didn't talk to me. What would I have said? The same as Gentry. *It's not your fault. Quit beating yourself up. You don't have to work so hard.*

What else had gone on that Aiden had weathered alone?

"You can talk to me, you know. I mean, really talk to me, Aiden."

He glanced at me, then slid his eyes back to the road. "I know."

Did he? "I don't mean that you tell me what happened and then give me all the reasons about why you made your decision while I argue how you're wrong. You can tell me how much it sucks to do the work of at least two people. You can tell me that fighting against your grams is exhausting and most of the time you wish she'd leave the company completely, but you can't change because you're worried about her health, and after everything, you're not going to have the weight of Grams's decline on your shoulders."

"Jesus, Kate." He released the wheel to scrub a hand over his face. "You nailed that one."

"You do the work of more than two people, don't you? You worry about your dad." How many of Aiden's duties were a CEO's, but Aiden intercepted them before they reached Gentry?

His expression softened. "It's better now that Kendall's working for him."

Except both Gentry and Kendall had bent and stretched as far as they could. They were at their breaking point. Aiden would shoulder more of the burden without a word. He'd do what he could to protect his dad and his stepmom and his grandmother. Just like he'd taken the position at the company. Someone had to do it and he wouldn't let his mama's memory down and coast through life. He'd ruin himself before he did that.

The magnitude of what my husband had been going through sank in. "I want to support you, listen to you, like you listen to me. But I don't know what you need if you don't talk to me."

"I need you, Kate. That's all I've needed."

The lights of Billings lit the clouds in the distance. A glow in the middle of nowhere. We were almost home. He'd drop me off at Mom and Randall's and then he'd go home. Alone. On Christmas, after he'd gotten into an argument with his dad.

"Can I stay with you tonight?"

His surprised gaze caught mine. "Of course."

Good.

I couldn't picture us walking into the

house and then Aiden spilling his guts about his feelings over the last four years, much less the last ten or twenty. That wasn't him. I'd have to be patient. I'd have to read him as well as he read me. Aiden didn't use words to show people how much he cared. He used actions, and I had to learn to listen.

iden

MY NEPHEWS' laughter drifted down the hall of the trailer and into the bedroom. I sat on the edge of Kate's bed with my arms propped on my legs, answering emails on my phone.

New Year's Eve wasn't a holiday. I'd gone to the office early in order to make Sharon's dinner on time. The McDonoughs celebrated New Year's Eve with pizza, but just because Sharon didn't cook it didn't mean I was going to be late. Other than not wishing to insult my mother-in-law, I had another reason to make sure I showed.

Tonight, Kate was coming home with me. Her bags were packed and by the bedroom door. Tomorrow morning, I'd wake up next to my wife.

This year was going to be different. I'd find a way to balance all the demands on my time. I'd make it work.

Violet hovered in the doorway.

I glanced up from my screen. "What's up?"

She looked around the room in a way that told me she didn't have a purpose for coming in here, but now that I'd asked her a question, she was determined to figure out an answer. "Um…what are you working on?"

"I'm analyzing the amounts we've contributed to non-petroleum-based energy research programs over the last five years and trying to project how much more we should contribute based on current findings."

"Oh," she said like she followed every word. "I'm almost eight." She kicked a foot up so only her toes were on the floor, then took a hop into the room.

I clicked off my phone. Solar energy returns could wait. Violet was usually in the thick of rowdiness with the boys. She seemed to need something quieter right now.

"Any birthday plans?"

She shook her head and wandered into the room, plopping on the bed, her little legs swinging off the side. "My dad said he'd take me wherever I want to go to eat."

"That'll be fun."

"Yeah," she said. "I told Mommy I wanted a watermelon cake."

"That sounds…" Would the cake look like a watermelon, or taste like it? Or both? "Good?"

She nodded. "Chocolate chips are going to be the seeds."

That answered one question. "How's wrestling?"

"Good." Violet's shoulders hunched.

What had I said? I nudged her with my elbow. "How good is good?"

"Grandpa tries to coach me, but there's a lot of kids."

"And not enough coaches?"

She nodded. "Think Aunt Kate will practice with me?"

The image of Kate wrestling with little Violet made me smile. How cute would that be? Seeing her mess around with the boys had shown me a whole new side of her. Violet was so much smaller, but with just as much determination. "There's nothing wrong with asking her."

Violet shifted from foot to foot, her expression unsure.

"Would you like me to talk to her?"

She brightened. "Could you?"

"Hmm…" I pretended to think about it. Violet's eyes widened as she waited for the answer. "I'll talk to her."

She grinned and threw her arms around me. "Thank you, Uncle Aiden." She jumped back. The wrestling crisis must be taken care of in her mind. "I brought my Old Maid cards but no one likes to play with me. Gramma said it was game night, but they're not playing games I like."

Kate had asked Violet to be her partner during Scrabble against Randall, but the girl had drifted away a little before I'd left for the bedroom. Jason and Sophie were each cleaning off their own six-pack and getting louder in a Cards Against Humanity game with Sharon. My mother-in-law was indulging in her second rum and Cherry Coke. The game was getting rowdy and full of jokes Violet shouldn't hear. Matt and Violet's mom, Ada, had plans with friends and had dropped Violet off to play with her cousins.

I could easily work another hour on my tiny screen, but I'd been sequestered in the bedroom long enough. I'd work longer tomorrow. "Why don't you grab your cards and bring them here?"

Her eyes brightened. "You know how to play Old Maid?"

"Kiddo, I grew up playing Old Maid." I hadn't played the game since I was old enough to tie my own shoes, but she didn't need to know that.

Violet ran off and was back within a minute, lugging a pink backpack covered in unicorns. She jumped onto the bed. I tucked my phone away in my pocket as she unloaded dolls and books from the backpack.

I picked up one of the books and paged through it. "You can read this stuff already?" My first-grade days were hazy, but I didn't recall reading books with this many words on the page. It was a cross between a graphic novel and a chapter book.

"Uh-huh." She found the cards and shoved everything else to the side. A fairy doll and a book similar to the one I was holding fell off the side. She ignored it. "So, I deal all the cards. Only put down pairs. If you get two school teachers, put those cards down. But if you have three school teachers, don't put all three down."

She spoke with the seriousness of Kendall running a meeting. I picked up my cards and arranged them, setting down each pair I found. Over the top of her cards, Violet watched me like a hawk, waiting for me to make a wrong move.

"Okay," I said. "Remind me how the rest of this goes again."

She smacked her lips, her expression full of ancient wisdom. "So. You pick a card from my hand, and if you get a pair, set it down. Whoever's left with the old maid loses."

"Got it."

I chose a card. Half my enjoyment from the simple game was watching Violet trying to control her poker face. I knew when I was picking the old maid or not by the way her eyes lightened or her mouth twisted, fighting a smile.

I wasn't a big believer in letting kids win—lord knew Mama never had. She'd been brutal to play cards with. But uncles were supposed to spoil their nieces and I'd done a shit job of it. When choosing between the last two of her cards, I deliberately chose the one that made her smile impossible to hide.

"Oh, no." I feigned disappointment. "I lost!"

She dissolved into giggles.

I grinned and shuffled the cards. "Play again?"

"What's the party like in here?" Kate leaned against the doorframe, her warm gaze taking in the cards.

"I'm getting my butt kicked. Wanna play?"

Kate's gaze landed on Violet. "I don't know. I've heard what a card shark she is."

Violet scooted over, sending more of

her books and dolls onto the floor. "We can play with three people."

Kate glanced down the hall. Thumps resonated from the living room. Shouts of *Why'd you do that?* mixed with accusations of cheating from Caleb and Corbin. Jason's boom cut through the noise. "Shut the hell up. The neighbors are gonna call the police."

Kate lifted a brow and eyed us. "I think cards is a safe choice."

"Are you guys staying overnight too?" Violet asked as I was dealing cards.

Kate smiled as she sat on the edge of the bed. "No. Jason and Sophie get the bedroom. You and the boys get to camp out in the living room."

If there was a living room left after tonight.

"Can I go home with you guys?"

I paused mid deal and caught Kate's gaze. She lifted her brows to ask if it was okay with me.

I'd imagined taking Kate home and

keeping her up until dawn doing wicked things I wouldn't feel right doing with a seven-year-old overnight guest.

Violet intently watched us silently communicate.

Kate wasn't answering, leaving it up to me. Which meant she didn't mind, but she worried I would.

We'd never had a kid stay overnight. None of my brothers had kids yet and Kate had rarely hosted her family for the holidays. From the ruckus, I could understand why. I couldn't imagine that in our quiet house.

A sense of loss tugged at my chest. Caleb and Corbin arguing was nothing like what Beck and I could do. Or Beck and Xander. Dawson and any of us. Sometimes all of us, and we hadn't needed to be fighting to be that loud.

The silence was as obvious as the lack of photos of Kate and me living our life.

"We'll have to ask your parents," I finally said.

Violet flung herself across the cards into my arms. I patted her back and met Kate's gaze. The wistfulness in her eyes disappeared as soon as she looked at me. Did it have to do with not having Violet or the boys over very often? Or did it have to do with not having kids of our own? Would she tell me what she'd been thinking?

I didn't think so. And that bothered me. We weren't moving forward with the divorce, but that didn't mean we were done working on our relationship.

Kate

I woke with a warm lump pressed into my back. It was too small to be my husband.

I blinked my eyes open. Aiden's side of the bed was empty. I closed my eyes and concentrated. Muffled, rhythmic thumps came from downstairs. He was in the gym, but he'd closed the door to keep from waking us up.

I shifted to my back. Violet uncoiled from her huddle and flung an arm and leg out, narrowly missing both my face and my bladder.

Chuckling, I rolled a little farther away. But the girl was a heat-seeking missile. She flopped into me.

What would we do today? I wasn't prepared for company. I'd felt like a failure of an aunt when I'd realized that I hadn't done an overnight with my niece and nephews since I'd been married.

Frowning, I rolled out of bed and dressed. I knew why I hadn't had sleepovers, but I'd never asked Aiden about it. I had assumed he'd be working and he'd want it quiet. Would he have minded? Could I have had the boys over, made popcorn, kept them from destroying the house, and then played with them the next morning? Would Aiden have joined in?

Would I have invited him to?

We had all this acreage and I rarely did more than grow a few flowers and take walks. It was made for kids to roam, build snowmen, and find frogs.

Violet sat up. Her fine blond hair stuck up in a million directions, a dandelion gone to seed and ready to blow away.

I rubbed her back and murmured for her to go back to sleep, but she shook her head and stumbled to the bathroom.

She'd managed to stay awake long enough to yell Happy New Year at midnight with my intoxicated family and her overstimulated brothers. Then she'd fallen asleep on the drive to the house.

I'd taken way too much pleasure watching Aiden lift her out of the pickup and cradle her into the house. We'd put her in the guest bedroom across from our room, but as soon as I'd wiggled between the covers next to Aiden in our bed, she'd cried out.

A strange room in a strange house.
I'd led her to our bed and she'd been

asleep before her head hit the pillow.

She trudged out of the bathroom. "Can we have pancakes for breakfast?"

"Absolutely."

I made Aiden's protein shake and left it on the island instead of taking it down to him. Violet helped me measure ingredients. Flour dusted the counter and the floor by the time we were done, along with the residue of an egg I'd swiped up right away.

Seeing my kitchen dirty like this filled me with a sense of rightness. And that gave me pause.

Aiden bounded up the stairs, wearing his usual workout gear plus a shirt, since we had company. He smiled at us. Lines of fatigue fanned around his eyes. He spotted his shake and beelined toward us.

"Thanks."

"Welcome." I peeked at him while pretending to watch Violet whisk the eggs. I loved seeing him after he worked out. Sweaty. Casual. His thoughts weren't as rigidly guarded. He usually smiled easier, laughed more. But this morning his shoulders hung lower, and when he closed his eyes to chug his shake, he left them closed a few heartbeats longer.

"Did you get enough sleep?" I asked.

"Yeah," was all he said. He put his empty shaker in the dishwasher. "I'm gonna shower. Let me know when breakfast is ready?"

Violet bounced on her toes. "I'll make you a special pancake, Uncle Aiden."

Another fatigue-lined smile. "Thanks, Petal."

She giggled. "Welcome, Bud."

The nickname was cute. They'd come up with it last night when Violet asked why people called her dad Mattie instead of Matt. *Could I be called Violetie?* Aiden had countered that nicknames could also be a play on a name. Like Flower, Petal, or Bud for Violet. She'd lobbied hard for Petal. Then started calling Aiden Bud.

With her help, making pancakes and eggs took longer than normal. Aiden hadn't come out of the bedroom yet. I wiped counters while Violet swept. Aiden still wasn't out.

"Do you mind getting silverware and napkins? I'll get Aiden."

Our bedroom door was closed. His voice drifted through the door. "I get it."

I hated to bug him, but I'd just signal him somehow that breakfast was ready. I cracked the door. He was on the edge of the bed, his head in his hand while he listened. His damp hair was pushed back like he'd run his fingers through it a few times since he'd gotten out of the shower.

"No, I know, but I'm going to be objective." He glanced at me. The resounding pressure in his eyes faded, but didn't disappear. "Yes, I'll get those too." His shoulders went rigid. "I remember what happened, Grams. All I'm doing is compiling numbers. Yes, I know we're on the downswing of a boom."

Aw, heck. Emilia had caught wind that the board was getting approached about adding high-level positions and she was readying herself. Why couldn't she see what it was doing to her family?

"Bye, Grams." He clicked off and tossed the phone aside. Scrubbing his face, he muttered, "I shouldn't have answered."

In all the years I'd witnessed him giving one thousand percent to that company, I'd never heard him say that. That he'd said it in regard to his grandmother was depressing. "How'd she hear of it?"

He reclined on his hands. "Kendall sent the agenda out yesterday, hoping Grams would think about it over the holiday before she bombarded us. We didn't want the board to think we were jumping them with this request. We want to be transparent."

"And what is your grandmother's problem with taking a day to think about it?"

He gave his head a little shake. "Unfortunately, they're valid concerns. Not insurmountable, but valid."

"Okay?" I took a seat next to him.

"How are current employees going to feel about new positions with market-comparable wages? New hires making more is never good for morale. Even if all current positions get the same bump, there are still those employees who will point out how much less they made when they started. Then there's the promotions. Could any in-house promotions cause declines in morale? Competition in the workplace can be good to a point, until an employee feels like they've lost a chance for upward mobility, or that the promotions weren't fair. If we hire outside of the firm instead of promoting from within, how will that look to lower-echelon employees? We could have a mass exodus, which would increase costs as we recruited, filled, and trained those positions." He dropped his head back. "I haven't even run the numbers for the meeting yet. It's in two weeks. I was going to do that today."

"Violet and I will stay out of your way."

"I know. I just wish…" He rolled to his hip to face me. "Why have we never had sleepovers?"

The sudden change in subject made my head spin. Sleepovers? "I don't know, but I've been wondering that. You were working. And I guess if you weren't, I wanted my time with you." I picked at the comforter. Brushed off invisible lint. I'd been greedy about my time with him, wanting him to myself for the scraps I was given.

He frowned and sat up. "Damn, Kate. I didn't know. I'm sorry. They're welcome whenever you want. I'll try to carve out time—" His frown deepened. "We haven't talked about kids since before we married."

No. We hadn't. I tried not to think about the march of time passing me by. The heaviness in my chest when I saw friends with their babies and kids. Coworkers sharing the trials of motherhood with each other.

"You said you wanted to settle into the

marriage first," I said carefully. "Do you feel like we're there?"

I squeezed air out of my lungs and wicked in another breath as he thought about the answer.

Violet leaned through the door, one hand clutching the doorknob and the other on the doorframe. Her little shoulders stuck out and she cleared her throat like we were the ones interrupting her. "Your special pancake is getting cold, Uncle Aiden."

His soft grin kept hope simmering in my heart. Was I still naïve, still thinking Aiden could strike the balance he was so certain of?

"Can't have that." He pushed off the bed and held out a hand for me.

I slipped my fingers into his strong grip. I met his gaze and smiled. I shouldn't slip into my default *nothing's wrong here* mode, but I did. For now.

CHAPTER 17

iden

KENDALL WAS SLUMPED in a chair across from me in my office, one booted leg crossed over the other as she leaned on the armrest. "That was a train wreck."

The office building was mostly empty, the board meeting over. Kendall, Dad, and I were in my office with the door closed. Emilia had said her piece. A long spiel about company integrity. A family-based business straying from its roots. How would it look?

Dad and Kendall had been prepared. Data. Figures. Projections. How our current efforts exceeded the grass roots of the place in all the best ways.

But Grams had a way of picking up on weaknesses and exploiting them with emotion. An amazing talent from a grandmother who'd never shown much emotion besides anger and derision.

It'd been enough to split the vote. Without a resounding yes, we had to come up with another proposition that included fewer positions and lower wages.

"She's always been resistant to change," Dad said. "We'll keep trying."

Kendall pressed her fingertips to her temples. "We're already close to bare minimum. Her morale argument is bullshit. We can promote from within for the marketing and human resources positions. Even for the more general VP and the finance VP."

"She's going to want that one cut." I shouldn't have spoken. Kendall and Dad had done all the talking during the meeting, presenting information, including detailed stats of the hours they worked in the office and out of it.

Grams had scrutinized me. Years ago, she'd been the one to back me when I'd proposed eliminating the financial VP position after Sebastian was fired. Today, Grams had perceived my silence as a lack of support for the proposition. Maybe she thought she was championing me. Did I want her to?

I didn't want to directly oversee anyone, but that didn't mean I thought our family company hadn't outgrown the constraints Grams had set decades ago.

I should appreciate the support, but my gut churned. I might need to stop after work and grab a few Tums.

Dad leveled a fatherly gaze on me. "Do you really think you can keep going like this?"

"I'm making it work."

"Life needs to be about more than making it work."

I spread my hands. "What do you want? You wanted numbers; I got you numbers. You wanted me to work things out with Kate; we're back together. You wanted me as CFO; I'm a damn good CFO that can do the job of three employees."

Kendall nibbled her lip while she watched us. I hadn't meant to get so defensive.

"I never wanted you to be the CFO if that wasn't what you wanted."

Shock kept my mouth shut for several moments. "What do you mean?"

He looked at me like I should already have a basic understanding of what he'd said. "You wanted to work at King Oil. I helped make it happen."

"You said…" What? I struggled to recall conversations we'd had before I left for college. They'd been superficial. Logistical. About what degree I should get. When I could start. What position would best benefit me until I became CEO. Anything to tap-dance over what we'd really been feeling in the moment.

Dad's mouth tightened. "All I wanted was for you to do something that made you happy. All of you. I was sucked into the business because I didn't have a choice. I was having a family before I graduated high school. My parents' health wasn't the best. Your grams and DB had all the answers. I was a scared kid who just wanted to ranch, but I had a baby on the way and no money. Then another baby." His lips quirked. "And another and another. I worked my ass off to provide so you and your brothers could do what you wanted in life. I've given everything to this company so all of you could have the choice in life I didn't." He reclined in his chair, realization dawning simultaneously with mine. "You didn't want to work here?"

I couldn't respond. Anything other than "Yes, I wanted to work here" would be a lie.

"Aiden?" Dad asked gently. "Did I make you feel like you had to?"

I shook my head and avoided his gaze—and Kendall's compassionate one. He hadn't made me feel like I *didn't* have to either. We hadn't gotten that in-depth in any of our discussions. If he'd spoken up, would I have let it sway me from Grams and DB's expectations? It didn't matter all these years later, so all I said was, "It's a good job."

"It's an excellent job," Dad agreed. "There are others out there who want to do it."

"I want to do it."

"Do you? Or since you're here, are you going to make sure you do the best job possible because that's your personality?"

"It's not a personality trait, it's expected. And it doesn't matter. I'm the King Oil CFO now."

But Dad wasn't to be brushed off. This wasn't the same dad from high school. This dad didn't give up. "Is that why you took the layoff incident so personally? Because you wanted to do something else and you thought that was what'd caused the oversight?"

Maybe because Dad had held the position open after the previous CFO resigned. He'd held the position open, hadn't promoted Sebastian, and slid me right in. I'd gotten the job over other qualified candidates. And I'd fucked up. Sebastian had fucked up, but he might not have if he'd been CFO and some other vice president had had to run the numbers and make their best educated guess.

"It's in the past," I said, my desperation to move beyond this conversation and never think about it again growing.

"It feels like it's firmly in the present, Aiden."

"Dammit, Dad." I jumped out of my chair and stalked to the window. Many days, this was my only dose of sunshine. The heat from the window eased the pressure in my head. Damn headaches. "Can you just fucking drop it?"

In the reflection of the glass, Kendall's wide gaze was on Dad, but his maddening, steady gaze was glued to my back.

"Do me a favor, Aiden." His calm tone only stoked the unreasonable anger coursing through my body. "Think about the opportunities your *neutral* stance on these positions are costing people. If the way it affects Kendall and me doesn't bother you, think about how Mrs. Chan might be job hunting because she's hit the top of the ladder. About the qualified, ambitious applicants out there who'd love to work with a company like ours but had to take jobs with corporate goliaths who only see them as a number and treat them worse. King Oil has been growing for over forty years. Society is going to be dependent on oil-based energy for decades to come, and not only that, we're uniquely situated to support and develop other energies. It's an exciting time. There are people out there who want to be a part of it. What's your part in that?"

I didn't turn around but watched in the window as he rose and held his hand out to Kendall. She stood and hugged his waist, leaning her head on his shoulder.

"It's not too late to do what you want in life, Aiden. If this is it, so be it. If it's not, you have an entire family willing to support you. But you need to tell us. You need to talk to us. You can't keep it all inside. You and I have both experienced the drawbacks of doing that."

I stuffed my hands in my pockets. Kate had said something similar not long ago. I was working on opening up with Kate. That was to secure a future with her. My future with the company was secured. I was roped to it no matter what I said.

He brushed a hand down Kendall's face and they turned to leave. By the time they reached my office door and opened it, they weren't touching. Professional coworkers.

Dad's words sank in, inch by inch, like a struggling man in quicksand.

You have an entire family willing to support

you. But you need to tell us.

What would I say? *Hey, Dad—can you work even harder than you have because I just want to check out? No, I don't have a plan. It's just that work has been an oppressive Groundhog Day since I started. Oh, and can you disrupt my brothers' lives like they don't have their own jobs and families who are counting on them?*

No.

You take after her.

I leaned my forehead against the cool glass. I was becoming Grams. Stubborn. Unwilling to ask for help. If I wasn't careful, I'd end up alone like Grams too.

PLANKS OF CORK flooring were piled at the edge of Xander's garage. He punched the button on the door and closed us in. Savvy and Kate had gone thrifting for office decor. My sister-in-law's new hobby, now that she had a big garage to work in and a home office that cut out commute time, was to repurpose items for home decorations and sell them at booths in the summer.

I stayed behind to help Xander put in the floor of her office. Savvy had liked the look of Xander's office so much, she'd asked him to do her office the same. I eyed the color. Not quite the same. She'd gotten a deal on stock that had been returned to the supplier. A contractor had ordered the wrong shade of walnut and his customer had been pissed. Sections had been trimmed already, and it was up to me and Xander to complete the puzzle in Savvy's office.

Just the challenge I needed to take my mind off the dismal talk in my office a few days ago.

Kate had sensed something was off, but I couldn't bring myself to tell her anything other than the meeting hadn't gone well but that we were going to keep working on it. I'd also said I'd add my support to getting an assistant at the very least, and for implementing a round-robin of VP positions.

During my research, I'd intentionally duplicated Kendall's attempts. I didn't second-guess her. I wasn't micromanaging her. But I'd stumbled across a topic I hadn't given much thought to.

Leadership styles. The bios of several of the execs in the companies I'd looked through had referenced transitional leadership. Transactional leadership. What worked better in which environment.

At no time did any of the execs claim to micromanage, nor did they discuss the long hours they put in. I didn't doubt that they did. What I doubted was that they were plugging away after everyone else had left because they were doing the tasks better suited for people under them.

Like I had been doing since Sebastian had been fired.

I might have the right to take responsibility for what had happened then, but as I read through company ethos, objectives, and mission statements, I could see that I had taken the wrong responsibility. I hadn't nurtured those under me. I'd let them do their job, but I hadn't stopped in and asked how they were doing. What they needed from me. What they liked or disliked about their job. Part of me—most of me—had sensed I was part of what they'd disliked. I'd gotten a top corporate gig straight out of college because of my last name. They didn't know what I'd sacrificed to stay on the fast track through college. I'd given up wrestling and a social life as I'd diligently chiseled away at the mountain of schoolwork to prove I deserved to be King Oil's CFO.

I had been glowering at the pile of floor planks several minutes before the burn of Xander's stare made it through to my consciousness.

I lifted a brow.

Xander shrugged. "I mean, we could glare it into place." He tossed a wrinkled sheet of paper onto the planks. "Or you could look at my sketch."

Fatigue weighed on me like I'd been putting down flooring for the last week, twelve hours a day. Though if I had, I'd probably feel better than being parked behind a desk for twelve hours a day. I'd feel like I'd accomplished more.

"Your sketch is fine."

He narrowed his eyes and propped his hands on his hips. "Or you could tell me what the hell has you spacing out."

Questions. Doubts. Fears. I had a lot flipping around in my mind like a pinball. I didn't want to talk about it, but the question escaped anyway. "Did you ever feel like you had to work at the company? Did Grams or DB ever talk to you?"

"No. Never." He blew out a laugh. "I didn't think for one moment Dad wanted me there."

"Because he thought you could do better."

Xander chuckled. "No. Because he

thought the company could do better."

"Ouch."

"That was how I felt, but Dad and I have talked a lot more this last year, you know." It was his turn to be captivated by the flooring. Maybe I needed a stack in my office to stare at. "You know what he told me?"

I shook my head. Dad had told me a lot lately, and he'd done it bluntly. Had my brothers had some eye-opening talks with him as well?

"He said Mama wanted to be a photographer."

"She was one." What was I missing?

"Professionally. I guess Grams was pissed Mama didn't want to follow in her footsteps and work in the oil business. Then she got pregnant, and her and Dad's fates were decided."

And Dad got pushed into the company. "Mama loved ranching though."

"She did. But she loved photography more. Dad said he never wanted me to give up what I was passionate about, he just wanted me to be smart about it. Build a good foundation, maybe get some business education so I could run a successful business in order to do photography as long as I wanted." Xander sucked in a breath. "But you know how it was after Mama died. We were kind of shit at communication and I took everything he said incorrectly and personally."

"I was told I was supposed to take over for Dad."

"We all knew you would. Wait—you were told?"

"DB laid it out pretty clearly." I looked at Xander. "What would you have done if he'd told you that?"

Xander frowned. He shifted his weight from one foot to another. "Well, he wouldn't have, for one. He made some comment once, about me being soft. I left for a long ride after that and didn't come back until after he was gone."

"Shit."

"Yeah. I don't remember DB very well. Just that he was always bitching about the Cartwrights, or telling you everything we weren't doing good enough at the ranch. He wasn't a happy man, but he didn't deal with Mama's death well."

"None of us did."

"You didn't want to work at King Oil?"

"More like I didn't realize I had a choice. Dad told me something similar. He worked hard so we wouldn't be shuffled into a life that we didn't get to choose, like him and Mama."

"Yet that's exactly what happened to you."

"We are shit at communication."

"So what now?"

I stooped and snagged the sketch of how we'd fit the planks into Savvy's office. "We put a new floor in."

"Aiden." He paused until I met his grave gaze. "You tell me that you never wanted the job you worked so hard for and then you want to drop the subject?" Xander had been the aloof one, but he wasn't letting this topic go. He wasn't avoiding the conversation and doing his own thing.

"It's done. I'm moving forward. We're talking about adding new positions and I'm going to propose a reorganization." Once that was done, Grams and the rest of the board willing, it'd get better. The demand on my time. The stress. The lack of enthusiasm for sitting through hours of meetings. I had no idea how long it would take, but I had to fix what I'd helped keep broken at King Oil. I had to do this for me and Kate.

Dad's question kept ricocheting through my head. How long could I keep doing this?

Xander pushed a hand through his hair, his movements rigid. "Look. King Oil did everything Dad wanted for us. Beyond that, you don't owe it anything." His tone grew heated. "Not a damn thing. Look what it did to Grams and DB's relationship with the Cartwrights." They'd all been friends before Grams and DB had gotten greedy.

"Yeah, Mama and Dad could build a nice house. Mama could stay at home and raise us, but we don't know that she wouldn't have chosen something else. Dad might've been able to ranch and be home more too. But he had to work at the company. Then you. You gave it half your life, Aiden. You almost lost your wife. Don't let it keep taking. It's just a company. You still have your health. You have Kate. You have money. A shit ton of money that was meant to give us the freedom Mama and Dad gave up."

My skin tightened. What he said resonated so soundly it took me a moment to realize that my younger brother was giving me advice. He was looking out for me. Our roles had reversed. The kid I had always been a little bit envious of because he could just leave when he was upset? He wasn't going anywhere now. He'd changed. He'd grown up. He was no longer stuck in the past and letting it decide his future. And he was telling me it was time I did the same.

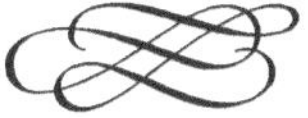

 ate

Violet hopped on the sidewalk. I opened my front door and she continued hopping like a bunny inside.

"Hey there, sweetie."

"Hi, Aunt Kate." She grinned at me and kicked her boots off. Bits of snow flew around her feet and a chunk landed on top of my socks.

Matt handed over a backpack emblazoned with a yellow *My Little Pony.*

He would head to his job delivering furniture after this. "Thanks, Katie. Telling her that she could hang with you all day helped her get over how upset she was that she couldn't do the wrestling tournament this week."

"She told me she wished she could practice more."

Matt rolled his eyes and yanked his gloves out of his pockets. "She's been bugging Randall. I've asked her to lay off. He's exhausted after work and a week of running practices."

"I'll wear her out." I would be the one worn out, but I'd looked forward to today as much as Violet. Once wrestling season and the endless tournaments were done, I would have the boys over. Then all three. I had lost time to make up for.

Matt stepped back like he was going to leave, but his gaze swept over the large picture windows, up to the roofline, then across the front yard. I knew the view he was seeing better than anyone, probably even Aiden. Gently rolling hills with scattered snow that was deeper than it looked. Dried brown broom grass sticking up through the white. The landscape was serene and peaceful with its own beauty in the winter.

"Damn," he said. "I forgot how big this house was."

Two of Matt's houses could fit into this place. "Want to come in?"

"Nah. I feel like a runaway steer in a ceramics shop when I'm in there."

"I don't have anything that's breakable. Why don't you and Ada come over for supper when you're both done with work?"

His light brows popped. "Seriously?"

I frowned. "Why would I be joking?"

"I've been to your place twice. Once when I helped you move and that one Thanksgiving when Mom brought all the pies."

Mom brought baked goods to other people's houses, said it helped her nerves when she was visiting a strange place. She'd brought five pies that Thanksgiving.

I lowered my voice. Only Matt could hear. "Hey, I'm not concerned about the house getting dirty or things getting broken. And I'm not ashamed of you guys. I appreciate that your 'fuck them' attitude stops with me, but it's not necessary." I poked Matt in the chest. "And you need to quit making comments about what I have to do to get his attention, or I'll go into graphic detail."

His eyes flared. "Katie-bear, that would give me nightmares, and then I'd have to kick my brother-in-law's ass. I ain't been to jail in years; I don't plan to go back." He flashed an unrepentant grin. "But hey, congrats on figuring out what he'd rather look at than his phone."

I swatted at his shoulder, but he danced out of the way.

"Ada's mom invited us over, so we'll have to come another time. Thanks again for taking Violet. I'm up for a promotion.

If I get it, I'll be on day shifts, in an office, and I won't be bone weary at the end of the day. Then I can help her wrestle. I hate when she feels…" He lifted a burly shoulder.

He didn't want to make Violet feel unwanted. Most shift-working parents didn't have to worry about it, but they hadn't grown up with a dad who'd rather work and fuck around than come home and spend time with his kids. "I get it."

Matt nodded and trotted to his pickup.

I shut the door and went to find Violet. She was sprawled across the couch.

"Where's Bud?" She hadn't given up the nickname, and Aiden hadn't discouraged her.

"He's downstairs in the office. You can pop down and say hi, but you have to knock quietly in case he's on the phone." For the last month, he'd been wrapped up in work. More like the Aiden I had served with divorce papers. Only this time, we talked. He explained his vision for the company and how, eventually, it'd help him with work--life balance.

He'd recommitted to the company, but he'd also recommitted to me.

I faced another weekend in a quiet house, but I'd take him lunch in the office. If Violet weren't here, that lunch break might turn into a quickie. If Violet weren't here, I'd find something to do. I'd been thinking about Aiden's comment about pets. Maybe I should get a dog. I could even get two. And a cat. I could start by fostering, and then stop if I started keeping too many animals.

Violet bounded downstairs. Her knock wasn't exactly quiet. Aiden answered right away. Even if he had been on a call, he'd mute it for her. He'd loosened up about the work he did at home. No more business wear in the home office. No more notifications, which I loved as much as he did. And he tried to arrange any virtual meetings during the week, claiming he could do desk work faster if he was uninterrupted.

Violet was already on his lap getting a tour of his desk by the time I entered. His office was as sparse as the one in the headquarters building. I'd put some of Xander's pictures on the walls, next to his mother's. But there were no shelves with trinkets. No photos on his desk. Just a computer and a second screen. He could play music from any of his devices but he never did. He worked in solitude, trying to make every second count.

I wished that it helped, but there was always more for him to do. Though I understood the pressure he was under better than I had before.

Violet's blond pigtails fluttered as she craned her neck left and right. "Where's the pictures of you and Aunt Kate?"

"Our wedding photo is upstairs," I answered.

Aiden looked at me when he spoke to Violet. "I noticed that too. We don't have enough pictures of us." He beckoned me over and dug his phone out. "Go stand by Kate."

Violet rushed me. I crouched and smoothed out her hair. Before I could look at Aiden, he snapped a picture.

"I wasn't ready!" Violet stuffed her hands on her hips for a Wonder Woman pose. I dropped to my knees and did the same.

Violet giggled and struck a red-carpet pose next—turned to the side and looking over her shoulder. Again, I copied her.

A few more shots and Violet stopped the show. "You need to be in the pictures too, Uncle Aiden."

I thought he'd refuse, but he spun his chair around and held the phone out to take a selfie. We crowded behind him until all of our faces were in the shot. He managed to get one with all of us smiling among all the silly-face shots—mostly from Violet.

"Okay." I took Violet's hand. "Let's let

him get back to work. I brought some craft kits home from the library. Want to see what we can make?"

"Sure!"

"You gonna have lunch with me, Petal?" Aiden asked before we left the office.

"Sammiches. Right, Aunt Kate?"

"That's the plan." I smiled at Aiden on the way out. He returned it, but I didn't miss the loss in his eyes. He wanted to come with us, make some crafts, and help prepare sandwiches.

I'd seen that look more often. When I picked up the boys from practice when both Jason and Sophie were working. When I let him know I was running errands on the weekend. When I went to bed and he stayed up late.

He claimed that his efforts would get him to a place where he could have a life, not that he'd described it like that. What would our life look like in another four years? And would I be okay if it looked the same?

Aiden

My mind was burned out from creating three different restructuring models to present to the board, all while keeping Grams's anticipated arguments in mind. All three of the models didn't include the founder of the company sticking around to make progress a pain in the ass.

It was late. Kate had to work in the morning. I had to work in the morning, and for the first time, I was considering skipping my morning workout. But if I did that, sitting at my desk would aggravate my back and make my sciatica flare up. Because that was what happened when I worked so damn much.

Violet had left hours ago. Kate had brought me supper, and I'd plugged through the rest of the evening. I left the office and slogged upstairs.

Kate was on the couch, her face lit by the light flickering from the TV. When she noticed me, she shut it off. She might be in her fluffy pajama pants and her sleep shirt, but I forgot about my fatigue when my gaze stuck on her pert nipples poking through the shirt.

Her breathing picked up. She'd noticed.

"You didn't have to wait up," I said as I slumped in the recliner. I was glad she had. I'd been home all damn day and hardly seen her.

"I know it's late, but I thought we should finish the conversation we started the last time Violet was here."

It only took a moment for me to recall what had been interrupted. "Kids."

She nodded. Her expression wasn't neutral, but it was guarded. "Kids. Do you want them?"

I scrubbed my face. "Yeah, I mean of course. It's just…a bad time." I winced. "God, I know I've said this before, but I'm working on it. I really am. If this goes through, if we can restructure the company, then it'll be different. It'll be different." Would saying it twice make it true?

Her gaze intensified, and her jaw worked like she was chewing the inside of her cheek. She could claim nothing had changed and she'd be right. I still worked long hours. I still hardly saw her. We talked more when I was around. That was about it.

I'd asked her for time once. She'd given it to me. And I was asking for more time again.

Her jaw quit moving. She'd come to a decision and her multifaceted eyes filled with resolve.

This was it. She had every right to issue an ultimatum. This relationship had been one-sided since the beginning, and I was asking her to stay the course.

But she didn't say anything. Instead, she eased off the couch to her knees and prowled toward me.

"Kate?"

She stopped at my feet. The heaviness of our conversation kept my body from fully reacting to her proximity, and especially her position. "I like where we're at. It's enough, Aiden. It's enough." She ran her hands up my legs and my restraint was obliterated. My erection went from a few extra pumps of blood to a raging hard-on. "I've been wanting to do this. Just this, just because."

She didn't initiate sex. I'd realized it, but I'd never wanted her to feel uncomfortable, so I'd never mentioned it. If she needed me to make the first move, I'd happily do it. She was my wife, of course she'd sucked my dick before, but it'd been during sex, as if she felt like returning the favor after I'd made her come on my tongue. I hadn't thought that she enjoyed it. I'd never asked for her to suck me off, and I hadn't dared let myself dream in case blow jobs were on her I'd-rather-not list.

And here I'd thought she'd call me out

for requesting more time, again. This was special. Just like her.

I kept my hands on the armrests, afraid sudden movement would turn her boldness into embarrassment. "I'm all yours."

She pulled her glasses off and set them on the end table. This was the sexiest foreplay of my life. When she curled her fingers under my waistband, I couldn't remember looking forward to something so much.

She yanked my waistband down. Cool air wafted over my rigid cock as it sprang free. The thing didn't bob though. I was too fucking hard for that.

Her hands hadn't left my waistband. She eyed my erection like she was afraid it'd bite back.

"Are you sure you want to, Kate?"

Her gaze popped up to mine. It wasn't trepidation I saw, but anticipation. "Yes," she breathed. "I want to. I just… I'm not good at it."

"The fuck you aren't."

Her brows lifted. "But I haven't really done anything like that for you."

The whole time we'd been together, she'd been afraid of disappointing me. I realized that now. "Kate." I ran my hands through her hair, letting the silky strands cool my fingers when the rest of me was a furnace.

"I figured you'd had"—she grimaced like she hated taking a highlighter to her perceived shortcomings—"*better*."

"Than you?" I said incredulously. "Get that shit out of your head. Everything's better with you. Everything." I pointed to my straining cock. "Especially when it comes to you touching me like that."

Her soft chuckle blew air across my heated flesh and I nearly groaned.

I cupped her chin. "Before you, my life was empty, including the sex."

She spread her hands out and ran them down my thighs. The horny guy inside me willed her to drift closer to my dick, but the married man trying to make sure his wife knew how much he desired her held it in.

She chewed the inside of her lip as she brushed a hand up my leg. I let out a ragged moan when her warm hand gripped the shaft. "I still don't have much experience with this. I should probably practice."

"As much as you want. I'm not going to complain."

She scooted closer and I widened my legs for her. Her mouth descended on the tip and I was riveted. Her lips opened and my lungs froze. She sucked me into her mouth and my head dropped back. "Kate. Goddamn."

She played. That was the only way I could describe it. I held back as much as I could to keep from choking her with wild, aimless thrusts. But she toyed with me. I didn't care if she was doing it intentionally or not. My balls were strung tight. My spine sizzled with unspent energy, but she didn't settle on a rhythm.

She was studying me. Pumping my shaft

while her head bobbed up and down. Another low groan eked out of me when she gave my balls a squeeze. She kept doing it. Pumping and squeezing and sucking.

I like where we're at. It's enough, Aiden. It's enough.

Had there been resignation in her words? Was she giving me a blow job because she didn't want me to question her easy acceptance? She'd tell me if she had an issue with waiting—

She swirled her tongue around the tip and licked all the way down.

"Kate." My fingers curled into the armrest.

She had free rein to do whatever the hell she wanted with me. I was getting close when she ran her tongue around the crown. My hips jacked up.

"I'm not going to last long," I warned her, but she didn't stop. My hips had a mind of their own, but she moved with me. I rolled my hips up and she sucked me down.

Fucking divine.

I did it again. And again.

"Kate—" That was all the warning I could get out, but she didn't stop.

Lightning gripped my body. I barked out her name, my back bowing as my balls drew impossibly tighter, and released into her hot mouth.

My wife was drinking me down. I was spasming too hard to stare, but I caught enough of the erotic picture to never forget it.

When I sagged, she released my cock with a pop and sat back, wiping off her mouth. The self-satisfied expression on her face would've made me chuckle if I'd had enough energy after the most amazing blow job.

I gathered her onto my lap, careful of my ultra-sensitive dick. To let her know that nothing she could do would turn me off, I brought her head down and kissed her. She stiffened for a heartbeat before she melted into me.

Her flannel-clad ass stroked against my

cock and the sensitivity changed from needing a moment to ready to go.

I broke the kiss to murmur a thank-you against her lips. I didn't just mean for the last few minutes, but for understanding me, for being patient.

She tucked her head under my chin. I couldn't see her expression. I was afraid to. What decision had she come to before she'd crawled toward me? It wasn't about whether or not to give me a blow job.

I needed time to prove to her that she'd made the right decision, whatever it was.

CHAPTER 19

ate

My birthdays were usually a quiet meal out. Aiden would take a couple of hours off and maybe work from home the rest of the night. He wasn't doing that tonight.

I was seated in the back room of a steak house, a boisterous place where my family could laugh and my mom's smoky cackle would get lost in the noise. Caleb and Corbin argued until baskets of warm buns were set in front of them. Then they argued over the last bun until Aiden ordered more.

Aiden, Jason, and Matt were engrossed in talks about the wrestling club. Jason and Matt peppered Randall with a million things they thought he should do to grow and expand the place. Randall asked each of them if they were going to help, and then the discussion dissolved into brainstorming. Aiden listened but didn't add much. He probably agreed with Jason and Matt, but his time reading people in the boardroom made him sensitive to Randall's weariness.

Aiden had asked once if money was the issue. Money was always an issue, but in Randall's case, it was the paperwork. The background checks on all the new coaches, the training, and keeping up with all the USA Wrestling rules. Randall wouldn't let just any coach near his kids. Families paid the club money and Randall took that responsibility seriously. His mission statement was about teaching and empowering kids through the sport of wrestling. The wrestling came last. Teaching and empowering would always be first.

My husband had heard a few of these discussions, but tonight was different. It was Aiden's mildly wistful expression. The arrogant tilt he had to his mouth was natural. It had nothing to do with arrogance and everything to do with genetics. I'd seen pictures of Sarah. Hers had probably come off as a secretive smile. On Aiden, I'd dubbed it resting business face. But that arrogant tilt was tipped back more tonight, like he was drawing into himself. Like he wanted to help, but he and Randall both only had twenty-four hours in a day. Time would always be an issue as long as King Oil was in his life.

It was his baby.

Violet tugged on my sleeve. "Aunt Katie, wanna play tic-tac-toe?" She shoved a blue crayon toward me and positioned the kids' menu between us.

I didn't have a choice, but I wanted to play with her. It'd keep my gaze off the absentminded way Sophie ran her hand through Corbin's hair as he played some sort of game against Caleb on their parents' phones. How Ada was attuned to Violet and her needs as she visited with me and Mom.

Violet put an *X* in the middle, and since I'd grown up with ruthless brothers, I put my *O* in the top corner. A few ticks later and I had two ways to win while Violet lost.

Instead of being scandalized, Violet's mouth hung open. "How does that work?"

"It doesn't all the time, but always start in the corner and your odds are better."

We played through the ready-made tic-tac-toe boards, then Violet drew a new one before each game.

After legitimately losing a round, I caught Ada grinning at us.

"Thanks for inviting us out," she said.

"Anytime." Aiden had made the arrangements but had asked me to contact everyone.

"It's been really nice," Sophie added. "Seeing you more. I know the boys enjoy it."

I'd been to their tournament last week. Aiden was crunching numbers and redesigning King Oil, so he'd missed it. He'd promised the boys he'd catch the next one, and he'd never made a promise like that. It'd be after the board meeting so perhaps he thought either way, he'd have time to get away.

I hoped so. I understood the rationale behind the extra work from the last two months, and that made it easier. I'd also needed the space. I didn't want him to see me grieving.

He wanted to wait for kids, but I'd seen the reality. His life wasn't changing. If I wanted to be with him, this was how it would be. No kids, him dedicated to his job. Some women might end the relationship and find someone else to have a family with.

I'd made my decision. When we'd discussed it again that night on the couch, and he'd said he wanted to wait, I knew that it'd never happen. And that I had a decision to make.

Aiden was it for me. I wanted my life with him. I had thought that life included trying to grow a family, but it didn't. No matter what Aiden thought, it didn't.

I had the urge to call Bisa. To sit on the phone with her while we each ate ice cream in our separate homes in our separate states, but her parents were visiting from Ghana. I wasn't going to intrude on her time with them. It wasn't like she could take regular international trips on a children's librarian's wage.

So I sucked it up. Truthfully, I'd had four years to come to the realization that it wasn't going to happen. After learning why Aiden was the way he was, how critical it was for him to fulfill his responsibilities, I understood.

Letting go of one dream in order to live another wasn't easy, but I had so much.

Trying not to dwell on what I didn't have would get easier. Some day.

Aiden

THE LAST OF my slides was on the smart screen mounted to the wall. The board considered my talk. Kendall gave me an encouraging smile.

My data had been all-encompassing. I'd interviewed the CEO and three VPs from a Canadian oil company, two more leadership teams from E&P companies in Texas, and even one in Saudi Arabia. I'd compiled data from three thesis papers about leadership styles in oil companies, and I'd interviewed the authors as well. I had data from publicly traded companies and from private firms like King Oil.

We were the only company that ran with a skeleton leadership crew. The only company where the leaders acted in a management role more than as mentors and figureheads. And the only company who'd caved to the whims of its original owner. That part I left unsaid. It would be obvious.

That original owner had pinched features and pursed lips. Her skin was tinged red.

I exchanged a look with Dad.

Grams was pissed.

Calvin, a longtime acquaintance of Grams and a board member who often followed her lead, tapped his pen. "What, exactly, are you asking for?"

For fuck's sake. "We want to restructure the company."

"And you told the world?" Grams snapped.

Ah hell. I'd plowed into my information gathering in order to be armed to the teeth against Grams's rebuttals, and I'd forgotten that I'd committed the unholiest sin of all.

I'd leaked our business.

Every other oil company was competition in Grams's eyes. She didn't believe in colleagues or camaraderie outside of King Oil. She'd grown up in a kill-or-be-eaten world. Business was cutthroat and those who slashed first stayed alive.

It was why the company had had to be restructured when Dad took over as CEO. He'd had a good reputation and so his last name had been plastered all over while Grams's had been moved to the background.

"I discussed leadership styles with them, yes," I answered evenly. "We didn't discuss business otherwise."

"Yet what are they going to think? King Oil is crumbling from the inside out."

Dad spoke up. "It's not unusual for companies to restructure." He gave Grams a knowing look. "I'm not talking about changing out people, but changing processes."

Her eyes narrowed. Calling her out like

that in front of the other four board members hadn't been a good idea. But the point had to be made.

Calvin tapped his pen. He did it every time he wanted to talk. The man had programmed us well. When that damn pen tapped, we shut up and waited for him to speak. "Do you think this is a good time for upheaval? Our wells in western North Dakota and eastern Montana are running at a quarter of what they were ten years ago."

"That would make it an ideal time," Kendall said as if Calvin had unknowingly answered the question himself. "When things in the field are quieter, we have more flexibility."

Grams pounced on Kendall before she could continue. "If you're so flexible, then why the need for restructuring?"

"Emilia." Dad folded his hands. "We're running the inner office with one more person than you and DB had when you started with a few wells on Cartwright land." It'd been Dad, Grams, and DB. Dad and I had Kendall and Phillip.

"And we've expanded into three states." Emilia looked at each person lining the table. "Now you have marketing departments. HR. IT. Accounting."

Calvin's pen tapped. I rolled my eyes. Kendall caught the move and her agreeing sigh was silent, but I saw it.

"Why don't we take some time to study your data, Aiden," Calvin said. "It's a lot of information for us to make such a major decision."

Except that was what the board did when they never wanted to make a decision. They kept putting us off until we quit asking. It'd been annoying before. It was enraging now.

"How much time?" I asked.

Grams lifted a manicured brow. "There's no need to rush on a matter like this."

Before Christmas, I'd used the same stalling tactic on Kendall. I needed to tell her that she ought to key my pickup for how I'd acted. I wanted a decision now. I didn't want to work eighty-hour weeks while they ignored all the data I'd compiled. Like the chart I had designed that showed how we could promote from within and recruit from outside, incorporating a new leadership style without disrupting the daily work of the rest of the staff.

That chart had taken me two full weekends to organize, and that had been done assuming the people we hoped would accept a promotion would actually want the job. Two full weekends I could've watched my niece and nephews wrestle, taken Kate to visit her brothers or mine, or just spent time talking to my wife.

The patience I usually armed myself with when dealing with the board and Grams wavered. "How about we set a deadline for when we want to make the final decision?"

Calvin's pen tapped and I envisioned

throwing it on the floor and stomping on it. "We can't be hasty."

"Calvin's right," Grams agreed. "But we can use the next month to review your presentation, Aiden. Send us a link." She scanned the room. "Do I have a motion to adjourn the meeting?"

I glowered at my tablet. The last slide showed on my screen. My work was impeccable. Kendall's was as well. I'd combined her plans to expand our staff with my leadership overhaul. If this worked, we'd have room to breathe. We'd be able to have a life outside of work. And for once in my life, that was becoming more and more important. I went from being afraid of having to manage someone again and failing, to wishing I had at least a vice president and an executive assistant working under me.

The entire time I'd worked on this damn project, I'd feared a resurgence of those divorce papers. We hadn't ripped them up. They were in a drawer. I'd tossed them in with the Scotch tape, the screwdriver, and the extra batteries I never knew were good or dead. The junk drawer. Where the papers deserved to be if they weren't going in the shredder.

Kate had been quiet for the last month. I hadn't come right out and asked her what was wrong, but something was. We talked. We had sex. A lot of it. But a part of her was distant from me and I wasn't sure how to ask. The problem in our marriage had been me not sharing. What did I do when it was Kate?

The words "meeting adjourned" rang through the room. I slammed my laptop shut and stuffed my notes inside my tablet sleeve.

Grams stood at my side, her fingertips pressed into the table top. "This company was supposed to remain a family company. For you and your brothers."

My patience snapped. I gave her a hard look. Her brows rose, and she studied me. I was so carefully neutral around Grams, and

I should still try to be. She hadn't directly crapped my plan out of existence, but she didn't like it. She didn't want to change, but the main difference was that now I was ready to.

I needed this to be different. All of it. "You can't create a company by devouring everything around you and then act shocked when that company starts devouring itself."

She recoiled. I didn't know if it was from what I'd said or the heat in my tone. I didn't care.

I gathered my things and stalked out of the meeting. I had work to do. No matter what, that didn't change.

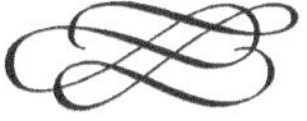

iden

PARENTS FILTERED OUT. One of the last tournaments of the season always drew a large crowd, but now it was done. I had watched the whole damn thing. I'd gone into work early to wrap up some reports and then met Kate here before the first match started. Those reports still weren't done, but the will to stay in my office wasn't there. I had more important places to be.

I'd seen Corbin wrestle. Violet too. She'd even waved at me, grinning with her little headgear over her ears, as she strutted onto the mat. Ada had warned me that Violet would hit me up for an after-action report of her performance.

Kate left the gymnasium with Violet so the girl could change out of her singlet. Ada had to go to work, but Kate said she'd wait with Violet until Matt picked her up.

I made my way to the gym floor. I'd help with the mats. The corner of my mouth ticked up. I couldn't enter the club room without thinking of how Kate and I had wrestled there.

Randall made sure to high-five or knuckle-bump every wrestler before they left. He told them something great they'd done that day, or a way they'd improved. He was a good coach, and he was going to miss this. He'd told Kate that he would've liked this year to be his last, but next year would definitely be it. As long as he found someone competent enough to run the club. The competent part was easier to find than someone with the time. It would be a part-time gig on top of whatever full-time job the new person would already be working, and for a few months of the year, the coaching side of the job kicked up to nearly full time. Running the club didn't pay enough to support a full-time position. Maybe he could've gotten it there, but he'd had the same roadblock. Not enough time.

Randall found me after all the attendees were gone. He clapped me on the back. "Thanks for coming. I think Corbin tried extra hard to live up to the tales his daddy told about you."

"Glad I could make it."

"You don't have to help. A few of the older kids volunteered. They get volunteer credits for some club they're in."

My disappointment surprised me. I wasn't ready to leave. The energy from the tournament still buzzed along the walls.

Excitement. Exhilaration. Support. I missed this feeling. This was part of what I'd given up when I'd walked away from the sport after high school.

I kept the resignation out of my voice. "I guess I can go find Kate."

"Violet told Katie she was starving. If they're not in the club room, they're in my office raiding my snack drawer."

The snack drawer he stocked for his grandkids. I gave him a nod and went in search of my wife and niece. The club room was bustling with activity. Jason and his boys were directing traffic for equipment return.

Randall's office was down the hall, a little-used space in the dark corner of the building that he'd been able to rent out.

Noise faded behind me the closer I got, and Violet and Kate's murmurs took over.

"I haven't seen that one," Kate said. "Is it the one with Ariel's daughter?"

"Mm-hmm." I could picture Violet's legs

swinging in Randall's rolling chair. "Why don't you want kids, Aunt Katie?"

My steps faltered. I hadn't meant to eavesdrop but I couldn't move.

"I did."

"Don't you still?"

"Yeah, but it's just not meant to be." The softness of Kate's voice wrenched my heart. We had no idea if it was meant to be. We hadn't tried to find out.

"Why not?" Violet asked with the innocent persistence kids had. She was seven and she'd thought to ask.

Kate was the most important person in my life and I'd never asked.

I'd asked her for time yet again and she'd given it to me. I wanted to think that she'd talk to me if she felt strongly about starting a family now. I hadn't pushed her to talk either. Was I afraid of what she'd say?

"Dreams change sometimes."

A vise tightened around my chest. I was a selfish bastard. I'd wanted my life with

Kate. I'd wanted her and I'd done what it took to get her. And she'd had to give up something she wanted. Kids. Her own family unit. Because of me.

"You gonna have that last cracker?" Violet asked. Normally, the way she pilfered food would've made me chuckle, but all humor had drained out of me.

I had to do something, and I hated the way my options were limited by what the board decided. There were still only twenty-four hours in a day. I couldn't find out that Kate dreamed of having kids only to leave her to raise them while I was in the office.

Maybe it was possible to parent while working as much as I did. I could finagle an assistant. Hire a personal assistant if Grams and the board refused additional positions.

I'd make it work. For Kate.

I rounded the corner and knocked on the doorframe.

Kate was hunched over the old metal desk, her hoodie pushing her hair around her face. She smiled. "Hey. Want a Cheez-It?"

"I'll pass." I hadn't eaten those since I was a kid.

"You ready to go?" she asked like she hadn't just confessed to giving up important dreams to stay with me. While I'd given up nothing but a few hours of work that I packed in during time I would've been working out.

"You two finish eating."

Kate dug into her tote at her feet. "Would you mind starting my car? My remote doesn't reach from in the building." She rose and walked toward me. "It really doesn't work unless you're standing right next to it. But I'm not parked far way. If you don't mind—"

I pressed my fingers against her plump lips. "Of course not."

Another problem she hadn't mentioned. Kate wouldn't give up the car and she wouldn't waste time getting a new auto start. They weren't critical to living in the north, but the other option was sitting in a frozen soda can when it was twenty below zero out, waiting for the heater to actually put out warm air.

I lifted my winter coat from where she'd set it with hers next to the desk and put it on. "I'll be right back."

I took the side exit to avoid the cleanup crew. As soon as I lost the protection of the building, the cold hit me and the fabric of my jacket crinkled like paper each time I moved. At Kate's car, I tested the distance. The damn thing didn't work even when I was twenty feet away. I got closer and tried. When it finally started, I peered in to make sure the locks hadn't disengaged while I messed with the remote.

I rarely drove Kate's car. She probably thought the inside of her vehicle would piss me off. Her passenger seat was littered with receipts. Some forms in the back stood out among the spare gloves and hats and an old pair of athletic shoes in case she went for a walk during her lunch hour. It was her car, but something prompted me to unlock the door and pick up the official-looking documents. I'd never been a nosy fucker in my life, but when it came to papers and Kate, I'd become quite sensitive. Besides, what if they were something important she'd forgotten?

I ignored the way the wind flayed the skin off my face as I read what was on the papers. An application for an apartment unit?

How old was this?

Sometime in the last four months. I let it fall back on the seat and shut the door. Locked the car.

She'd gone apartment hunting.

My wife had served me divorce papers, but after months of talking and growing closer, my mind had chosen to consider those documents as more of a warning. But an application for an apartment? With a year-long lease?

Damn.

Cold snaked through my jacket, its

frigid fingers wrapping around my chest. I'd almost lost her. I could still lose her. The balance I'd worked so hard for was a mirage. She was sacrificing to stay with me.

I rushed inside. She wasn't in the office, but I found her at the front door, waving to Matt and Violet as they left.

"I'll walk you out."

"Sure." She went to the side door I'd used before.

I snagged her hand. We were alone on this side of the building, though Randall would come around soon to lock up. But I couldn't wait to speak to her. "Do you want kids, Kate?"

"We agreed we'd wait." Her tone was light and neutral.

"And we agreed to really talk to each other."

Her mouth tightened and she nodded. "Right. You're right. Yes, I was disappointed when you said you weren't ready, that your job was still too much. And that's okay. I've realized that your company is your priority and that's okay. I love you. I love my life with you."

"It won't be forever—"

"Aiden." Sadness leaked into her small smile. "I don't want to raise a kid who wonders why a parent is never around, like my brothers and I did. You don't want that either, and it's okay." She moved closer to me and put her hands on my shoulders. "You wouldn't forgive yourself if you made your kids feel like they weren't enough. We have nieces and nephews and we're only going to get more. It's okay. I'm okay with it."

Dreams change sometimes.

I wasn't okay with it. She loved her dad, but she was constantly left wanting more. Then she dealt with her guilt for what paltry attention he gave her when her brothers were lucky to get a birthday card. I'd spent too many years missing Mama and wishing Dad were around more. It was why I'd wanted to wait to have kids of my own. For the reasons Kate had said.

But later had turned into years. What did I expect another "later" would do? What happened when Dad retired? If I took over as CEO, my time would be in even shorter supply.

That was my future. That was what was expected of me.

And my wife was willing to give up something as significant as kids to stay with me, and to save our hypothetical kids from experiencing what we had.

Was that what I wanted our future to be? If it wasn't, what was I prepared to do about it?

"I need to run back to work. Just for a little bit."

Disappointment flickered in her eyes.

"I'll be home in an hour. I promise."

She nodded and I rushed out the door. The next few calls I made would be some of the most important of my life.

Kate

CAN you come to the office as soon as you're done with work?

Aiden had been quiet all weekend since the tournament. He'd worked at the home office all day yesterday, and he'd been a driven man. I hadn't thought he could level up after the last month, but there he was, growling into his phone and pacing the home office. He hadn't even worked out.

Would I find out what was up? Pulling into a parking spot at King Oil headquarters, my gaze caught on a familiar pickup. Was Dawson here too?

I had gotten done at five and come straight here. The lot was over half empty. All but the inner office got to work their eight hours and go home.

I got out and gave the familiar pickup another look. The one parked next to it looked like Xander's. That was too much of a coincidence.

I scanned the lot for Gentry's pickup. Yep, in the farthest corner. Gentry probably parked there to leave open closer spots for the rest of his employees, but Kendall likely reinforced it to add more steps into their day.

Was Beck here too? If all three brothers were at King Oil, and Aiden wanted me here, what did that mean?

I was about to walk in when Lauren breezed out. "Oh! Kate!" She threw her arms open, then froze. "I never hugged you at the library. Am I allowed to hug the boss's wife here?"

I grinned and stepped into her firm embrace. "You can hug me anywhere. I've missed you, but I'm so glad I don't see you for all the right reasons."

"This job is the best." She nodded toward the door, then tucked her chin into the collar of her black dress jacket. "Was that the rest of the family I saw walk in earlier? Talk about a serious case of the nerves. All the Kings are in the castle."

I didn't mention that I had no clue why they were there. "Nothing to be nervous about. You do good work."

Lauren's nod was solemn. "I'll continue to be the best assistant they ever hired. Frigid days like this, I'm grateful for a job with a roof over my head and heat pumping through the vents." She squeezed my arm. "I'd better let you go. Something important's going on and I'm not going to be the one holding you up."

Something important. I rushed to the elevator and hit the button. On the ride up, I took my coat off. The doors opened and I frowned. The floor was quiet. Gentry's office door was open but the lights were off, same with Kendall's office, and Phillip wasn't at his desk.

Aiden's door was open and his light was on, but I didn't hear voices. Where were the others?

My husband was at his desk, but he wasn't working. He was doing the slouchy thing that made him look so damn good.

His suit coat hung on the chair behind him and he was missing his tie. The top buttons of his mauve shirt were undone, his cowlick was sticking up, and he was contemplating the top of his desk. As for the desk, it was empty. There was no tablet. His phone was nowhere to be seen and he wasn't looking at his computer screen. Was it even on?

I'd never seen him like this. Not in his work office or at home. "Aiden?"

He lifted his dark gaze but I couldn't read his expression. "Hey. You can set your coat in here."

"What's going on? Your brothers are here?"

"Yes. We're having a meeting before the board gets here."

"There's a board meeting tonight?" What was going on? His brothers had no power over the board. Were they coming to work here? Beck, maybe. He could sell his tech company, or heck, run both, but I doubted he wanted to. He loved his job and he loved Eva more. Xander didn't hate the company, but his attitude was live and let live. Dawson wasn't leaving the ranch.

"Yes." Aiden rose and rounded his desk. Putting his hand on my lower back, he led me toward the stairwell. The conference room was down one level. "I have something to tell you, and to tell the others."

He stayed quiet and I kept my questions to myself. Aiden was half in his head and half with me. He led me through the open office space that was normally bright with natural light during the day.

My stomach fluttered as several pairs of eyes watched us enter the conference room. It wasn't just Aiden's brothers. Their wives were here too, and they were as quiet as me, their curious gazes following us to the head of the table by the mantel.

Gentry's brow was furrowed. Didn't he know what this pre-meeting was about?

What the hell was going on?

Aiden pulled out a rolling chair for me.

When I was settled, he sat and folded his arms on the table.

"When I married Kate, you thought it was for the money." He looked at his dad first. Gentry didn't avoid his gaze, just dipped his head. The brothers' gazes brushed across me before they nodded too.

"We know you love her," Beck said.

"Right," Aiden said quietly. "I can't deny the trust was my original motivation. There was a lot riding on my decision, for all of us. As for how I felt about Kate, my private life was just that—mine." He cleared his throat. "But I realize that I've kept a lot to myself over the years, and all it's done is hurt me and those closest to me. And that's gotta stop."

Several bodies shifting in their seats filled the silence.

"I want to tell you all why I married Kate, and when I'm done, you'll know why I've made the decision I have."

Curiosity and anxiety mingled in my gut. I'd never seen Aiden so open with his family. I treasured the times he could be himself and joke around with them, but he was never this earnest.

He worked his jaw. The rest of the room stayed quiet, all sensing the weight of his decision and his determination.

He lifted his gaze to mine and held his hand out. I slipped my fingers into his warm hand.

His gaze softened but couldn't hide the underlying concern. "I have a story I need to tell you."

CHAPTER 21

iden

EIGHTEEN YEARS AGO...

MY NEXT OPPONENT'S details ran through my head as I sat with my teammates in a high school gymnasium in Billings. Jason McDonough. Sophomore. Fifteen like me. I hadn't faced him before. He'd hit a growth spurt and was now in my weight class.

Running through the data took my mind off what was missing about today. My dad had to fly to a meeting in Dallas. My brothers were home doing chores. I'd ridden the bus to the meet with the rest of my team. Grams never came to my competitions and I doubted it would change since DB had passed away. I had no one in the stands.

Mama had never missed one of my matches. Acid clawed its way up my throat as I struggled to direct my attention away from the gaping hole in the bleachers. I couldn't stop Mama's voice from flitting through my mind.

You can do this, Aiden.

Don't underestimate your opponent.

The only thing you have to prove is that you tried your hardest.

She would watch me and support the rest of my team, cheering for them through wins and losses. She'd study the weight class above me in case I wrestled up. Then I'd catch a ride home with her instead of taking the bus and she'd talk strategy.

That wouldn't happen anymore. It wouldn't happen ever again.

The longer she was gone, the more DB's voice infiltrated my thoughts. *If you're wasting time wrestling, you'd better make damn sure you're winning.*

I swallowed hard. Jason McDonough. Ranked eighth in the state. He'd won his last match with a 5–3 decision against Miles City last week. I forced my gaze to the two bodies grappling on the mat. I cheered when the rest of my team cheered, echoing whatever they said, floating through this night on autopilot, like I'd done all last year.

My attention caught on a girl about my age watching the pair wrestling. My gaze drifted away, then returned. She must be a team manager. But there was something about her. Several team managers I'd come across in my time wrestling were girls. Some wanted to wrestle but didn't want the

BS that came with a girl wrestling in the sport. Some were girlfriends of wrestlers on the team. Others just loved the sport and being a part of a team.

This girl was evaluating. The air around her was more serious than the others.

Plain brown hair with blond highlights that could just be from the gym's lighting hung past her shoulders, fluffing out at the ends, like she brushed it once in the morning and forgot about it. She didn't wear any makeup that I could tell, but I never noticed those types of things. Weird that I'd start today.

Did I need to be distracted that badly?

I must've. I couldn't quit watching her. She was across from me. I could cheer on my teammates while still watching her beyond the pair on the mat.

She shifted, her intelligent eyes studying the ref now. Her change in position allowed me to read her shirt. *I'd rather be reading.*

The corner of my mouth tipped up. A saying so at odds with her intensity.

Perhaps it was true for her the rest of the day, but the way her hands clenched…no. She wanted to be here.

The match wrapped up. The two guys stood side by side until the ref came over and raised one boy's arm. The wrestler from Billings had won that one.

The pressure was on me even more.

The girl wandered to where her team waited. The guys moved and shifted to let her through but didn't give her any more attention than that. They were used to her presence, but she wasn't quite one of them. She stopped by my opponent, Jason McDonough.

My eyes narrowed. Tingles of awareness traced down my spine. Had the other guys ignored her because she was with Jason?

She murmured to him. His gaze flicked across to my teammate. Jason's and the girl's profiles were the same. A little upturn at the end of the nose. Round cheeks that had probably been cherubic until puberty. They even crossed their arms the same.

A beat of relief had my mouth tipping up again. Siblings.

Jason nodded, his gaze growing shrewd. I knew the expression on the girl's face. It was the same Mama used to have when she'd talk wrestling on the drive home.

The relief I'd just experienced morphed into longing. Lucky bastard. Did Jason realize how fortunate he was to have someone, a person beyond his team, who supported him?

I ground my teeth together as my name was announced. It was time to compete. I walked out to the center of the circle on the mat. Licks of heat burned over my face, my shoulders. She was watching me. She'd study me, and then she'd talk to Jason about my techniques, my strengths, my weaknesses. She wouldn't judge me on my last name or what I could do for her. She wouldn't hold what I was doing today against what I was supposed to be as an adult. She'd see me on this mat. The real me that put his heart into wrestling because

Mama had thought I was good at it. And the girl would be oblivious. She'd have no clue that she'd made a sad, lonely boy from King's Creek feel seen again.

THE NIGHT of the library tour...

THIS WAS IT. Tonight was the night.

My heart raced. The crowd from the public library gathered. They'd met in town and driven here as a group, walked in as a group, and stayed a tight little community as they gathered in the meeting room.

Damn them.

Faces blended in front of me. Men and women avidly listening to a spiel I'd given several times before. All of it had been a cover for tonight.

My gaze jumped over the group. I tried not to linger on the women, but I had to know if she'd showed.

Had she changed? Had I looked right at her and not recognized her?

This was a long shot. I wasn't a gambling man. I worked for what I had and I didn't take chances. What needed to be done, I did.

The trust wasn't any different. It *shouldn't* be any different. But it was. I'd turned my career over to King Oil. But now I was supposed to turn my future over to a trust? To marry someone just to get some money?

I had responsibilities, but this felt invasive. This felt like a line had gotten crossed. Yet it had also gotten me thinking.

If I hadn't kept my head down and my mind on my job, what would my life have been like? Who would I have dated long enough to form a relationship with? Who would I have wanted to date?

When I was a teenager, there'd been one girl who'd fascinated me, and I had one final question. Would she have the same effect on me as an adult?

My gaze skipped over a pair of intelligent hazel eyes. I swallowed my triumph and forced myself to keep scanning as I spoke.

Kate McDonough.

The rest of the tour took forever. Dad and I took turns leading the tour. The entire time, Kate hovered at the back, on the fringes, like she'd done at the wrestling tournaments. Tonight her hair was sleeker and her lips were full of gloss, but she was the same girl. Watching everyone. Studying them. She'd watched her brother's opponents wrestle, then she'd talked to him.

No one else had spotted what she was doing, but she'd been as responsible for Jason's success in the sport as his coach had been. Jason, of course, had done the hard work, but she'd helped him strategize. She'd gotten his head in the sport and helped him focus.

What would it be like to have someone like that at my side?

I'd wanted to know then, and I wanted to know now.

I hadn't pursued her back then. She'd lived in a different town. I'd been college-bound on the fast track into King Oil. I could've wrestled on scholarships, but I couldn't have split myself between a sport and school. So I hadn't asked her out. I'd assumed her life had gone in a direction away from mine.

Then I'd been told I had six months to marry. And the first woman I'd thought of was her. What were the chances she was still in Billings? What were the odds she was single? What were the odds we were even compatible? A fascination from a distance as a teenager hardly made a valid foundation for marriage.

But if I had to marry, then I was going to give it a shot with the only girl who'd ever seen the real me. When I'd learned she worked in town and still went by her maiden name, I'd had to officially meet her.

It wouldn't do to go into the library and

pretend to check out a book. What department did she work in? What were her hours? A guy like me couldn't roam the library without getting noticed. I didn't know anything about her social life or how I could "run into her" otherwise. I couldn't look up Jason after ten years and ask about his sister that I'd never talked to.

So, I had devised a plan. I'd pitched it to Dad and he'd taken the bait. We'd give local municipal bodies tours after work hours and host an open house just for them. *Let's invite some city departments first.*

And tonight was finally library night. Like I'd planned.

And there she was. Going after the muffins. I'd asked the caterers to provide mini muffins. Jumbo muffins would've garnered too many questions. She'd always had a chocolate muffin the size of her head at the tournaments. Other wrestlers might've noticed the forbidden carbs, but I'd noticed *her* hunched over her food, meticulously dismantling the muffin in bite-sized chunks.

I prowled around the room. If anyone was trying to get my attention, I didn't care. I had eyes for one person. The floral top she wore swayed with her movements, hugging her full hips as she reached forward, and the leggings she wore outlined the rest of her lush, curvy body. She'd shed her youth and was in curvy, sexy woman territory.

Could the whole room hear my heart thud?

I'd never been this nervous before. Not before any of my matches, not with any opponent, and not before any meeting. All I had to do was talk to her to see if she still affected me. If she responded, then I could ask her out, and fate would take it from there.

What good was all this money and status if I couldn't use it to win the woman of my dreams?

Kate

THE ROOM STARED AT AIDEN. I wasn't the only one who couldn't believe his confession.

He'd set up the tours just to meet me? Not only had he remembered me, but he'd…thought about me when we were kids? He'd wanted to ask me out?

Gentry shook his head like his ears were full of water. "The tour idea wasn't community outreach? It was so you could ask Kate out?"

Aiden nodded. His jaw clenched and he stared at the top of the table. His thumb ran across the top of my hand, like it'd done while he'd told his story.

"Why wouldn't you tell me?" Aiden King had hunted me down?

"I manipulated you. I used the company to get you here to see if I could marry you for money. And when you talked about your dad when I proposed… I didn't feel like I was any better. I felt worse, because I still went ahead and rushed the wedding for the trust. I should've been honest."

"Yes, you should've, but it doesn't change how I feel about you."

"You were the one thing I'd done for myself in a long time. I was selfish. It was easier to shut my mind off and do what had to be done than think about where I'd rather be or who I'd rather be with. When I was tempted to speak up, the thought of losing you kept my mouth shut. I wasted four years together. I'm sorry."

"Oh, Aiden." The shame in his eyes tore at my heart. I squeezed his hand, wishing I could just crawl into his lap and hold him for hours.

"You did it for us, didn't you?" Beck asked. "You tracked Kate down because you knew that if you didn't marry and Danny learned about the trust, all hell would break loose. We'd be in a media shitstorm and the three of us would still have a trust to deal with, this time publicly."

Aiden's jaw flexed as he tipped his head.

"Just like you bit the bullet when it came to King Oil," Xander said. "You did it so the rest of us wouldn't get pressure from Grams and DB to work here."

"Damn, Aiden." Dawson shook his head. "No wonder you never really talked to us. You spent years bossing us around and getting attitude right back, then we got to do whatever we wanted while you were tied up here."

"I didn't realize, Aiden," Beck said. "I'm sorry."

"None of you are at fault." Gentry's forehead creased. I couldn't see his hands, but the way Kendall was angled, she must be clutching his under the table. "I've made a lot of mistakes in life, and the worst ones were after your mom died. I should've been there for all of you. But I'm here now, and I swear to God, son, if you don't quit, I'm firing you. Don't think I haven't figured out that you've been taking on so many duties to keep me from overworking. I'm healthier than I've ever been and Kendall makes sure my ticker gets a gold star from the doctor regularly. Aiden, you don't have to keep protecting us."

Aiden didn't let go of me as he faced his family. "I am quitting."

I let out a gasp. "You are?" This job was his life. He couldn't just walk away and be okay knowing he was leaving a mess.

"I want to be with you. I want to have kids with you. I want to teach them how to ride horse, how to wrestle, whatever they want to do." He looked at his dad. "You are right. There are others out there who want this job, and who'd be good at it. I asked you all here so you'd know everything, and to help us deal with Grams."

The fantasy I'd had all those years ago had been shattered—and now he was putting it back together. I wasn't deluding myself this time. There was a roomful of witnesses.

"But before we talk about Grams, I have something important to do." Aiden dropped to his knees and spun my chair toward him. The rest of the room stayed quiet. "This was Mama's ring. I told myself that I never gave it to you when I proposed because I wanted to win you over. I wanted you to know that I could give you the world. But the real reason was that I was ashamed. I hadn't been honest and Mama wouldn't have approved. I know now that this ring suits you better."

He took my shaking hand and slid the ring on. The small round diamond was tucked into a gold band. Simple. Beautiful. It fit like it was destiny.

"I meant everything I said the first time I proposed to you." Aiden gazed up at me. "But this time I'm going to be the husband you deserve."

I threw my arms around him. "I love you so much."

He rocked back on his heels, clinging to me. "I love you too, Kate."

By the time we quit hugging and kissing,

we were surrounded. He stood, still holding me to him.

His brothers smacked him on the back and offered their congratulations. When Gentry stood in front of us, he held his hand close to mine. "May I?"

I lifted my hand, the light catching the diamond, making it shine.

Gentry's brown eyes filled with nostalgia. "That ring was all a stupid kid could afford. After all the boys were born and I'd been working for Emilia and DB for a while, I asked Sarah if she wanted a different one." His lips twitched. "She said if I wanted it to sit in the jewelry box while she ignored it, I could buy her a new one." He released my hand and lifted his gaze to Aiden. "I'm proud of you."

After he finished hugging his dad, Aiden drew me into his side. "You mind staying and helping us face the board—and Grams?"

"Not at all." I rose on my tiptoes and whispered into his ear. "Afterward, I think there are some fantasies on your desk that we need to fulfill before you're officially done."

He groaned. "I'll make this meeting quick."

CHAPTER 22

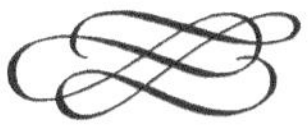

ate

Six months later...

I WAVED my free hand toward the counter. My other hand was propped on the toilet seat. "Grab the phone."

"What?" Aiden had a hold of my hair. I hadn't thrown up yet, but it was better safe than sorry.

"It's a—" A wave of nausea rolled

through me and I groaned. "Trust me."

"Okay…" He picked up my phone up off the counter. "Now what?"

I exhaled and slowly inhaled. The wave rolled through me. "Take a picture of us."

"Kate. You're bent over the toilet," he said as if it wasn't my head that was half a foot from the water.

"I'll tell you about a conversation I had with Sophie later. I just need a picture of you holding my hair while I vomit."

Another wave crashed into me and I heaved right when he was taking the photo. He dumped my phone on the counter and crowded behind me again. I took the damp washcloth he offered.

I'd been battling these bouts for the last couple of months, but this was the first time I had both Aiden and my phone with me. I leaned back on my heels. I thought I'd be okay, but I didn't want to leave the safety zone of the porcelain throne.

Aiden kneeled behind me. "Isn't this supposed to get better?"

"Maybe? The first trimester is almost done." I was taking my prenatal vitamin at night like Sophie suggested. She fawned over me as badly as Aiden.

We'd started trying immediately after the board meeting where Aiden had told his grams and the board that he was quitting. Gentry and Kendall had backed him up and said nothing was holding them to the company. Gentry could retire early and Kendall could take a job anywhere in the world she wanted. Only that part was a bluff. They weren't moving far from their families.

Grams had stayed silent for several minutes. Then she'd dipped her chin and tears had glittered in her eyes. She'd told the board that she should be the one to go.

Aiden had stayed long enough to help with the transition and train his replacement, but he'd militantly stuck to a forty-hour workweek. He'd been officially done at King Oil for three months. I was fairly certain this baby had been conceived on the company plane, in the back bedroom we'd never used before, on the way to Denver to stay with Beck and Eva.

Gentry would step down at King Oil after the new leadership was trained in. They'd hired a vice president from an oil company out of North Dakota: Barron Oil. Another family company, it was also headed by a workaholic CEO who was trying to recruit his oldest as his successor. Gentry had gotten the story out of the new hire and was glad to give him the upward mobility he wouldn't get at Barron Oil.

Then Gentry would take his place on the board, probably as president. Kendall was leaving too. She'd found a nonprofit in town that could use her expertise, expertise that usually came with a high wage. But she was working for a fraction of what she used to make and she and Gentry were traveling all over. *Before the grandkids start dropping,* Kendall had said, dancing and clapping after I told her Aiden and I were expecting.

Ours would be the first, but I wouldn't

be shocked if Aiden's brothers had announcements by the end of the year.

I tossed the washcloth in the dirty laundry and stood up.

Aiden was at my side. "It's passed?"

"For now." I washed my hands and took a swig of mouthwash.

After I was done, I slogged to the bed with Aiden hovering behind me. My nightstand had a picture of Aiden and me with the Colorado mountains behind us. A bigger photo that included his entire family at Beck's cabin in Aspen was mounted in the living room next to pictures of my niece and nephews. We now had as many pictures of people as we did of landscapes in our home.

Our beagle—crossed with who knows what—rescue puppy that Violet had insisted we name Bud jumped on the bed, his tail wagging. The kitten we'd adopted at the same time—named Petal, also suggested by Violet—swatted at Bud, then started grooming the puppy's little ear.

I sank into bed with a sigh, loving that my days off involved my husband and our pets. Aiden had all the days off, but his evenings would soon be a different story.

"Randall call you yet?" My stepfather had been calling every day since Aiden had approached him about taking over the wrestling club.

Aiden chuckled. "I think I have a missed call. He's going with me to talk to a builder. I want his insight on the design."

The club would have its own space and year-round wrestling. Violet would have her uncle as a coach—Aiden would make sure of it. Both Violet and my nephews would get free lessons if they wanted. Jason had tried to object, but Aiden had said the family discount was nonnegotiable. Aiden planned to lease some space for other club programs. He had ideas for creating scholarship programs. We'd talked a lot about how we wanted to use the trust money.

We didn't need it. I liked working at the

library. That was how I wanted to contribute to the community. Aiden would be a stay-at-home dad and run some of our own nonprofits. I met with Lauren a couple of times a month for coffee. She gave me her thoughts for programs that might help the not-quite-retired crowd learn new skills to finish out those last years of work, or because they couldn't afford to retire. Between Lauren and the library director, they'd identified technology as a huge pain point. Aiden and I had set up an annual donation to the library's technology and career outreach programs.

I stretched out while Aiden grabbed a Tums for the low-level heartburn I couldn't shake. Aiden lay next to me, his body as sinfully powerful as it'd always been. The only thing different was the expression he wore. His resting business face was softer, a little less arrogant without stress tightening his lips.

I brushed my fingers down the scruff on

his face. I liked how it felt—everywhere on my body. So he only shaved every few days.

He kissed my fingers. "How many are we having?"

I chuckled. "I think we should find out how much the first one turns our world upside down before we talk numbers."

"Deal." He rolled to his back and laid his arm out.

I curled into his side. We had nothing to do today and nowhere to be—unless we wanted to. If I wanted to nap in the middle of the damn day, he'd help me.

I put my hand on his chest. The diamond on my ring glittered. I never took it off. And I never would. I kept the old one in its own special jewelry box, and I'd pass it on to our kids after we told them the story of our not-quite-textbook romance. "I love you, Aiden King."

"I love you, Kate King." His hold around me tightened. "You're my queen."

GENTRY

FIVE YEARS LATER...

I LEANED against my pickup and soaked it in. In front of me was Dawson's place. The house I'd built with Sarah. She and I had barely entered adulthood when kid after kid had arrived. We'd hoped this place could contain our big dreams. For so many years, I'd worried that those hopes had been buried with her. Our boys had scattered, isolating themselves and burying themselves in their work.

Then their mother's crazy idea had prodded them into being adults that would have made her heart burst with pride.

I know mine did on a daily basis.

Emilia's had as well. I knew that now. And I was grateful that I'd learned it before we'd had to bury her just hours ago. Right next to Sarah and DB.

She would've hated a formal reception where everyone talked about her, so after the family had finished at the gravesite, we'd come back to Dawson's for a large barbecue.

I inhaled the mix of fresh spring air mingling with the subtle scents of dirt and manure. Dawson had a few extra guys working for him nowadays, but he always made room for me and his brothers and our wives to help work cattle. Though, we couldn't spare everyone these days.

Too many kids to keep track of.

My mouth tipped up as my oldest granddaughter sprinted through the yard. Sera's long hair trailed behind her as she chased Beck and Eva's oldest, three-year-old Maddie. Sera took after Aiden. A permanent solemn expression that broke into a grin when she was around her cousins. But around her two-year-old brother, Rand, and six-month-old sister, Lily, she took her big-sister responsibility seriously. As for Maddie, that girl took after

Beck—she was an angel when we were looking and liked to get into trouble when we weren't. One thing I was certain of was that Maddie would be able to reprogram my computer by the time she was ten.

Bristol and Dawson's boy, Daniel, tried to join in on the fun with Sera and Maddie but kept getting distracted by bugs crawling on the ground. His coppery hair gleamed under the May sun as he bent to inspect his new find. Bristol stepped out of the house with baby Emmaline strapped to her chest. Bright orange hair stuck out of the navy-blue baby wrap. She handed Daniel a cup of milk and wandered to the flower beds. Squatting, one arm wrapped around her precious bundle, she pulled a few weeds.

For years, those flower beds had sat empty. Dawson and Bristol might not care one bit about flowers, but with Savvy's help, they now had basil, oregano, tomatoes, mint, peppers, and whatever else Dawson had requested.

As if my thought conjured her, Savvy

stepped out of the back of the house with Kendall trailing her. Savvy carried one of her and Xander's one-year-old twins and Kendall carried the other. Jasper had my name as his middle name. Jet's middle name was Savvy's dad's name, Walter. The son I worried I'd never connect with had named a son after me.

My chest got tight and it had nothing to do with clogged arteries.

Kendall spotted me and set Jet down next to where Savvy was letting Jasper play in the grass. She strutted over to me, her hips swaying, a warm smile on her face.

"The service was beautiful."

I dipped my head. "Emilia would've hated it."

"Yep. But she would've secretly thought she deserved it."

"You know… I resented her a lot more than I thought." All those years getting driven into the ground by the company. The drama around each and every trust because she couldn't stand to lose the money. The way she'd never seemed to want to be close to us, her only living relatives. She'd done it all for her family. I saw that now. "But I owe her everything."

"None of us agreed with how she fought for the company and the money, but we've sure reaped the rewards."

"It took me decades to understand what she was doing." My kids and their kids could do whatever they wanted in life, but they'd chosen to pay it forward, each family in their own way. "I'm going to honor what she's left us by being there with you and the rest of our family."

"I'll miss her." Kendall stepped into me and I folded my arms around her. She liked to put her ear against my heart and listen to its rhythmic thud.

"Me too." I hugged my wife and watched my family. My kids. More grandkids than I'd ever thought I'd be surrounded by. For so many years, I'd wondered what the hell Sarah had been thinking.

When she died, I had wondered what I'd

do without her. But she'd made sure we were all taken care of.

Kendall spun in my hold and we watched our family. When we came here, we all stayed at the lodge Dawson and Bristol had built for us between our properties. My favorite days were lounging on the porch with Kendall and watching the sun rise or set.

"Are we brave enough for the big sleepover tonight?"

I chuckled. "Brave? Or stupid?" Kendall's idea. We'd watch all the grandkids while the couples got away for a night out.

"Naïve." She laughed and draped her arms over mine. "I love our life together, Gentry."

"Me too." I'd spent my life digging up what I'd thought was one of the world's richest resources, when it was really this. My family.

ABOUT THE AUTHOR

Marie Johnston writes paranormal and contemporary romance and has collected several awards in both genres. Before she was a writer, she was a microbiologist. Depending on the situation, she can be oddly unconcerned about germs or weirdly phobic. She's also a licensed medical technician and has worked as a public health microbiologist and as a lab tech in hospital and clinic labs. Marie's been a volunteer EMT, a college instructor, a security guard, a phlebotomist, a hotel clerk, and a coffee pourer in a bingo hall. All fodder for a writer!! She has four kids, an old cat, and a puppy that's bigger than half her kids.

mariejohnstonwriter.com

Follow me:

ALSO BY MARIE JOHNSTON

<u>Oil Barrons</u>
<u>Make Me Whole</u>

<u>Oil Kings</u>
King's Crown
King's Ransom
King's Treasure
King's Country
King's Queen

www.ingramcontent.com/pod-product-compliance
Lightning Source LLC
Chambersburg PA
CBHW060938190726

48286CB00005B/1321